Years to Savor

STEPHANIE FLYNN

Small Fish Publishing
USA

First edition
Cover design by Stephanie Flynn

ISBN large print edition: 9781952372209

Special Note

Time travel is real.
For a few short hours, you will be transported to 1995
and back again.
Enjoy the ride.

For the best experience, please read Kiko and Eric's backstory in **Minutes to Live, Matchmaker in Time 0.5.**

Chapter 1
Present Day, Green Bay, Wisconsin

Chaos was coming.

The unpredictable and uncontrollable phenomenon swirled through Kiko Takai's living room. She strained to keep her feet in place, while butterflies attacked her stomach and waves sloshed her brain. She had questions, and only her boss had answers, so she planted her feet and gritted her teeth against the psychic attack. What she'd affectionately called the Mystic Cloud of Dread was none other than her boss's micro body parts arriving like a storm and chasing off unwanted spectators, slowly assembling his corporeal embodiment. She'd never been susceptible to his...charms...before.

During her last few matches through time, Kiko's abilities had glitched. One match, Dr. Mathew McCall, received an extra trip because it was her fault she'd almost had him killed. Others were shorted their needed time to accomplish the mission Kiko had given them. Thankfully, they all worked out in the end. But slowly the headaches started.

At first they were a minor annoyance like eye strain that she could wait-out or nap-away, but the last one built into a skull-splitting migraine, leaving her curled on the floor in the fetal position. She'd experienced such pain only once before, and she would've been happy to never relive it. Just like the headaches before, it faded away, but when this one did, it took her abilities with it. She'd tried every which way to use them again, but they'd vanished—no more matches and their destinies, no more tunnels through time. Kiko wouldn't complain about having normal sensation in her hand again. She didn't exactly love having her hand tingle like it was waking up for a century. If she'd known the side effects of the job, she might've passed on the opportunity.

She was kidding. That wouldn't have made her decline the offer.

Although, Chaos's micro body parts swirling around her living room was close.

At twenty years old, Kiko Takai had been a newlywed, and while the ink was still drying on her marriage license to Kiyoshi Takai, she became a widow. Deep in the bowels of grief, she had been approached by Chaos with the job of a lifetime. Nothing he'd said made sense, but her head was a churning mess, and the promise he'd made was as attractive as light to a moth—healing from her tragic loss. She grabbed onto that promise like her life depended on its warmth.

Kiko wanted to escape her devastating, meaningless existence and experience firsthand other people's true happiness. Only days had passed before her head cleared enough to realize her mistake, and then it was too late. Unlike her matches, where she gave them three chances to figure things out, Kiko would get no second chance. She didn't regret much in her long life, but she'd screwed up with Eric Woodson. Kiko wanted a chance to explain everything to him. After all he'd done for her, she owed him that much.

Abruptly, the Mystic Cloud of Dread ended its assault on her senses. Kiko panted and pressed a palm to her forehead in relief. She could live the rest of her life without experiencing that again.

Chaos was here.

"You're finished, kid," the deep rumbling voice of her boss said. No doors opened or closed, no footsteps nor doorbells. Chaos in the flesh—sort of—stood in her living room—all jade green eyes and clean-shaven jaw. He still wore the trench coat, and it was still ridiculous now during a scorching July summer as it had been during a snowy March.

"My abilities are gone. Am I fired?" Kiko asked.

"More like retired," Chaos said gently.

She'd never left a job from an inhuman...being...before, and it was terrifying. "Now what? Am I going to age rapidly and die? I know a hundred and twenty years is more than what humans usually get, but it still feels like...not enough."

"Just as your contract has been fulfilled, your pause on aging has ended. You'll resume a normal life span."

"After a century of doing and seeing things humans couldn't even dream of, I can't 'retire', but life has moved on without me. I'm a ghost, effectively dead, to the people who knew me. Where do I fit in? What am I going to do now?" Since the pause on her humanity ended, her emotions—starting with panic—were crawling out of a dusty locked box in her head. Kiko didn't like the feeling of lost control.

Chaos's lips pulled into a smile. His celebrity-white teeth had never changed. "Do whatever humans do."

Not one for overexplaining, as usual. "So that means my periods are returning?" Kiko grumbled to herself.

Chaos lifted his brows but didn't respond.

Kiko had passed the decades as the visions directed her from one pair of clients to the next, strolling through time as she'd needed and sometimes as she'd wanted. No matter how many futures she saw, her own and her loved ones were blocked—probably to spare her the pain she'd been promised would heal away. She'd visited her parents a few times to keep their suspicions at bay. She'd visited Yoshi's grave, but he never responded to her ramblings, naturally.

The one person she wanted to visit was her closest friend, and after Yoshi's death, her best supporter. Every time she'd appeared on his doorstep, she'd been unable to decide how to explain her new reality to him. She visualized disbelief, panic, and anger at imagined lies. Then one day, when she decided not to be afraid any longer, she found out he had gotten married. The news struck her with a surprising pain, which confused her more than anything because they were just friends. Since then, she'd left Eric alone to respect his new happy life.

"So now what?" Kiko asked, drawing a blank on what was to come.

"I will send you whenever you want, but not before the time you were recruited."

Kiko frowned. The thought hadn't occurred to her to change her own past, to save Yoshi's life and rewrite her own history. She dug around for the right feeling but couldn't quite stick a finger on it. Was she upset by having to move on from her short marriage or relieved to never see Roger Meyer again? Deep down she knew going back wasn't possible with time paradoxes—never mind her goof with Dr. Mathew McCall. Chaos hadn't reprimanded her for it, and she had no intention of admitting her mistake. "I understand. Otherwise there'd be two Kikos running around. On second thought, that might be really handy."

Chaos gave her a knowing smile. "Always the quick one."

"You know what I'm going to say, so why ask?"

Chaos had given her the ability to see into the future, and he'd taken it away, so it was reasonable to assume he knew everything. Amusement danced on his lips. "You know my stance on free will. I need you to verbalize your request."

Something something in the fight against his brother Order, who was strictly into fascism. Kiko's Love Curator position entitled her to no pay, as she'd been warned, but she'd figured out a way to sustain herself with choice investments and timing. But now she had the rest of her mortal life to support herself without her abilities. She'd made a nice chunk of change, but if she wanted to be fully secure and have the freedom to explore her new life, she knew just the right time to go. "Nineteen ninety-five." The dot com bubble was just forming.

"As you request—"

"Wait." She cut him off. "Can I settle my affairs in 1988 first? I have a rental to empty, professors to acknowledge, bills to pay. A life to clean up."

The corner of his lips lifted, and he snapped his fingers.

Kiko's vision wavered like a pebble tossed into a calm pond

while her stomach roiled. She forcefully exhaled while bending at the waist, pressing her hands just above her knees. She hadn't experienced it from this side before, but once was enough to satisfy the curiosity.

After a blink, the living room she used to share with her roommate April McCall, flipped from white walls and mismatched college furniture into lime green with orange accents, doilies, bronze sconces, and way too many overgrown plants. Oh, shit.

In 1988, her rental house belonged to someone else.

Chapter 2

1988, Green Bay, Wisconsin

Kɪᴋᴏ ᴛɪᴘᴛᴏᴇᴅ ᴏᴜᴛ ᴛʜᴇ front door while listening and watching for witnesses. Last thing she needed was to be arrested and tossed in jail for breaking and entering. She should have seen that coming, but with her visions gone, the obvious was no longer obvious. The safety net of vanishing into different times when trouble appeared was gone. Kiko needed to be very careful.

With keys, wallet, and two different generations of cell phones in her pockets, she called a local cab and hitched a ride to the airport. Traveling in the slow mortal fashion would take some frustrating time to get used to, but any flight was more pleasant than a three-hour cab ride. Once she landed in Milwaukee, she hailed another cab. Tires rumbled over the uneven pavement, and a dreadful mix of affection and fear swirled through her as she approached the house she'd shared with her husband, Yoshi. Her hands trembled in anticipation of memories becoming fresh all over again.

"Hey, what day is it?" Kiko asked the driver.

"Thursday," he responded with a glance in his rearview mirror.

"The date, I mean."

He quirked a brow at her and said, "April twenty-second."

"Thanks." According to the cab driver, it had been one month of linear time since Chaos visited her with the job opportunity of a lifetime. Now she knew what to expect. Kiko tossed a few bills at the driver and hopped out.

The light blue house on the corner lot was the same as she remembered it. The shrubs were still overgrown, the creepy house next door was still empty, and the sidewalk still uneven. Kiko watched her footing on the jagged sidewalk and remembered when she'd first come to Yoshi's house. In the dark, she had tripped on one of the raised concrete squares, and he'd caught her by the hand. It was the first contact they'd made, and her heart skipped a beat like a nervous teenager. Instead of those flutters of excitement, a hollowness of dread filled her as she approached the house she once considered home. Stepping inside would be the hardest thing she would've done in decades.

Kiko squeezed her eyes shut and unlocked the door. Stale air choked her lungs, and the scent of Yoshi's dilapidated carpet rushed her nose. She forced her hand to flick on the light switch, and her eyes darted to the space above the mantle, where Yoshi's prized katana had been displayed. The space was empty, the sword likely still in police custody. Her gaze shifted to the spot on the linoleum where Yoshi had been impaled through the chest, bleeding, dying. This part of her was so long ago. She felt detached, like she was reliving someone else's life and memories or like a bad dream that wouldn't go away.

Near the fireplace hung a framed photo collage of her, Yoshi, and their best friend Eric Woodson. That night bowling was one of her favorite memories, and Eric thoughtfully gifted her the collection of photographs after Yoshi's death. Eric's glossy smile on three-by-fives curved her melancholy lips. She shifted her gaze to the kitchen table, where they'd had a store-bought, super late Thanksgiving dinner. He was so thoughtful. He'd supported her and held her through the pain until Chaos appeared. Eric was something special, and although they had been friends, his marriage still stung.

If she hadn't disappeared, would Kiko have been invited?

If she hadn't disappeared, would it have been his and hers instead?

Kiko brushed away those stupid thoughts. Friends, bonded over the loss of a person they both held dear. He'd kissed her lightly on her cheek. Kiko's fingers found just the spot. It was a kiss of desperation, of thanks, of who-knew-what, but she never forgot it.

Eric had a girlfriend at the time.

Dwelling on things she couldn't change was pointless. Time to get to work. She collected leftover empty boxes from the closet and packed her own stuff separate from what remained of Yoshi's. His parents took everything they wanted of his, leaving her with clothes, personal items, and a few pictures and books. She kept a couple mementos and pictures and piled up the rest for donation.

After Yoshi passed, Kiko couldn't handle taking the bus—too many memories and too many episodes of her breaking down in public, so she bought a baby blue Bronco. It still sat in the driveway. She loaded up the donations and delivered them to the local Salvation Army. When she returned, she hauled all their mismatched college-special furniture curbside.

Kiko wrote a letter with the next month's rent check describing her intent to move out with the expiring lease. After the crime scene cleaners had left, the place was spotless. With her living alone and frequent visits from Eric, the place was only dusty. Kiko loaded her personal belongings into the Bronco, ready to say goodbye to this life. Kiko flicked off all the light switches, left behind her keys, and mailed her notice. While driving, Kiko left voicemails for her instructors, explaining she couldn't finish classes and apologizing for waiting so long to drop the semester.

It was too late for a refund, but Kiko didn't need it.

Her parents were still here in Milwaukee. An urge to say goodbye in person nagged at her. She hadn't seen them in eighty years, but to them, she had visited about two months ago. Still, Kiko wasn't sure she wanted to see them, but the dutiful daughter prevailed, and she drove to their house and rang the doorbell unannounced.

THE SIMPLEST PECK ON the cheek haunted him. Not that Eric Woodson shouldn't have done it. No, he wanted Kiko to know the faintest dusting of how he felt about her, but he could no longer look his girlfriend in the eye. Eric was no cheater. He should've ended things before his feelings for Kiko grew so far, but he was caught off-guard. From the moment Yoshi had introduced Eric to Kiko, he'd been drawn to her. But as his best friend's girlfriend, he kept his heart walled against what it wanted.

He respected Yoshi too much.

But after he'd tragically died, Eric could think of nothing else but being at Kiko's side, helping her through the pain, pulling her back above the drowning despair, and showing her beautiful things could still happen in the face of such misery.

He wanted Kiko Takai to be happy. That was his greatest wish.

Eric walked out of his door as a freshly single man, energy pumping through him. That wall he'd built over his heart shattered into bits and blew away with the breeze tousling his hair. Despite Kiko's current state and her not answering the phone, despite Yoshi's death still hurting, Eric found a sliver of hope.

He expected Kiko to be in another fit of uncontrollable pain. Rather than disturb her with another attempt at calling, Eric drove to the nearest grocery store and bought her favorite—broccoli and steak. Would it be too much for her if he had a brand new grill delivered to her house?

He pictured her trying to drag herself out of bed to answer the delivery man's arrival, and Eric couldn't do that to her. With food in hand, he went straight to her house. The sight squeezed his chest. Kiko and Yoshi's furniture was lined up along the curb of their front yard, and a little at the corner. He parked in their driveway, and her Bronco was gone.

Eric's breaths tore from his chest. Leaving the food behind, he rushed up to her front door and knocked. "Kiko? Kiko are you in there?"

No answer.

"Kiko? I need to see you."

Still no answer.

Eric lifted a rock and used the spare key to open the door. He called into the darkened space. "It's just me. Everything's going to be okay. I haven't heard from you, and I'm worried. I hope classes aren't that brutal."

Eric turned on the lights, and he sucked in a breath.

He shouldn't have kissed her. At her most vulnerable point, he'd gone too far, and now he was too late.

Kiko was gone.

She'd left without saying goodbye.

Eric's arms fell to his sides, and he focused on trying to breathe.

KIKO SHIFTED HER WEIGHT from one foot to the other. As her mom opened the door, it was too late to run. Kiko's spine stiffened.

Mom brightened. "Hi, honey. Good to see you out and about. Come on inside."

Kiko followed her mom into the living room. The house smelled foreign to her—a seasoning blend, perhaps. There was a perfectly good reason why Kiko had subsisted on Pop-Tarts when she'd lived with her parents. Mom couldn't cook unless the preferred temperature was well-burned and the flavor on the wrong side of charred. The guilt over staying for dinner was one reason why she never wanted to visit.

Dad was becoming one with the recliner as usual, and some basketball game made a racket on the TV. "Kiko, how're you holding up?" he asked, keeping his eyes on the screen.

Kiko's parents pitied her loss, but since they thought she was too young to marry, their apologies were superficial, and the sooner she 'got over it', the better. Minutes after leaving the past behind her, Dad had to drag it back up. Thankfully, she'd had a century to 'get over it'. This callousness would be another reason why she never wanted to visit.

"I'm doing okay."

"How's school?" Mom asked. "I haven't heard about your grades. Did you hear back from any grad schools yet?"

And there was the next reason why she didn't want to visit. Her parents both inspired and hindered her career dreams by encouraging her to apply herself, while fighting so much Kiko couldn't study. She should've completed undergrad next month, but Kiko saw no point in finishing. Yoshi's death left her brain a mushy haze, incapable of attending classes and working on her senior project. She could hardly smile for the customers at the Gap. "I dropped out."

Three simple words transformed Kiko from a child back on the track of obedience to the black sheep of the family. Mom gasped and covered her open mouth with her hand, while Dad's gaping flytrap was left on full display.

"You've been pushing toward grad school for years. Why on earth would you quit during your last semester of undergrad?" Mom asked.

Because she'd become a time traveler, matchmaking couples through history for a century while becoming a multi-millionaire. After that, school seemed so...unsatisfying. What would they say to that? "I'm going a new route."

Mom popped a disapproving brow. "And what's that?"

During her temporary immortality, Kiko had plenty of time to explore all the subjects that interested her. Some lasted a few weeks, others much longer, but none stuck around longer than a decade. The one thing still of interest she hadn't yet tried was finding a home for all the wonderful romance stories she'd transcribed as they happened before her eyes. She kept the stack of red journals in storage. Publishing was her new goal, a chance to show the world she made a difference, that she mattered. But Kiko couldn't tell her mother she wanted to publish all her manuscripts, because where did she find the time to write so many? "Writing."

"Like newspaper articles?" Mom asked.

"Close enough."

"That's interesting," Dad said without any enthusiasm. "Stay for dinner?"

Kiko's stomach knotted. She checked her watch, being careful with her technology for the time she was in. A promise of several hours was several hours too long to spend catching up in an area of her life she wanted to forget. Besides, the topic of conversation wouldn't be conducive to choking down unappetizing char. "I'm between places at the moment, and I need to find somewhere to settle."

"You never told us you were moving," Dad said, finally peeling his eyes from the screen. "But makes sense you don't want to stay in your house."

"Is that what you've been up to these last few months?" Mom asked.

"Just looking for a fresh start. The Bronco's all packed."

"Okay, honey," Mom said. "Keep in touch."

Kiko gave her parents a sad smile. In their eyes, she was a twenty-year-old college dropout, but even when she wasn't, they never showed any support beyond requiring career success. Without that, she was less than nothing. Case in point: they didn't offer Kiko her old bedroom to get her bearings after Yoshi's death. They didn't wish her well or say they were proud of her for finding the strength to move on. They didn't offer to help carry boxes or furniture. They didn't even offer leftovers, but she wouldn't have accepted them anyway.

The only time her parents were happy and not fighting was after she'd moved out. Mom even praised Yoshi for sweeping Kiko out of their house. With a choked voice, Kiko waved and said, "Will do. 'Bye."

Mom went to the kitchen, where dinner definitely smelled long-overdone, and Dad returned his attention to the screen.

Kiko let herself out the front door and climbed into the Bronco. They didn't even ask where she was going. Kiko was ready to move on to her new life, and her parents weren't going to be a part of it. A weight lifted off her shoulders as she backed the Bronco out of the driveway. There was only one person in Milwaukee she hated to leave, but after Eric Woodson got married, she'd promised herself she wouldn't bother him, and just because that hadn't happened yet, who was she to interfere with the future destined for him?

While Kiko gassed up the SUV for the drive north to Green Bay, the tiny embellishment she'd given her parents popped back into her head. She really did need to find a publisher for her stories. Then she'd continue to write, because she had a few of her own to tell.

Maybe on her journey to return to a normal human life, she'd even make some friends or find someone...more.

Chapter 3

1995, Green Bay, Wisconsin

Eric Woodson was not a gambling man. As the vice president of finance, he trusted numbers; the math always made sense. But today, he considered buying a lottery ticket.

Eric dropped his presentation documents onto his desk and eased into his chair. Instead of frantically assembling new charts with several scenarios to vouch for his data, Eric threaded his fingers together and marveled at his luck. He'd just given the budget for a client's debut novel, and his wife, the director of marketing, hadn't fought him on it. Eric couldn't think of a single time in their history that had happened.

Then the Chief Executive Officer of Blue Feather Publishing, Paul Woodson, kept quiet. His dad hadn't argued with him or sided with Amanda. Eric's stern old man had been genuinely accepting and calm over the figures and projections. This kind of luck had never happened before, and although his flush bank account wasn't hurting, a lottery ticket seemed like a wise choice today. He still had a mortgage on the palatial suburban home Amanda had wanted.

That thought brought a cloud over Eric's mini celebration. Eight years ago, Eric pictured his life much differently than it turned out. But wasn't that always the case? Big dreams died hard, and Eric's were no exception. When his father bought this publishing house and insisted Eric move to Green Bay and put his new college skills to use, Eric struggled. He'd already had a new phone number, a new address, and a new vehicle. How was Kiko Takai ever going to find him?

Then Dad wanted to move across the state to a smaller city.

But Kiko wouldn't answer Eric's calls. She'd packed up and vanished without a word. Eric thought their friendship meant he deserved at least a goodbye, but he'd crossed a line and chased her away. Seven years had passed since he last saw her, and not a day went by without him thinking of her...of regretting kissing her.

Not the kiss itself, but the timing.

Eric leaned forward and lifted his most treasured possession—a photograph. Eric affectionately rubbed his thumb along the frame of one of his happiest memories. Eight years ago, he, Kiyoshi Takai, and Kiko Hada were arm in arm at the bowling alley, all smiles of youthful innocence. Kiko's radiant face with a beaming smile held center stage. Eric's gaze was turned toward her with a big goofy grin, and Yoshi made a silly face while extending his arm up to take the photo. That night, he and Yoshi were neck-and-neck on the scoreboard. Despite warning them both of her bumper-friendly skills, Kiko knocked down pins without one.

Everything had been perfect, except Yoshi and Kiko were in love, and Eric was the good friend—the backup protector, only admiring her from afar.

His office door swung wide, and the snarl on Amanda's face meant the uncharacteristic amiability was over. This was rampage Amanda, arms full of papers and clearly on a mission.

Eric had everything most people could ask for—a status car, a motorcycle to drool over, a house with its own zip code, and fat bank accounts. Although he'd prefer a career where he wasn't under his dad's thumb, he couldn't complain. He was envied by those who wished to have what he possessed. He was respected by those in the same tax bracket. But since Eric had grown up affluent, he didn't measure success by things.

There were some things money couldn't buy.

As his wife approached, Eric set the photograph safely back on his desk so she wouldn't notice it and grow angrier.

Amanda flung the papers at his desk, almost like a Frisbee, knocking over his most treasured photograph. Eric frowned, made a point to slide the papers aside, and settled the photo frame back on its legs where it belonged.

The regular Mr. Hyde somehow transformed into Dr. Jekyll

for a morning. Eric wanted to know what the secret serum was. He said carefully, "So, you and Dad were both unusually...agreeable this morning. What happened?"

Amanda pointed to the papers with a smile on her face. "Consider yourself served."

Served with what? Eric spun the stack around and skimmed. Petition to File Divorce. His eyes searched for the named petitioners. Good thing he didn't waste money on a lottery ticket after all. "What's this?"

"I saved myself the process server fee, because I was curious how you'd react," Amanda said.

Eric blinked. So many thoughts wanted to rush through his mind all at once they snagged. He croaked out the first thing he could, "You served me at work?"

Amanda looked him up and down, lips twisted in disappointment. "I should've paid the fee." She spun on her high heels and slammed his office door shut on her way out, rattling the frames on the walls.

Eric looked at the papers again in disbelief. They were here, and they were real. He'd always made her happy. Whatever she wanted, she got. It didn't make sense. What did he do wrong?

Three years ago, when he'd first met the new director of

marketing, he'd been unable to resist the statuesque blonde with drive and charisma. Amanda Carter was beautiful, and she was forward in her desire for him. He'd pictured them as a power couple living in a penthouse with a scenic view of the city, taking global vacations every few months with a private nanny for their children.

Not long after they'd gotten together, his dad pulled him into his office and said, "Son, trust me from experience, don't dip your pen in company ink."

Mom, who used to be Dad's secretary, ran off with the pool boy, claiming Dad was too busy during the day and never home at night to give her the attention she needed. Dad's experience with interoffice relationships was different. Mom worked for Dad to be supportive, while Amanda worked alongside Eric competitively. Therefore, to a late twenty-something with a high-powered career and more money than brains—hey, he was mature enough to recognize it—Dad's experience had been irrelevant. A starry-eyed Eric ignored the warning, and now he could hear the 'I told you' so ringing in his ears.

Just like Mom and Dad's split, now the awkwardness of Eric and Amanda divorcing would threaten their professional relationship. One of them was going to have to leave, and just like Mom, it would have to be Amanda. Maybe that was why she'd been amiable this morning. With her resignation looming, she had no reason to fight any longer.

An alert chimed on his desktop.

Pushing the documents aside and opening the shared server directory on his computer, Eric scrolled through the latest report of revenues from the month's new releases, and his projections had been spot-on. After a quick self-pat on the back, he opened the Expenses by Department file. Blue Feather Publishing was well into the black. Dad had made the right choice in buying this place. But one department above all others had costs out of control—a column filled with red cells in the spreadsheet.

Eric rubbed the crease forming across his forehead. Dealing with Amanda's departmental spending was like bashing his head against the wall and expecting it to move. Useless. Painful. Frustrating. A waste of time. As much as he looked forward to the life he wanted, a piece of him—an enormous piece—missed the old carefree days of going to college, breaking kendo shinais at the dojo, and bowling with his best friend Yoshi. Eric gazed at his treasured photo and smiled as memories of them laughing, talking, and sharing meals warmed his heart. Then the visions darkened to Roger Meyer making advances...Eric shook his head, refusing to allow that...that man to ruin his day. Eric used the term very loosely.

Amanda had questioned his love for the photo several times, but Eric brushed her intrusion off. At least he wouldn't have to defend himself any longer. Eric lifted his twenty-four-karat gold pen, a work anniversary gift, while he read through the documents, ready to start his life—not over, but fresher and wiser.

Maybe he should get that lottery ticket after all.

Chapter 4

1988, Green Bay, Wisconsin

AT A STORAGE RENTAL place she knew would survive many decades into the future, Kiko climbed out of the Bronco and stretched her sore legs and aching back. Songbirds chirped overhead and several doves perched on the powerlines. It was a warm spring afternoon, and the grass had just turned green. Many trees still hadn't opened their leaves yet. Mother Nature was just waking up to her full potential. Kiko entered the claustrophobic office.

A radio played rock and roll music from the 1950s. An elderly man sat behind the front desk, bobbing his head with the rhythm, lips silently forming the words. And then came the air guitar. Kiko smiled. He reminded her of a fun-loving grandpa, something she'd never experienced firsthand. A thread of loneliness wove through her.

"Good afternoon, miss. What can I do ya for?" he asked, dropping his fingers from the imaginary fret.

"Can I rent one of the smallest units you have?"

"Five by ten it is. How long do you want?" The wrinkly old man smiled with loose jowls.

Kiko counted on her fingers the months and years to cover the bill until 1995. She hoped the man would live that long. "Eighty-five months."

His bushy gray brows popped, showing faded gray eyes. "That's a mighty long time there, miss. Are you sure?"

Kiko chuckled to herself. In modern times, that was a standard car loan. "I'm sure."

"If you insist."

Kiko wrote him a check and drove her Bronco down to her assigned door. She unloaded the boxes of things she hadn't needed for nearly a century—pots and pans and extra clothes, namely. The old photos and her favorite Michael J. Fox poster were pieces of her that hadn't existed for so long. She was a different person now, but she didn't have the heart to trash them, and she didn't want to. For some reason those parts of her life still clung to her.

An image of Eric Woodson popped into her mind.

It had nothing to do with him! she internally yelled at herself.

Because it did.

Kiko sighed. With the Bronco unloaded, she slipped into the driver's seat and steered toward her and April's rental house in the present year. The historic district in Green Bay was a sight to behold. Victorian-age homes dotted the landscape, right next to gas stations, parks, hospitals, and fast food restaurants. She parked at the curb and hoped the occupants hadn't seen her or remembered her mysteriously sneaking through their orange and lime green living room. The house's sunshine color with ornate trim reminded Kiko of quieter times—not that she'd give up modern convenience for that—no way. After experiencing life at so many social and technological advancements as a figurative ghost, Kiko preferred city life. She didn't want to be invisible anymore.

She didn't want to be alone anymore.

Kiko stepped out of the Bronco and put her hands on her hips. "Now what?" she said to herself. The rest of her stuff was in that house, but over thirty years into the future. As if a beacon was activated, her vision blurred, and her stomach flipped around. Kiko closed her eyes and pressed a palm against her Bronco for stability. In a blink, she tipped off balance. Her Bronco was gone, but she was still at the curb.

Present Day, Green Bay, Wisconsin

KIKO TURNED IN PLACE as if some thief stood nearby cackling, but it wasn't no thief. "What the hell?" she asked nothing and everything at once.

"It's not hell." Chaos appeared before her and handed her a ticket. "But this bill might be. Your Bronco was towed a while ago, but with the power of time travel at your fingertips for a century, I bet you can handle it." Chaos pointed to the space where her now-missing vehicle had been.

"It wasn't sold at auction?"

"I made sure it wasn't."

Grumbling under her breath, Kiko said, "Yeah, I can cover it, but I need a ride."

"I think you can handle that too."

Chaos was an immortal with debatable tangibility and far more important matters to attend than Kiko's retirement. "Yeah, I can. I appreciate the favor, but why are you here?"

"I thought I'd give you the same courtesy you gave your clients."

Understanding the implications, Kiko's blood chilled. "Are you saying I have three tries to save my true love?"

"I promised you the time to heal and a reward at the end of your service. The game you made was creative, but since we're both fully aware of it, yes, three tries there and back again. But you already used one and you haven't even found him yet."

Chaos's promises had been a major factor in her accepting the job, but now she had to earn her reward. Figures. But knowing a second chance was within grasp had her heart soaring with excitement. There was a true love out there for her. Just the thought was overwhelming—to experience the touch and love of another, to share lives and memories, and especially to not be lonely anymore. Watching matches screw up thousands of different ways, she was a master of the game she'd created. "I told my clients who they needed to save. Will I get the same courtesy?"

He chuckled, his deep bass rumbling in her ears. "That's too easy for you, and not so much fun for me."

"You get enjoyment out of this?" Kiko was horrified.

"Didn't you?"

"I hated to see them suffer. I gave them the chances they needed to fight through the pain and find love. I cheered for that happy ending."

"And that's what makes you human." Chaos smiled reassuringly. "You win. I'll give you a clue, but you're not going to like it."

Kiko didn't like anything about this except the promise of a second chance at happiness.

"The man of interest to you has an enemy. If you leave

him be, you'll both be miserable but alive. Seeking your happily ever after will risk both your lives. So that's your first choice—whether you want to risk your life for love."

A long pause followed. That was nothing to go on. Kiko asked, "That's it?"

"When the time comes, you'll figure it out. You were one of my favorite Love Curators, and I'd hate to lose you to a pair of vengeful humans."

That was another clue. If she kept asking questions, maybe more would come out. "I'd hate to lose me too. Putting your favorite Curator in danger must keep you up at night."

"I don't sleep, kid, but you did a great job with those matches. Almost no one had a psychotic episode."

Kiko bit her lower lip. "Oh. That's good, I suppose."

"Better statistics than most. So, I'll see you next time you need me."

"Wait," she said. "Can I have an emergency responder?"

Chaos smiled. "Not yet. I'll be watching." With a single blink he was gone.

Kiko dragged out her smartphone and used an app to catch a ride over to the impound lot. It would've been cheaper to buy a new Bronco, but she paid the ridiculous fee for the convenience. She drove back to her rental house, now hers and April's, and packed up her stuff there too. Luckily, a previous client, Mathew McCall, had already emptied out all his sister's things after he'd found out where April went. Now both siblings were living their happily ever afters with great jobs and families of their own—in two different centuries. Kiko was happy for them, for all her matches.

With her next rental all packed, Kiko went online to pay her last month's rent and give notice that she wasn't renewing their lease. Smartphones were leagues better than old flip phones, but she'd endure the nineties for a shot at the dot com bubble.

Kiko loaded up the Bronco with the rest of her stuff, and she stared down the heavy boxes full of books she'd written. After taking a breather, she started the arduous process of hauling them all into the Bronco. She drove her stuff to the same storage unit rental facility. The same old fun-loving grandpa was perched behind the desk, the same old 1950s music thrumming behind him. This time the music was louder, his hair thinner, and his brows bushier.

She renewed the rental for just a month and left herself a note that in about thirty years, her rental would expire. Kiko had every intention of emptying it long before then. With a friendly nod, and a second's glance of recognition on the old man's part, Kiko ducked out of the office and drove her second life's stuff around the corner to the same storage unit. Everything she'd packed in here from 1988 was so dusty. Where she was going, the mess wouldn't be so bad.

Kiko unloaded everything but the books. If she was going to publish them, how was she going to get them back to 1995? This was beyond Mathew's dirt, April's manacles, and Becca's duffel bag of books going through the time tunnel. Verity and Jonathan Arris each crossed over by hugging the person holding the emergency transponder. Kiko didn't have one, and how was she going to hug hundreds of books?

Kiko climbed in next to them, and bear-hugged the stacks of boxes, feeling like an idiot. But before she went to her 'retirement' year, she needed to know something. Her ability to sleep at night depended on it. Kiko slipped her smartphone out of her pocket and ran an internet search for her husband's murderer. She tapped the newspaper article with her finger.

"Greenleaf, Wisconsin. Convicted felon Roger Meyer from Milwaukee, Wisconsin, was shot dead at The Wounded Soldier during a fight. Meyer had served seven years in prison for the slaying of Kiyoshi Takai. Three suspects were arrested..." Kiko trailed off and squeezed her phone.

The murderer only serving seven years of his sentence pissed her off, but at least he got what he deserved in the end. Kiko checked the year on the article—1995. Shit. Well, she only needed to avoid that bar and she'd have no troubles.

Kiko replaced her phone in her pocket and hugged the boxes again. "Chaos? If you can hear me, 1995, as requested."

Kiko's vision rippled, and her stomach quivered. She pinched her eyes shut, and when she opened them, a gun pointed at her through the window of her Bronco's tailgate.

Chapter 5
1995, Green Bay, Wisconsin

In the middle of unshackling himself from his unpredictable wife, a tapping at his office door lifted Eric's head. He'd been too blindsided by the whole thing to be angry at the disruption. "Come in."

Eric's assistant, sweet and shy Caroline, with her short pixie hair, wide doe eyes, and small curvy lips, popped through his doorway. Amanda had always been sharp with her, which for the longest time Eric thought was female rivalry in the male-dominated corporate ladder. But Eric couldn't figure out why Amanda would want to harm Caroline's career. An office assistant didn't threaten a director of marketing. He could only guess his wife was jealous of Caroline's time with him, which was nonsense.

"The two p.m. is starting soon," Caroline said, blinking her big doe eyes. She popped her hip toward him with a hand on the curve to accent her delicate waist, but he ignored the unusually flirty body language. She added, "Do you want me to delay them?"

Eric checked the clock on his desktop. He had one minute to get over to the conference room. It wasn't like him to get distracted, but he had a damned good excuse today. "Cece's? No, I'll be there in a flash."

Amanda wasn't much for privacy if the information could get her something. Caroline's blatant message proved the corporate grapevine was healthy and well-fed, and very soon the whole building would find out. The sooner Amanda quit, the sooner the grapevine would nourish itself on someone else's private problems.

Eric collected armfuls of paperwork and rushed down the hall, blowing past his assistant. The conference room seated four important people. Paul Woodson sat at the head of the table. Fred Carter, vice president of marketing, whose daughter Eric was in the process of divorcing, had seated himself on the left. Amanda Carter sat next to him with a smug smile on her lips, and finally Todd Stammer, the agent representing a future bestselling author on the right. Eric nodded to everyone and slipped into the seat across from his dad at the foot of the table.

"Nice of you to join us," Dad said, and Eric didn't miss the undertone of annoyance.

Eric arranged his handouts and passed them around the table. He flicked on the laptop wired to the table, and the PowerPoint on the white projection screen lit up the room.

Caroline poked her head inside and flicked the lights off with a wink. Steam came from Amanda's ears, and Eric suppressed a chuckle, relieved to have someone else be the target of Amanda's ire for the moment.

"Todd, thank you for coming," Eric said. "Shame Cece couldn't make it."

Todd acknowledged his pleasantries with a nod, and Eric continued, "I'll be presenting the budget we have assembled for Cece's latest novel, and afterward, Amanda will go over the marketing plan using my projections." He intoned the 'my' just enough as a statement for Amanda, but the others didn't notice.

Amanda crossed her arms and shot daggers at him with her eyes.

Eric walked through the presentation figures based on projected sales and predicted expenses. "Here's the juicy part," Eric said and Todd chuckled. The others weren't amused. "Cece will receive her advance delivered in three equal payments on the following three dates, provided all contract terms have been met."

Todd's gaze followed the pointer on the screen. "Looks good. Cece will be pleased."

Eric tipped his head to Amanda. "And now for the marketing plan. Amanda?"

His future ex-wife took the floor. "Good afternoon, Todd. It is too bad Cece couldn't be here today, because I have exciting news for you and her. We've secured orders from a couple of national department store chains and confirmed our printers can handle the quantity. For ads, we have a full-page spread planned in Newsweek magazine, several newspaper interviews scheduled, and a book tour." She babbled on, and Eric watched her mouth move, but he didn't listen to her words. It was always the same plan with minor changes depending on the genre and number of orders.

Todd nodded in key areas and scribbled notes on a pad of paper.

Blue Feather Publishing, a small fish in the publishing world, was currently at its peak in gross revenues since Dad bought it out and turned it around. Eric was expected to take over when Dad retired someday, but he was a numbers guy through and through. He didn't want to be CEO, but he couldn't disappoint Dad and spit on the privilege he'd been gifted. All day long the employees were busy, phones rang, and printers hummed. There was a life force in this building. Even Amanda seemed in her element here, where her excitement and charisma shined, so Eric was surprised she'd be willing to quit to save face. She technically hadn't admitted her intentions, but there was no other option here.

"Eric," Amanda said with a scowl.

Everyone stared at him. "What?"

"We don't agree with your projections. To market Cece to her fullest potential and maximize revenues, I need a bigger budget," Amanda said with a glint in her devious eye.

"We've done this before, Amanda. The orders from the stores are not final. If we get returns...that cuts into the budget. We can reevaluate after initial sales reports are in."

Todd's brow furrowed.

"Cece is under contract for a trilogy. Book one needs a bigger budget." Amanda crossed her arms.

"The number of books expected to go to market doesn't change what the numbers are today."

Dad said, "Meeting adjourned. Thanks for coming, Todd. We'll keep you posted." Dad glared at Eric but said nothing.

Amanda was reckless, and Eric wanted to keep Blue Feather's doors open. Why he hadn't seen it before baffled him. He should've served her with divorce, but he was glad she pulled the trigger and opened his eyes.

Eric returned to his office, closed the door behind him, and sat at his desk. He sought Kiko's smiling face, and he relaxed. Now he was ready. Eric lifted his gold pen and scribbled out the remaining signatures at the tagged places before the next interruption delayed his freedom.

WITH THE BLANKET OF his life unraveling, Eric wanted to preserve some threads, while others he gladly snipped himself. Eric's soon-to-be-ex-wife had requested a last-minute Friday off, and like always, Amanda's dad had granted it to her. While she left for another girlfriend's retreat somewhere, Eric packed her things. Hey, he could be a nice guy. The divorce documents specified he kept the house, but he had to buy out her half of the equity. No problem. He had his upcoming bonus from Cece's launch to pay her off. Eric was surprised she'd rather have the cash, considering this was the house she'd chosen, but she was hardly home. Eric was the one who'd spent late nights and early mornings working to afford it for her. It was a classic sunk cost fallacy, but he didn't want all that time spent to be for nothing.

Giving her half the savings account stung a little more, but it was fair and a worthy sacrifice to remove her from his life. Snip, snip.

Boxes of clothes filled the foyer, and Eric needed a break. He had no idea she owned so many, since she had her own closet and they maintained separate finances, which turned out to be damned good luck now.

The doorbell rang, and Eric swung the front door wide, surprised to see his dad standing there. Dad didn't pay many social calls.

"Can I come in?" Dad asked.

Eric reluctantly stepped aside, not wanting to hear Dad's comments on the mess, and skeptical of the reason for his visit.

Dad's lips quirked into a smug smile. "I told you so."

Eric groaned and dragged a hand down his face. "If you came here to gloat, save it."

"I saw right through that girl, but you wouldn't listen. Look what it got you."

Dad's insults were like barbs yanking on raw flesh. "She works under you. If you could see through it all, why is she still employed at Blue Feather?"

Dad shrugged. "She does good work, and she looks good."

Eric was not going to dive into his Dad checking out his wife. That was one thread in the unraveling blanket he needed to spare.

"Besides," Dad continued. "It keeps Fred Carter satisfied, and I don't need to be on her father's bad side."

Eric frowned at the pathetic excuses. "You sound like they own you."

"See, son, that's what you haven't learned yet. If you treat your people well, they do good things for you, but if you dismiss what's happening under your nose, you create enemies."

"You're keeping the Carters happy because you're afraid of them?" Even more pathetic. The strong, cold, business-savvy image Eric had always held was beginning to unravel. What else had he been blind to?

"Don't dismiss fear as a weakness. It's intuition. Pay attention to it. Your gut just might save your life."

"Business isn't life and death. You take this all way too seriously." Images of his mother popped into his head. "Is that the real reason Mom left? She didn't share your...questionable...business ideas?"

"Leave your mother out of this," Dad warned.

Eric gritted his teeth. "What are you doing here?"

"I came to give you a warning, and ask a favor."

"Little late." Eric's hand waved over his packing progress. "And I'm busy."

"This isn't about that, but since you didn't heed my first

warning, maybe you'll listen this time."

Eric raked a hand through his hair, resigned to listen to whatever the newest office gossip entailed. "Want a drink?"

"Miller Lite, if you got it."

His dad followed him through the tiled foyer, down the hall, and into his expansive kitchen. He didn't know why Amanda insisted on remodeling it. Most of the shiny stainless steel appliances went unused. He opened the fridge door and tossed a can through the air, and Dad caught it. They both guzzled half their drinks before speaking.

"So what's the big warning this time?" Eric asked, more wanting the conversation over than actually caring what the scoop was.

"Something fishy is going down at Blue Feather. I only caught snippets here and there, but I'm listening to my gut and something isn't right. I want you to poke around, and tell me anything unusual that catches your ear."

"Care to share with the class what you've heard?"

Dad stood and settled the empty on the marble countertop. "Good luck packing up." He swiftly took his leave.

Well, Eric didn't put much stock in the company grapevine anyway, but if Dad was worried... Whatever. He had bigger fish to fry than whatever hot gossip Dad wasted time with.

Eric closed the door behind his dad and returned to packing. He had her dresser remaining and whatever accumulated under his bed. Yep, his bed. For the last several months, she'd been staying in one of the guest bedrooms, because she'd claimed he snored. At the time, he apologized and tried to make her as comfortable as possible, but after she'd handed him divorce paperwork, he wondered the real reason.

Eric scooped a handful of clothes from the bottom drawer of her dresser, and a plastic rectangle clattered to the floor. He dropped the clothes and turned the plastic container over in his hands. All the tiny foil squares were punched through. He popped open the lid with dread and checked the date on the prescription label inside the cover. This was a pack of birth control pills dated last month. Eric sucked in a deep breath, tears welling in his eyes, and he brought the empty pill pack to the foyer and placed it on top of the boxes. He wanted an explanation, and if she were home, he would demand it.

Since their wedding night, they'd tried to have children. Amanda knew he wanted a bunch of kids, a fabulous nanny to spoil them, and a penthouse condo he'd go home to after long nights at the office. He'd compromised on two of the three, and Amanda assured him she wanted the same crew of kids.

He could handle and dismiss so many things in the name of making Amanda happy, but this was the worst she'd ever done to him. Lying to his face all this time. The only thing keeping him on his feet was physically working to remove her from his life. He balled up her clothes and shoved them into more boxes while swiping away tears.

When she finally submitted her resignation, Eric was going to celebrate.

Chapter 6
1995, Green Bay, Wisconsin

THE STORAGE UNIT FACILITY hadn't changed much, except for a shaky pistol aimed at her through the back window of her Bronco. A man, perhaps in his early twenties, with a bandanna covering the lower half of his face and a backward baseball cap, stared at her with wide frightened eyes, but not as frightened as hers.

"What the hell just happened?" he yelled through the glass, voice breaking in panic. "Where did you come from? How did this car get here? Why is no one driving?" he turned his head, addressing someone else. "Travis, did you see this shit?"

Kiko followed his gaze.

Another young man, heavier-set, with his face and head just as obscured, ran past the terrified armed man, but this guy had his arms full of something. Kiko could only guess they robbed a storage unit. She had nothing of value to them in her Bronco, but she was a witness and Chaos hadn't given her an emergency responder.

"Why are you standing there, Sean?" Travis, the heavier-set man yelled, panting and struggling to keep everything in his arms. "Let's get out of here."

Warily, Sean lowered his trembling gun, and the two young men dashed to a waiting cranberry Geo Metro further down the row of storage units. When they slammed their car doors shut, the getaway driver squealed the wheels on the pavement.

Before Kiko could catch her breath, the fun-loving grandpa, with a snarl on his face to scare the socks off any child, rushed around her Bronco wielding a rifle. He released a single round, blowing out the back window of the Metro.

Kiko blew out her held breath and scrambled over the back seat and slipped behind the wheel. An emergency responder appeared on the passenger seat. Finally! Kiko slipped it into her pocket.

The not-so-fun-loving grandpa slammed his palm on the hood of her Bronco. "Where did you come from?" He moved to her driver's side window and tapped on the glass with the barrel of his gun, trying to make out her features through the tinted glass.

Reluctantly, Kiko rolled down the window and smiled awkwardly. "I was just stopping in to renew my rental. I don't have anything to do with whatever that was, and I didn't see anything."

Wise eyes studied her, and his brows lifted with recognition. "I remember you. Ya haven't aged a day. Well, come on in then."

Kiko climbed out of the Bronco, trembling, and she followed him inside.

"I was chasing those thieves and then you just...appeared...somehow. A solid few minutes of my memory blinked away at me. Seems to happen more often these days. Scary stuff, I tell ya. A piece of advice, young lady? Don't get old."

Kiko smiled. "I'll try not to." She never had aged, but after a century on this planet, growing old wasn't so scary anymore. She looked forward to experiencing and understanding the natural process while avoiding the frustrating ageism. Being treated as less than for simply being born a woman was one thing, but being treated as damned-near a child was a whole other beast she'd like off her back.

"You're lucky I saw you, or I might've shot those men right through your vehicle." The grandpa settled the rifle out of sight and perched behind the desk again. "And I'm sorry about the hood of your car. I'm just frustrated those hooligans have broken into the same storage unit three times now. If I can't stop them, everyone's going to collect their stuff and run, and I'll be out of business. They trust me with security. If I don't have their trust, I have nothing."

"You could retire and save yourself the stress."

The grandpa swatted at the air dismissively. "Retirement's for the birds."

Kiko understood that sentiment. At the counter, she renewed her storage unit for the next eighty-five months to get her through her earlier visit in the present year, and the grandpa gave her a discount in apology for the dent on her Bronco's hood.

With a friendly wave goodbye, Kiko jumped back into her Bronco, thankful it—and its battery—time jumped with her. Kiko started up the engine, and she cruised along the city streets. When she chose 1995 as her retirement gift from Chaos, she'd intended to make choice stock purchases just prior to build of the dot com bubble. But if her old boss tossed her into the game she'd created to find true happiness, she wasn't going to be hopping around in time as she'd wanted. Three chances, there and back again, and she'd already used one. That meant Kiko was going to need to be a functional human, and that meant she needed a home to go to. Kiko had been a transient for so many decades the idea of staying put both scared and excited her.

But this time, she'd find her own rental. Memories of Yoshi flashed through her mind, and Kiko couldn't help a small smile. Then Eric's face appeared in her mind, and instead of smiling, her chest squeezed with an ache of loneliness. She missed him. He was her best friend. Was she right to leave him? Could married people have friends of the same sex? Would Kiko be okay just as friends? Her trail of questions was pointless. She was moving forward.

Kiko drove toward the nearest gas station to pick up the day's classified ads, wishing her smartphone worked in this time for the convenience, when red and blue lights reflected into her eyes from the rearview mirror. Kiko couldn't think of anything she'd done wrong. Driving wasn't that hard, and she wasn't distracted...much. Kiko stopped at the curb and rolled down her window. She dug in the glove box for the documents the officer was going to ask for. That she didn't need the power of future sight to know.

The officer closed the distance and eyeballed her interior. "License and registration."

Kiko passed them through the window, completely puzzled about what she'd done wrong.

He read the information and added, "Do you know why I pulled you over?"

"No, sir."

"Driving is a privilege, and to do so requires drivers to pay fees in order to prove they're safe on the roads. Other fees, like your registration here, are required to help pay for the roads you drive on, and it also ensures the vehicle matches its plate, discouraging theft."

Kiko's stomach sank. Her registration was long since expired and her license pretty close to it. Passing an inane test in an office didn't prove she was a safe driver. The state just wanted money, but Kiko grumbled under her breath rather than argue the point.

"Registration isn't a fee you can pick and choose which years you pay. Frankly, I'm appalled no one caught you yet. Pay your fees or get off the road. This is your only warning. Next time I'm taking away your license."

"Yes, sir." Kiko accepted the ticket, and after he returned her documents, she drove off.

Now detoured from finding a home, Kiko drove to her bank for a new debit card. Then she went to the courthouse to pay the fine. After spending most of the day in her Bronco, she just wanted to crash on a comfortable bed and take a nap. But she still had to sit in line at the Department of Motor Vehicles for the next—she didn't know, three hours?—to get an updated registration sticker.

By the time she left the DMV and received plenty of tongue lashing from the clerk, the sky darkened. Kiko activated her smartphone's flashlight and attached the new sticker to her plate. Her arms pimpled with gooseflesh in the chilly summer night breeze.

At the nearest gas station, she finally collected the newspaper. Using the vehicle's interior light, she circled a few ads for apartments, and after a few phone calls, she had one appointment to view a place the next day.

In the meantime, Kiko found a motel with the vacancy sign lit, and she crashed on a smelly, scratchy bed. Before drifting off to sleep, Yoshi returned to her mind again. Kiko resolved to visit Yoshi tomorrow all the way back in Milwaukee.

Chapter 7

1995, Milwaukee, Wisconsin

In his best suit and holding a bouquet of flowers, Eric stood before the best friend he ever had. No matter where the winds of time swept him off to, Eric was still stuck in his head, haunted by the past. The summer air was unseasonably chilly, and the sun had been blotted out by clouds. It was fitting, the gloom of nature following him into the cemetery. The lines marking the perimeter of the rectangular hole had long since been grown over. Eric leaned down and placed the bouquet in the holder alongside the headstone. The florist had picked a cheery monochrome palate of purple this month, but Eric wasn't feeling cheery, and he was certain Yoshi wasn't either.

Eric's personal life was a mess. The problem was people divorced all the time; it was normal. Eric couldn't move on from the disappearing Kiko or murdered Yoshi, and he didn't know whether to laugh at the insanity or cry at the heartbreak. That wasn't normal. There, he acknowledged it, but he had no plans to deal with it.

"Another month has passed, Yoshi. The florist chose purple this time. I hope you like it. So how've you been?" Eric flicked a stray leaf aside, hoping, unreasonably, for an answer.

"I'm guessing you heard the news, but if not, Roger Meyer was released from prison. I couldn't believe it either, but at least he can't hurt you again. I think what bothers me the most—besides vigilante justice being a tad bit illegal—" Eric paused and allowed himself a smile of amusement, but it only lasted a few seconds, "is I wish I knew you were at peace on the other side."

A small breeze ruffled Eric's hair.

"I've got more news for you. It's happier news than a convicted murderer going free, I suppose. Amanda and I are splitting up. I just...I don't know. Now don't tell me 'I told you so'. I can't handle hearing that again."

No response, as expected.

Eric sighed. "All these years go by, and I keep striking out. How were you so lucky when we were so young?" Eric lowered a hand on the gravestone, aware of how idiotic that sounded. "Sorry, buddy. I didn't mean it that way."

Yoshi had been like a brother to Eric, two peas from the same pod—best friends, who spent years training in kendo together and sharing the triumphs and failures in their love lives. So it only made sense the day Kiko Hada walked into Yoshi's life, both of them were smitten. When Eric had met her, she'd been wearing her work uniform, a polo and khaki pants, while folding clothes at her retail job. The moment her gaze locked on his, Eric was lost, but since she was his best friend's girl, he'd respectfully held it all in. He'd constructed a wall to prevent her from reaching the full depths of his heart.

But Eric was no engineer. The wall had crumbled despite his best efforts. And when Yoshi died, he flew to her side. Eric helped Kiko through the tears, the pain, the questions, the longing. And her touch helped soothe him too. After a couple months, he could fight his feelings no longer, and he'd kissed her. He'd had a girlfriend at the time, and it was completely out of line. In embarrassment and shame, he bolted, and out of respect to his girlfriend, he dumped her.

When Eric returned to apologize to Kiko for being out of line, she'd disappeared. That haunted him still. What if he hadn't kissed her? Would they still be friends or would they be more? Eric didn't believe in fate or destiny, but there was something about that woman he couldn't shake.

He never got closure, but he believed that wasn't the real reason he held on.

He did wonder how much of his marriage to Amanda was affected by Kiko. Hard to say. He'd been genuinely attracted to the leggy blonde when he'd met her, but still, his mind kept returning to the one who got away. Maybe Amanda was justified in her jealousy. Still, if she'd just asked, Eric would've granted her an amicable divorce long ago.

In the end, he wished Kiko was in his life with her soft hands around Yoshi's neck while Eric longingly watched from afar, rather than have her missing and him dead. Was she suffering? Was she dead? He didn't know, and that was part of his fixation.

"From all the incredible luck you had in life and all your infinite wisdom on the other side, do you have any pointers for me?" Eric asked his silent friend.

Another breeze kicked up, giving Eric the chills. He stood. "I miss you, buddy. I hope everything is well for you down there or up above or wherever you are."

A soft gasp behind him turned Eric's head.

The sun's rays broke through the stifling clouds, lighting her raven hair like a dark halo. Her glistening eyes bore into his soul, and her lips parted just slightly with the same familiar shock he felt. Yoshi had finally answered his wishes. Yoshi had somehow found Kiko on the other side and delivered her to Eric for one last goodbye. Eric never believed in ghosts before, but he was damned well believing now.

Or had he finally lost his mind in his grief?

Not wanting to explore the truth, Eric only gazed upon her beautiful face, trying to hold back the tears of gratitude.

"Eric?" the angelic voice of Kiko asked.

He only stared. The sunlight blurred the edges of her smooth face. After all these years, she looked exactly the same as when he last saw her. He didn't know how to thank Yoshi enough, but this would have to do, "Thanks, buddy. I owe you one." Tears shamelessly fell down his cheeks.

"Eric, are you okay?" Kiko asked and stepped closer.

He didn't move, afraid the hallucination would vanish all over again.

Kiko's hand reached out and squeezed his forearm.

Eric stared at her delicate fingers in amazement. Could it be he could touch her? He lifted his own hand to test her corporeal strength. His cold skin landed directly on her hand, and the electric charge he felt every time he touched her returned.

It was almost as if she were...real.

"Kiko?" he whispered.

The corner of her lips lifted just a little. "It's me."

"You're alive?" As the thought registered and before she could answer the dumb question, Eric pulled her into a bear hug. Her scent filled his nose. Her hair tickled his face. Her body pressed tight up against his. She was here. "I never thought I'd see you again. I'm so sorry about everything." About Yoshi's death, about scaring her away, about not confessing his feelings, and probably a few other things he hadn't processed yet. Thank you, Yoshi, for sending her back to me, he thought.

Her arms squeezed him back, and a warmth flooded his body. He had a chance to explain everything to her.

"It's been a long time. Don't be sorry anymore." Kiko pushed him back to arm's reach and studied him. "Do you want to join me for coffee?"

"That sounds great."

Eric slowed his stride to keep pace with her, and his limbs tingled in hyperawareness. His brain failed to comprehend she was right next to him after all these years. They approached a Bronco straight out of the late eighties, and recognition kicked his brain. "Is this the same Bronco you bought after Yoshi died?"

"Same one."

Eric slipped into the passenger seat. "It's in perfect shape."

Kiko drove them to a local coffee shop, Espress Your Beans. "Some things never change."

Eric gazed upon her timeless face, uncertain where to begin with all the questions he had. He didn't want to scare her off right as he got her back. Kiko parked at the curb, and Eric opened the coffee shop door for her.

Kiko ordered a cappuccino while Eric just ordered a cup black, and all the while he couldn't help staring at her. He paid for their drinks, despite her objections. It was the least he could do.

They shared a small round table together, and his knees brushed against hers. Sparks of energy buzzed him wide awake long before the caffeine traveled to his brain.

"So what have you been up to?" he asked.

Kiko smiled and swirled her drink with a straw. "Working."

She didn't elaborate, and he couldn't help the disappointment. Why not a simple phone call or email? He hoped whatever work it was had been so demanding on her time that even one message to reassure him she was alive would've been impossible. "That's it? Just working?"

"I tinkered in hobbies, too. Mostly I worked and wrote."

The magic word she used sparked his interest, and a tendril of heat rolled through him. "What kind of writing?"

"I wrote books full of adventure stories. Uh, science fiction or fantasy romance..." she trailed off as if uncertain. "I haven't quite figured it all out yet, but I am working on getting them published."

"Do you have an agent?" Eric leaned forward, captivated at his luck, but he kept a lid on his excitement. He didn't want to overwhelm her. A lot could've happened in seven years.

Kiko shook her head. "I haven't got that far."

He pictured her lit up on a red carpet, light bulbs flashing, a dazzling smile on her face. "Well then, you're in luck. I happen to work at a publishing house."

"You do?" Her eyes widened in absolute shock. "I didn't know that. Last I knew you were…" she trailed off again.

A stab of pain hit his chest. She'd looked him up but never bothered to say hello. Had his kiss embarrassed her that deeply?

They exchanged glances, and she cast her gaze aside.

"I was what?" Eric prompted.

"Married." She stated it as a fact without emotion, and that told Eric all he needed to know. She was ambivalent about his love life, and he was firmly in the friend zone.

Still.

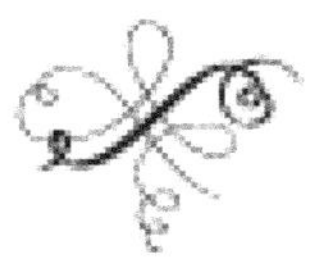

Kiko fought hard to spit out the word without choking up. She had to think it through, clear her head, and focus. It wasn't her place to interfere with his marriage. Eric ran a hand through his sandy blond hair and his bright green eyes were fixed on her. Small lines formed at the corners, making him more handsome with age. His sharp black suit covered his tall and lean frame. She didn't know what Eric had apologized for, but she owed him an apology. She appreciated his friendship, she really did, but her inability to function after Yoshi's death wasted Eric's time when he should've been moving on with his own life, with his girlfriend, even if they weren't destined to be together.

Eric had done nothing wrong. Quite the opposite. He'd done more than she could've asked.

But diving into a conversation that deeply minutes after reconnecting felt inappropriate. She didn't want to chase him off. Eric's presence made every cell in her body feel alive, while also making her feel grounded, reminding her she was a normal human again, not some immortal floating through time doing Chaos's work keeping the planet in turmoil—the good kind—where people maintained their free will. People loved, they fought, they chose, or so it went. From Kiko's point of view, there wasn't much choice in it.

Last time she'd seen Eric, they'd embraced in her living room, and he'd given her a quick kiss on the cheek. She wasn't ready then, but she wanted more now, and her chest burned with heat.

Married.

She met his gaze for an instant and retreated to the swirls in her cappuccino. This large chasm between them was unresolved, and she didn't know where to begin. She couldn't explain where she'd been. Telling him the truth of where she'd been 'working' would only split that chasm irreparably and impassably. At her first foray back into the human world, she couldn't handle the laughter or irritation on Eric's face if he didn't believe her.

And how could he?

Time travel wasn't real to humans.

Immortality was the stuff of fiction.

She couldn't tell him, but she wanted someone to understand. To know her. She wanted to connect.

Eric's interest in her stories was obvious, but she had to lie to him already. If she told Eric they were biographies, he'd probably shake his head, get up, and walk away.

Kiko opened her mouth to say something, anything to fill the awkward space between them. "We never had a void to fill before," Kiko said with a soft chuckle.

"Some things do change," Eric said sadly.

Kiko didn't like that tone. It was one of defeat, resignation, or an early goodbye.

Kiko wasn't ready for that yet.

The door to the coffee shop swung wide open, blowing a gust of cool air inside.

Kiko shivered, but a glimpse of fluffy blond hair circa 1988 and a reflective flicker from designer shades drained the blood from her limbs. Kiko sucked in a breath, eyes wide in absolute terror, and Eric scanned her face in alarm and followed her gaze.

Roger Meyer strutted inside with a beige polo shirt and an apron over black jeans. His head swung toward her table as if he sensed her, too. At once she saw the Roger monster holding a bloody katana and heading for her in a jealous rage, now filled with vengeance. It wasn't logical, but it was so foreign to her—the worst of human emotions. Kiko was paralyzed.

ROGER MEYER HAD BEEN released from prison early for good behavior, but old man Meyer declined to reinstate his son's position at the commercial real estate company he owned. Turned out, clients were afraid to visit empty buildings with a convicted murderer. Since then, Eric hadn't followed up with his current place of employment. In a city of half a million, three hours from his home, he shouldn't have had to. Of all the coffee shops in all of Milwaukee, what were the odds Roger Meyer worked here?

A thread in his frayed life just tore free and drifted to the floor.

Eric tensed.

A smirk crossed Roger's lips, and his eyes groped her body. "I spent years trapped in a shoebox waiting for you. I like surprises, especially beautiful unannounced surprises."

The hairs stood up on the back of Eric's neck. He stood up to block Roger from reaching her. "We aren't here for you. Leave us alone."

Roger's dark gaze turned on him.

Eric balled his hands and clenched his body rigid and ready. He'd never fought Roger at their dojo, since the men were in different weight classes, but if necessary, Eric wouldn't hesitate.

Roger chuckled. "You expect me to believe that, man? Because there are how many coffee shops in this shit town, and you two just happen to visit the only place I've been working since my release? I smell bullshit."

Eric spoke for him and Kiko. "We didn't know you worked here, but we're happy to leave. Kiko?" Eric held out his hand for her.

Roger shoved his shoulder, and Eric lost his balance and

banged his hip into the table. Their coffees spilled, pouring over the table and dripping onto the floor. Two customers waiting in line gawked, and one of the employees whispered to another. Trouble was arriving soon.

Eric needed to shut this down and get out of here before Roger escalated. "Leave us alone, Rodg. Don't you have work to do?" Eric didn't mean for it to sound like a taunt, but it might've come out that way. Eric shook coffee off his hand and with regret, wiped the dampness onto his suit.

Roger returned his attention to Kiko. "I'm not going to leave you alone. I've been waiting for a chance to talk to you for seven years and here you are, but you"—Roger jabbed Eric in the shoulder again—"are in my way."

Eric gritted his teeth. He'd waited all these years too, but he was nothing like Roger. No one was.

The murderer continued, "Kiko, come with me for a few minutes, and after we're done having a civil chat, you're free to go."

Both men waited for Kiko's answer. Her gaze bounced from Eric, who shook his head to discourage the ridiculous idea, to Roger and back. He knew what Roger was capable of, and one wrong move or word, and Eric would have two graves to visit.

Kiko stood and Eric held his breath.

Chapter 8

THE LAST TIME KIKO had been alone with Roger, she'd buried a steak knife in his gut, and if it weren't for a lucky aim dropping him to the floor, she'd be dead. Following him anywhere gave her fifty-fifty odds of getting killed, but not going with Roger was a guarantee many people would get hurt. Or at a minimum, lots of property damage.

Eric, a prized kendo fighter, wouldn't back down from a threat, but Kiko feared a cup full of crazy and sixty extra pounds gave Roger an advantage, and she refused to risk Eric's life. She'd just gotten him back for however long she had him, and she couldn't lose him now. While he had a wife, a great job, a beautiful home—a life, she had nothing, and that meant nothing to lose. Besides, she had Chaos watching out for her, and an emergency responder in her pocket.

Kiko stood. "Sure, Roger."

Eric's mouth gaped open, and he hissed in her ear, "You can't be serious. You know what he can do."

"Just wait here, okay?" Kiko asked with a reassuring touch on his arm.

Eric's gritted jaw flickered, but he nodded. He was primed to attack Roger, and she didn't blame him, but this was something she needed to smooth over herself. She was confident in her decision, since Roger would die in a shooting at The Wounded Soldier. She only had to wait him out until then.

A barista brought a towel, busying herself with the mess on the floor, and Eric stepped away to give her space. The fire in his eyes could burn down the building, and Kiko wanted to be in his arms more than anywhere else. But she couldn't always get what she wanted—that was real life.

Roger grasped Kiko's wrist painfully, but she hid the wince, and he dragged her behind the counter. Kiko exhaled a deep breath and stole a final glance at Eric. He was pissed, hurt, worried, and she hated that her choice stressed him. But Kiko was comforted knowing he was waiting for her. She could handle this. She could face her husband's murderer and her own attacker.

They wove through the back and into the employees' break room. The cheap hollow door closed behind them. Blocking the only exit with his bulk, Roger released her wrist, and without a word, he untucked his shirt.

Kiko stepped back. She'd expected any number of things, but not where this was going. There were no windows. No other doors.

Roger lifted the fabric to reveal the scar she'd left on his abdomen. A pink line marred his flesh as long as her hand was wide.

"You did this. Do you see it? Do you remember?" He released his shirt and placed a gentle hand on her shoulder. "Kiko, I'm sorry."

Her eyes popped wide. This was absolutely not where she thought this was going. Her tongue was glued to her mouth. An apology from Roger? Unheard of.

"I just snapped," he continued. "I didn't mean for it to go so far. I didn't mean for him to die." His hand slipped off her shoulder, and he tucked his shirt back in. "I only needed an outlet, and the situation had too many variables. I lost control, and I'm sorry."

He sounded sincere, but Kiko didn't buy it. "I don't know what to say."

"Forgive me?" Roger flashed his manipulative million-dollar smile.

He couldn't be serious. Roger didn't care about her enough to need forgiveness. Something else was going on. "Why?"

Roger paced the small room like a tiger in a constricting cage. He blew out a breath and raked his fingers through his fluffy hair, agitation growing by the minute. Roger had served most of his time, but that didn't mean he was any better now. Or had getting knocked from his millionaire lifestyle taught him something? After all, he was voluntarily showing up for work as a barista in an apron. Roger might've changed.

Her musings filled the time while she waited for the door to be free.

"I'm in this program, man," Roger said, standing still. "You know, I didn't want to. Group therapy is for losers, but it was that or go back to prison, so whatever. I went, and we had meetings, and they gave us books about these steps. So, I read some." He shrugged, as if self-improvement was a waste of time.

Kiko didn't move a muscle.

Roger said, "I determined I hurt a lot of people in my life, and I needed to make amends. You were on my list, but I couldn't find you until today. So I'm trying to say I need you to forgive me so I can continue my healing process."

Not in a million years if they were the last two people alive. If she lied, he would sleep better at night, but she didn't owe him that. If she spat the truth in his face, 'never', he could snap again, and she didn't need a repeat of her own past. Weighing the options and with bitterness on her tongue, she said, "Then I forgive you."

Roger lit up like a live wire and placed both his hands on her upper arms. Leaning down to meet her eyes, he said, "You have no idea what that means to me. Thank you."

Fearing he would kiss her, Kiko tilted her face away. "Can I go now?"

Roger released her arms and resumed pacing. The most important thing was, he no longer blocked the door. While his hand reached into the apron-covered front of his waistband, Kiko inched toward the exit. "There's something else I need to ask you."

Kiko swallowed a thick lump in her throat while she tracked his hand. "What is it?"

He stopped and loomed over her. "Will you go on a date with me?"

Kiko's face scrunched in disgust without her meaning to show it, and his features twisted in a rage, turning his head and neck bright red. Roger hadn't changed. Kiko skimmed for anything useful in defense—or offense. She only saw boxes, which she wasn't strong enough to hurl at him with any impact. A hook full of spare aprons hung on a wall. A broom leaned against the corner of the small storage room. Nothing she could use.

"Uh, Roger," she said, trying to calm the incoming explosion. "I think maybe—"

A growl came from deep inside his throat.

Kiko held her breath, and her heart pounded in her ears. What could she do? Something completely repulsive. "Sure, okay. Yeah, Roger, I'll go out with you." The words fired out in a panic, and flashes of Roger forcing a kiss on her, like he had in her parents' living room, spun her insides.

As her words registered, the red drained from his face, and his posture relaxed—from angry grizzly to fluffy teddy bear just like that. Roger smiled. If she didn't know the type of man he was, Kiko would almost think the smile was sweet. "Wow, really? Great. Where should I pick you up?"

"I'm between places right now, so, where do you want to meet?" Kiko inched her way toward the door while he was distracted by the sudden good news.

"You know, I used to do real estate. I can help you find a pile of bricks, or I have lots of room at my place."

"Thanks for the offer, Rodg, but I've got it handled."

"If you insist. We can meet here if it makes you more comfortable." He swaggered toward her.

"I don't think management would like that."

Roger stopped and smiled. "You always were quick. I meant—"

Eric had taught her long ago to use distraction to her

advantage. Kiko flung open the unguarded door and dashed right into Eric, who may have been eavesdropping. She found comfort in that. She grasped Eric's hand and pulled him into a weaving run toward the front door.

Roger snarled behind her, and a terrifying pop rang through the small coffee shop. Eric's hand slipped from her grasp.

Eric? Kiko skidded to a stop and turned. At the sight of Eric sprawled on the tile floor, Kiko's hands covered her mouth. This can't be happening.

Chapter 9

Tables knocked over, drinks spilled, chairs shoved and slid around, screaming. So much screaming. Employees hid in the back and hopefully called for emergency services. Kiko collapsed at Eric's side while the pungent scent of blood filled her nose and spread beneath him, coating the tile floor in a puddle. The wound on his back must've penetrated straight through. She checked his pulse, and it raced in a desperate attempt to pump oxygen through his system, but with each thump of his heart, more poured onto the floor. This wasn't a survivable wound, but she slipped her hands into his soft blond locks and covered his head in protection.

Roger approached, carrying a pistol in his meaty fist and a grisly snarl on his lips. "That was the last time you will ever say no to me." He leveled the handgun at her and squeezed the trigger.

Disbelief and utter terror froze her in place, while a scream exploded from her mouth. Despite what she knew, she couldn't prevent the monster from striking again.

Her stomach convulsed, and Kiko's vision rippled. She was too distraught to feel any physical pain, but she knew she would collapse—from a bullet wound or from fainting, she didn't know, and she didn't care. No matter the game Chaos sent her back to play, she didn't have anything to live for without Eric in her life.

The cappuccino was coming back. Kiko rested a hand for balance against the side of a brick building in an unfamiliar alley and vomited. She didn't care how she got here. Tears ran down her face, stale coffee clung to her mouth, and her nose ran, but still the scent of blood lingered. Kiko wiped her mouth and face with her sleeve, and tears blurred her already wavy vision. Sobs choked her throat.

Kiko stepped away from her mess and slid down against the brick wall. She never had a chance to reunite with her best friend, to see how he was doing, to reminisce about what they'd lost. Any chance she had of reconnecting had been ripped from her. The two best men in her life were taken from her too soon. Yoshi's death stole her future, but Eric's death stole his and his wife's. He was her only friend.

Eric was dead. Even if by some miracle he would survive that gunshot, he was married. And why did that word haunt her so much?

The answer came to her, lifting her spirits for just an instant before crushing her against the alley's cold, hard grime. Kiko wanted more, but she could never have it.

Anger tore through her. She didn't feel 'healed', and there was no peace. Where was the 'reward' Chaos had promised?

Boots appeared in front of her, and she wasn't sure if she cared whether Roger wanted to finish what he'd started. There was nothing left for her to live for. Detached from what was to come, Kiko looked up.

Chaos loomed above her, features grim. He had pulled her before Roger's bullet connected. "Hey, kid." He held out a hand, which she took, and he hoisted her off the ground. "I gave you the emergency responder for situations just like this. You know better. Why didn't you use it?"

Kiko had sent hundreds of people through time to experience a soul-crushing test of their will to live and to love. Being on this human side, fighting firsthand and watching people she cared about getting killed was so much more painful than she'd ever guessed. Usually, she pulled her present-day match before they saw the carnage. Chaos hadn't given her that. She'd been unable to think straight, and even if the lifeline had come to mind, she didn't think she could've left him.

Kiko said softly, "I don't know whether to thank you or beat you with my fists. It's so much worse on this side."

Chaos nodded in agreement.

"Did you ever have chances to fix your future?"

The corner of his lips lifted. "If I did, those memories were long gone thousands of years ago. Now, pull yourself together for your last chance."

Kiko never wondered until now what happened if all three chances were lost. It never happened to any of her matches. "What if I fail?"

Chaos rested a comforting hand on her shoulder. "Then you have to find your own way through life, like most folk."

"And Eric stays dead?"

He pressed his lips to a thin line. "I'm afraid so."

Her lower lip trembled, threatening her composure. She sucked in a raggedy breath and blew it out forcefully. Her hands were stained with Eric's blood. "I need to wash up."

"I'll send you back a little earlier. You'll have time to get yourself situated. I recommend avoiding the coffee shop."

"Thanks for the tip," she said dryly. Since Eric was married, he wasn't her match. She had only one try left to find and save her true love, but she still hadn't figured out who it was. "Can you tell me now who I'm meant to be with?"

"You'll figure it out," Chaos said with an amused smile.

What a frustrating ancient immortal. Without another word, her vision rippled again. Her stomach played cartwheels, and she felt sympathy for all the hundreds of people who'd experienced this many times. It was like getting slapped in the face with a four-minute flu.

When Kiko opened her eyes, she stood in front of Espress Your Beans back in 1995, but her Bronco was gone. She didn't know what day or time it was, but she couldn't wait around for a cab. Kiko glanced through the shop's windows but didn't see Roger. She craned her neck up and down the sidewalk, and thankfully no faces matched his. Roger could screw up his own life and get killed at The Wounded Soldier in Greenleaf like fate had designed.

She didn't see Eric either. Hopefully, he was safe somewhere. Kiko jogged the mile through the city and found her Bronco at the cemetery. Eric wasn't here either, and not wanting a repeat of that horrific experience, she popped into the driver's seat with breath panting, double checked all her red journals were still stacked in the back, and hit the gas.

After some needful hours of quiet on the long ride back to Green Bay, the shaking of her hands subsided. Kiko pulled the Bronco over at the curb across the street from a little house in a residential neighborhood with a For Rent sign stabbed in the grass. The single story had a door off to the right side and a picture window large enough to make it look like a cute little cyclops. Matching balls of shrubbery adorned the front corners. Kiko checked her watch, wondering if the meeting had been scheduled or not, and dialed the number anyway.

A woman picked up, and Kiko introduced herself and explained the sign.

"Yes, it's available."

"Can I meet you to see it? I'm looking for a place as soon as possible."

"Sure, missy. I'll be right over. Make sure you have ID on you." The polite woman's voice explained the rent amount and required deposit, and then reiterated the no pets policy. So she hadn't made the appointment yet. How much earlier was she?

Kiko agreed to the woman's terms, and she'd be right over. Kiko ended the call, finger combed her hair in the vanity mirror, and spit in her hands to wash the blood off against her dark wash jeans. She collected her purse, slung it over her shoulder, and stepped outside the vehicle to check her registration. It was current. That narrowed down the window significantly.

Kiko leaned against the Bronco and watched the neighborhood for alarming activity, suspicious people, or dangerous squirrels, until the woman arrived.

The tour was quick and the landlord easy-going, so Kiko signed a three-month lease on the spot. Thrilled with a place to call home, Kiko carried her journals inside in a painstakingly slow process and then brought in her single box of personal items. She tore into the box for toiletries to take a long-awaited shower. Eric's blood was still sticky on her hands.

Kiko never visited with Yoshi, but she couldn't risk returning to him and repeating Eric's nightmare murder. In the meantime, she had a few stocks to purchase. Kiko dragged out and setup her laptop. She logged into her stock trading website and bought thousands of shares of key companies in the future. She set a reminder for herself to sell the ones that wouldn't survive the dot com bubble bust in the year 2000.

Settled in a home, clean, and financially set for life, Kiko was ready for the next step in reclaiming her human life. She needed a daily distraction, a sense of camaraderie and normalcy—a job. Eric would publish her, she had no doubt, but she couldn't go anywhere near him. And knowing she had a better chance at winning the lottery than getting published otherwise, Kiko figured finding some entry level job at a publishing house would be her best bet—rub shoulders with the bigwigs and eventually ask for a favor.

She searched online for open jobs at publishing houses, avoiding Blue Feather Publishing, but there weren't any nearby or any available exclusively online. She cold called a

New York City publishing house on a whim.

Lacking furniture, she sat on top of her journal pile while her call was transferred a few times.

"You want what?" the man's voice asked.

"An entry level job."

"Do you have any industry experience?" he asked.

"No," Kiko answered honestly.

"Well, I know someone who's right up your alley." Kiko heard a snicker over the line, but it could've been static. "I'll transfer you. Hold, please."

Kiko waited and the line rang again.

"Hello?" That voice. Hearing it after what she'd seen jolted her.

Kiko's breath caught in her throat. She forced a whisper, "Eric?"

"Kiko, is that you?" Eric asked in disbelief.

"It's me. Are...are you in New York City?"

"Not right now. I'm in Green Bay. How have you been after all this time?"

Hearing his voice again calmed her. He was alive, and he had his family again. Selfishly, she wanted to see him, but she wouldn't go anywhere near a coffee shop, especially not three hours away. "I'm actually looking for a job."

"You're a marriage and family counselor. What kind of job would you want here?"

"I didn't finish school," Kiko said shamefully.

"In that case, I can find something for you. What's your specialty?" The purring warmth in his voice made her tremble.

Kiko didn't have any skills a publishing house would need that she was aware of. "Uh, the mail room is good."

"After all these years you don't have any experience? I can't believe that."

Kiko's cheeks heated with the praise. "Mr. Spreadsheets, the mail room is fine."

Eric chuckled at her old nickname for him. "Can you use Excel—pivot tables, graphs, and formulas? Because that's what my department does."

"Yeah, I can do that."

"Great. I'll transfer you to Caroline, and she'll fit you right in for an interview. I can't wait to see you again. I miss you, Kiko." The line beeped in her hands, and Caroline answered.

Eric missed her? Her mind went where it didn't belong before she pulled it back to earth. Of course he missed her. They had been best friends.

"Yes, an interview with Eric," Kiko said as Caroline's words cleared in her head.

"He has an opening this afternoon, and it's the only one for the next couple weeks. Can you take it?"

"Absolutely. I'll be there."

Caroline read off the address, and Kiko repeated it in her head half a dozen times to memorize it. Then she remembered she could just search it on the internet. After living in various decades for over a hundred years, she liked the technology of the present year best, but the mid-nineties were a very close second.

Less advertisements.

Kiko whipped up a mostly-bogus resume including the fuzzy tasks she'd completed while working at the Gap. Then she ran out to the mall and bought an armful of business clothes, dropped them onto her bedspread, and slipped into the most reasonable outfit she picked—a black skirt suit. She parked in a vast surface lot adjacent to a five-story building and exhaled a deep breath.

She would see Eric again, but she couldn't show any emotion from his murder earlier today.

Chapter 10

ERIC'S LEG BOUNCED UNDER his desk, shaking his tie, and a pen wagged between his fingertips. Kiko Takai, the woman he'd admired from afar, who disappeared for the last seven years, was due to stroll into his office in a few minutes for an interview. Frankly, he was shocked she was alive. So many calls and voicemails went unanswered. His guts swirled like clam chowder in a blender. He hoped he didn't make a nervous fool of himself.

A gentle knocking at his door stilled his jittery fingers.

"Come on in," he said hoarsely and cleared his throat.

Caroline opened the door with a pinched frown and waved her hand in a gesture for his guest to enter.

A nervous wreck, Eric stood, and as Kiko stepped into his office, his breath caught. She was more beautiful than he remembered, if that was possible. He wanted to run his fingers through her long black hair, sleek over her shoulders. The stunning skirt suit hugged her body and sent blood pounding through his veins. Under his gaze, Kiko's cheeks flushed pink, her delicate lips parted, and her mesmerizing eyes widened.

She didn't appear to have aged a day, and she looked good, so very good.

Caroline closed the door behind her.

Eric's foggy brain made connections to his limbs, and he moved across the room to her. The intoxicating scent of sweet tropical flowers reached his nose, and he savored the memory while lust soared through him. "Kiko, how've you been?"

"I'm okay. I see you've been successful. Vice president? I'm impressed." She smiled at him and blinked a few times as if she had something stuck in her eye. Her curled index finger pressed at her lower lid.

"It can get dusty in here. Contacts dry?"

"Dusty, like you said."

He wanted to squeeze her close, to feel her skin, to believe he wasn't hallucinating. He wanted to hold the life of her against his chest and never let go, but it wasn't appropriate to hug his future employee. He held out a hand, and she shook it.

Warmth rushed through him, curling down low.

"Have a seat." Eric gestured to a chair facing his desk, and he dropped into his own chair. The photo of smiling Kiko stared back at him. He focused on her real face, live and in person. He hadn't been imagining it—she really hadn't aged a day. "So you just pop into my office after seven years."

Kiko sat prim and proper—formal—her legs crossed at the ankles, back ramrod straight. "I thought I was here for an interview."

"You got the job. Talk to me."

Kiko blinked. "But I didn't... You didn't..."

He smiled. "You can use Excel. That's all the job requires. What I want to know is where you've been. I've tried to find you, to talk to you, but...everywhere I looked was a dead end. Even your parents haven't seen you in years." He interlaced his fingers to stop from fidgeting.

Kiko's cheeks blushed bright pink, and her eyes cast aside.

His need for closure blinded him to the intrusion. Not knowing hurt, but she didn't owe him an explanation just to make him feel better. "If you don't want to tell me, you don't have to. Answering is not a condition of the job. I'm sorry for pushing."

Kiko opted not to answer.

Perspiration beaded against his skin, and he feared he chased her off all over again. Eric stood. "Walk with me. I'll show you to your office."

Kiko followed him into the hallway. The urge to hold her hand was so overpowering he could hardly think straight. Instead, he guided her by the small of the back, relishing in the touch of the fabric under his fingertips. Her black high heels lifted her up. She'd fit perfectly against him, and her nose would reach his ear. Eric needed to stop these thoughts before they got him in trouble.

Focus on the work, he scolded himself. Keep her happy and make her want the offer.

Eric would've put her right across the hall from him, but Dan had claimed that space, so he guided her a few doors down to an unused office. "Here it is. I'll have it all set up and squeaky clean for you. Can you start tomorrow?"

A shy smile graced her lips. "Tomorrow works for me."

"Great." Eric inspected the room more closely. The window was too small, the square footage pitiful, and the lighting wasn't quite right. "On second thought, maybe I can find you a better space."

"This is fine, really. It's far more than I was expecting. The mail room would've been okay with me," Kiko said.

"You're not working in the basement—" Eric started.

"What's going on in here?" Amanda's grating voice interrupted, and the blonde stepped inside the cramped space.

Eric had never told Amanda the details about Kiko, but his wife was familiar enough with his prized photograph on his desk to make the connection, and the moment Amanda recognized Kiko's face was apparent on her features—the last thing he wanted to deal with right now.

He didn't want to scare Kiko off. Politely, Eric said, "Kiko, this is Amanda Carter, director of marketing. Amanda, this is Kiko Takai, and from what I can tell, the perfect candidate for my financial analyst position."

Amanda crossed her arms over her chest and twisted her lips. "There are no job openings."

"It's a good thing you don't know everything," Eric said, letting a shade of condescension slip out.

"Don't give me your lip." Amanda pointed at Kiko in accusation. "That's the girl from your photo. You told me she was dead."

Eric glanced at Kiko in shame. It was true, but only because he thought she was, and it stopped Amanda's relentless questions. The familiar tone boiled his blood. "Treat our newest employee with respect, Amanda."

"You can't hire just anyone you want."

Eric frowned. "The board of directors doesn't govern the hiring of operations employees, only management."

Amanda lifted her nose, and her glare jumped from him to Kiko and back. She narrowed her eyes, and Eric wanted to throw a book at her. "Just remember you're at the office. Nothing's private here." Amanda stormed out the door.

Kiko's eyes widened to saucers. "That was intense."

"I'm so sorry about that. She's always testy, but she's good at her job, otherwise I'd never let her within a hundred yards of you." Eric blurted the words and then thought about them. They were true too. Amanda was high maintenance, sure a bit catty, but as they said, opposites attract. He didn't trust her around Kiko, and he already regretted the introduction.

Eric personally escorted Kiko to the elevator, just in case Amanda tried something stupid, and with spying eyes on them, he resisted the urge to touch her lower back while they walked. The elevator dinged with the doors opening. Kiko stepped inside, and as the distance between them increased, a piece of him was torn away all over again. Would she show up tomorrow, or would she disappear into the ether for another seven years? "I'll see you bright and early tomorrow morning. As I said, your office will be ready for you."

"I can't wait," Kiko said with a sweet curve of her lips. She waved goodbye as the elevator doors closed. Her flowery scent faded, and a dull ache filled his chest.

I can't wait either, Eric thought.

He dragged his heavy feet back to his office to finish a couple reports. His eyes blurred over the spreadsheet columns. His wife's request for a divorce had serendipitous timing, and he was glad to grant it no matter what his future entailed. But with

Kiko back in his life, memories of her flooded his brain—from the happiest to the devastating, and everything in between.

He realized after all this time, he still wanted her. She was it for him—had been since the day they'd met. All those buried feelings rushed from his brain to his toes, hitting every necessary spot in between with a heat of desire. That crumbling wall around his heart had grown weeds among the ruins, but now flowers sprouted on the vines.

Not five minutes of reflection, while analyzing trends through a swimmy unfocused brain, his office door burst open, startling him as if he was guilty of something.

Amanda stood with her hands on her hips, fury twisting her features. "Liar," she said. "You little liar."

Eric bristled. He was not in the mood for her games. "What now?"

"Why did you say she was dead? What are you hiding?"

Eric sighed, not wanting to waste effort arguing. "I said she was probably dead. You filed for divorce, so what's it to you anyway?"

"She's the girl in your precious photograph. You can't deny it. Who is she? Why is she here now?"

Eric hated when Amanda picked a fight. It reminded him of his parents arguing. Besides, the walls in this office weren't soundproof, as she'd already reminded him. Eric kept his voice reasonable for privacy. "Yes, she's the woman in the photograph and an old friend, like I'd said. And now she's an employee, equal as everyone else. If you haven't read the employee handbook, harassment is a valid reason for termination."

"Are you threatening me?"

"I am reminding you of company policy."

She parked a hip on top of his desk, squishing some of his paperwork and shifting a stack. Her deliberate destruction of his organized space showed him how blind he had been to her charms.

"Have you been cheating on me?" she whispered her next accusation.

"I won't dignify that with an answer. Get out of my office."

"You will answer me!" she hissed.

Eric sprung up, chair rolling from the force, and he planted his open palms on his desk. "It is none of your business what I do with my free time. You're on the clock, Carter, so show some professional respect."

"Just because your daddy is CEO doesn't give you the right to boss me around, and don't call me by my last name."

"If you hate your last name so much, you could've taken mine. And two, I don't boss you around. You do whatever you want every weekend and most nights without so much as a 'bye honey, I'm going out with friends or random men. Toodles!' So, don't tell me what I can and can't do. While I packed your stuff, I found your birth control pills. Care to explain that?"

Amanda growled, and Eric smiled smugly despite his low punch.

"I hate you," she growled through her clenched teeth.

That should've hurt, but for some reason, Eric was relieved. Would that make the divorce easier? Faster? "I've already signed the documents. Derek will send them to your attorney when he's finished," he said calmly.

As if she fed on fighting, her steam dissipated. She asked with disbelief, "Today? That soon?"

There was no way she could change her mind now. "You spend more time out of our house than in it. With the empty pack of birth control pills, clearly we're heading in two different directions. You served me, and now I've come to see it was for the best."

"Can you just tell me who she really is?" Amanda asked sweetly. The master manipulator was back. How did he ever marry her in the first place?

Eric sighed. "She's a friend, like I told you. My best friend's wife."

Amanda quirked a brow. "You don't have a best friend."

"I did."

Amanda removed her butt from his desk. "In that case, why didn't you just say so? All this bickering for nothing."

"Because, as I explained already, it's none of your business."

"Of course it's my business, we're married."

"Only until the judge gives his stamp of approval."

"If this friend of yours is promising, perhaps she can be the bridge between our departments, a mediator, if you will. And we can figure out the divorce another time, or maybe not at all. What do you say?"

There was no going back to Amanda Carter, director of marketing, but an uncontested divorce sounded as nice as a free trip to Tahiti, and it would buy him time to gather the funds to buy her out. "We can discuss this another time."

Satisfied, she blew him a kiss and left, clicking the door shut gently behind her.

Eric Woodson, most desperate man alive for getting mixed up with Amanda Carter, biggest goddamn idiot for marrying her, but smartest man ever for not falling for her charms again. He wasn't sure if the last one really canceled out the first two, but that was semantics.

All he could think about was Kiko. They never got a chance to catch up. What was her life like now? Was she married? Did she have kids? Did he introduce her with the wrong last name? The thought never occurred to him before, but the idea of a family waiting for her back home sunk a rock in his gut like a gutter ball on the tenth frame.

He buried himself in his stack of reports.

Chapter 11

Night had fallen, and Kiko was tired. Her flat pouch of popcorn spun while the microwave hummed, lulling her back to today's 'interview'. It was one thing to watch your best friend's murder inches from your face. It was another thing entirely to smile and pretend it didn't happen. Because in this time, it didn't. The images of Roger's snarling face, the ear-splitting blast of the pistol, the horrific thump of an unconscious body hitting tile, the screaming customers, the blood pooling—all rushed her brain the moment she saw Eric alive again. Every ounce of strength in her body was used to bottle the emotion during her visit with him.

Suppressing the pain became much easier when Amanda Carter had entered the room. Kiko recognized her name from the wedding announcement—his wife, and the initial shock of being next to her stymied the images, but hearing Amanda's jealous snark put Kiko on the defense. How had Eric wound up with a woman like that? Kiko sensed he wasn't pleased with his wife's behavior, and Kiko didn't blame him. She couldn't imagine having a spouse so jealous she would belittle and berate a stranger.

After the embarrassing interview, Kiko went shopping for more essentials. She brought a television home in her Bronco and set it on a small stand—not as nice as the LED flat screens of the future, but it would do. And then she had a couch, coffee table, a small kitchen table and chairs, a queen-sized bed, and a dresser all delivered. It was almost like home. Her eyes darted to her framed collage from Eric. While the turnstile continued to work its magic, Kiko picked up her treasured gift, smiled at Eric's smiling at her in the photo, and set it down, planning to hang it later.

She'd wanted a nine-to-five sorting mail to keep her mind busy. She didn't plan on being a financial analyst for Eric, who clearly had close business relations with his feisty wife. At least Kiko wouldn't be bored. Instead, she'd have to watch him and Amanda getting cozy all day. Maybe she could transfer to the mail room after getting settled.

The microwave beeped, and she collected the bag, shaking it to cool while heading into the living room. In the large picture window, against the dark sky and streetlight, a shape caught her eye. A knock on her front door startled her.

Kiko set down the steaming bag and yelled, "Who is it?"

She moved to the side of the door and paused before checking the peephole. She'd seen too many people blown away through a door to stick her body in front of it. With no answer, she leaned over to see through the peephole, and no one was there. Hairs lifted on the back of her neck. Kiko opened the front door, just a little, with her foot wedged behind it for extra strength against a potential intruder.

Still no one.

Kiko opened it wide, and a sticky note on the door fluttered. She lifted the yellow square and closed the door. She turned the deadbolt, slipped the chain in place, and flipped the knob lock. Kiko wasn't paranoid or anything. It was just one of those days...filled with murder.

The handwriting leaned to the left in a half-cursive half-printed mess, resembling a stereotypical doctor's scratch. She didn't recognize who it belonged to. "Been hiding in plain sight all these years," she read aloud.

Why would someone leave a sticky note on her door? Why not knock and visit? She tried to remember everyone she knew in this year—her parents were still alive in Milwaukee, but they normally called, if they ever bothered at all. There was Eric, but she was at his office today. Amanda definitely held some animosity toward Kiko, but she had only just met her. Kiko's matches weren't in this city, and this wasn't Roger's usual calling card. He was a knock-on-the-door or knock-down-the-door kind of guy.

Kiko shivered.

She stuck the note to the kitchen table and sunk into the couch with the popcorn, and she clicked on the television, thankful for some background noise making her feel less alone.

Halfway through a trash reality television show, her older model cell phone rang, and the screen showed a familiar number.

"Hello?" Kiko answered.

"Kiko." It was Eric, and his warm voice filled the hollow emptiness inside. Her lips tugged at the corners. "I'm not keeping you from any…family business, am I?"

"Not at all. How are things going?" That was smooth, very smooth. She didn't want him to know how he affected her. She couldn't be responsible for ruining his marriage.

"I'm doing great, actually. I just received updated sales forecasts, and on your first day tomorrow, I want you to join me in the meeting at eight."

A web of nerves knitted through her. "Just received?" she repeated. "Tell me you're not working this late."

Eric laughed. "It happens."

Kiko didn't know whether to feel sorry for his hours keeping him from home, or grateful he'd spent some of that time to call her. "Do I need anything to prepare?"

"No, but I wanted to warn you my plans for the meeting will probably anger Amanda, and I don't want her to frighten you."

Why did he marry someone who needed a disclaimer? "I'll be wearing my iron suit."

A small groan reached her ear.

"Everything okay over there?" she asked.

Eric cleared his throat. "I'm…I'm good. Don't be late."

Kiko pressed the end button on her older phone and tossed it next to her on the cushion. She unmuted her show, now half over, and dug into her perfect-temperature popcorn with a smile on her face, curious about the upcoming drama tomorrow. One big benefit to working for Eric instead of the mail room was she didn't have to worry about mindless work inviting a tidal storm of bad memories.

It pained her to see Eric so miserable with his wife, though. Perhaps they could use some help. In her previous life, she would've offered pro bono. After all, she'd wanted to be a marriage and family counselor, but that previous life was way too long ago, and she wasn't licensed.

THE NEXT MORNING, KIKO pressed a notebook and clipboard

against her chest, wishing briefly for a tablet, and walked into the conference room. A long, lacquered table had suits dotted around it. Everyone stared at her, the newcomer. Kiko wasn't used to being the center of attention, and these high-powered people made her legs wobble. She clearly didn't belong, but Eric wanted her here, and she wouldn't let him down.

Paul Woodson, CEO and Eric's dad, made her the most uncomfortable. She wanted to impress him, but he had the presence of an experienced and hungry shark. "Welcome to Blue Feather. Eric filled us in on the situation, so make yourself at home. You've met Amanda Carter, director of marketing." Amanda glared. "This is Fred Carter, vice president of marketing." Fred nodded politely. "Caroline, Eric's secretary, will be taking the minutes today." Caroline ignored Kiko entirely. "And the shy one here in the corner is Josie, the intern. Please have a seat."

Josie blushed and dropped her eyes.

At least Kiko wasn't alone in her discomfort. Feeling like she was intruding on an unhappy Thanksgiving dinner table, her stomach knotted. She had no information about the meeting besides Eric's warning, so she didn't know what to do or what input she'd have. She slipped into the corner seat near Eric but across from Fred Carter and Amanda Carter. The resemblance made Kiko assume they were father and daughter. They both had the wide set eyes and light blond hair. Eric had many dashing features of his father as well. Paul was the image Eric would be in his sixties, and Kiko didn't mind what she saw—strong features, thick gray hair, and striking green eyes. Nepotism was alive and well here—typically something Kiko didn't agree with, but she made an exception for Eric. He was too sweet to see his privilege.

Caroline's fingers hovered over a boxy laptop, annoyance twisting her upper lip.

"So, we received news that Cece's upcoming release has surpassed expected preorders," Amanda said with a sneer at Eric. "I need the previously requested bigger budget to grow the buzz surrounding the release."

Kiko had an excuse to look at Eric finally. The sight of him calmed her, excited her, and pulled her in half. How was she going to establish a long-lasting business relationship with a man who made her skin tingle? She stole a glance at his lips and wanted to slap herself. Eric was...unhappily...married. Why couldn't her brain accept that?

Eric cleared his throat and his jaw flickered. "Preorders are twice what the figures projected, but I will not grant you a bigger budget."

Amanda leaned forward, finger pointing at his face. "I'm right on this and you know it. A bigger budget means more eyeballs and more sales. You're deliberately undermining this company." Amanda turned to the CEO. "Paul, can't you see? I was right, and he's—"

Paul pressed his lips together, and that alone made Kiko slide lower in her seat.

"You already went over budget without approval," Eric cut her off with clipped words. "The increase you're requesting has already been spent."

His wife shot death daggers at him, and Caroline the secretary looked at Amanda like she smelled a fart. What on earth was going on in this office?

"I did have approval," Amanda said, throwing someone under the bus.

Eric's eyebrows rose, and he turned to Fred Carter.

The vice president of marketing said, "I allowed her to run with it. Her explanation made sense, and like she said, she's right."

"Being right after the fact doesn't prove being reckless in the first place is reasonable," Eric said. "We have a budget we all agreed on, and we have to stick with it. We're growing Blue Feather in a reasonable and sustainable pattern. Reckless spending is akin to gambling, and since I happen to enjoy being employed, I'm not willing to risk Blue Feather's future on a whim."

"Reckless!" Amanda abruptly stood, chair rolling away behind her.

Fred Carter stood and wrapped an arm around her shoulders to guide her away. "I think we're done here."

"Yeah, we'll leave the loons to squawk at each other," Amanda said. Loons had a haunting wail, not a squawk, but Kiko didn't dare correct her. As her father dragged her to the door, she turned and said, "Pick sides, and when you choose me, we can move forward with maximizing the profits of this place. I happen to enjoy being employed too, but I'm willing to take a risk to capture a bigger market share."

Paul's lips pressed to a thin line again. The intern slipped low in her chair, probably debating her career choice at this point. Caroline watched the married couple with curious eyes.

The Eric she knew didn't deserve all this animosity, and Kiko felt like she was drowning—silent and helpless to stop it. As much as she wanted to defend him, Eric didn't need saving. One, Amanda was a little hotheaded, but Kiko didn't believe for a second she'd return with a gun, and two, Roger was far, far away. This was merely a battle of wills, wits, and words.

When the duo left, Eric shook his head and sent an apologetic glance Kiko's way. That he thought of her comfort while he was the target of the drama made her swell with warmth.

"In light of recent news," Paul said, "perhaps we should amend the policy to have two managers approve expenditures above the initial estimates."

"Agreed," Eric said.

"Caroline, can you whip that up and email the memo to me for approval?" Paul folded his hands together.

"Yes, sir," she replied quickly. "Eric, can I have a private meeting with you to outline the change in procedures?" A hopeful note played on her tongue. "I don't want to get something wrong and leave a loophole behind."

Eric dragged a frustrated hand down his face. "Sure, Caroline. Book it."

The secretary's face lit up with a broad grin, and Kiko couldn't help feeling a stab of jealousy—a little one, nothing like Amanda's raging tantrum.

Eric stood and held out a large hand toward Kiko. "Meeting adjourned."

She accepted his invitation, and comfort and protection enveloped her. His smile smoldered in her chest while he whisked her out of the room. In the hallway, muffled screaming escaped a room nearby. Kiko startled at what she thought was Amanda's voice.

"Don't worry about her, short stuff," Eric said, using an old nickname for her as he guided her down the hall. "She's just...I don't know."

"Noisy?" Kiko supplied. She didn't want to offend him by insulting his wife, but she wanted him to know she understood.

Eric chuckled. He led her out the front door of the building, and a black limo was parked at the curb. A tuxedoed driver opened the back door for her, and they both climbed inside.

"You keep a limo on standby?" Kiko asked.

"You never know when you need to escape."

When the driver slipped into his seat, Eric said, "Stan, take us to the Commodore."

Kiko was glad she wore a suit, even if it was a little stuffy for the Commodore. Her first day had been a whirlwind of entertainment and office gossip, and it wasn't even over yet. But rather than being an invisible, timeless bystander, Eric made her feel a part of it all, and she wouldn't change that for anything.

Even a little of her own Amanda animosity.

Chapter 12

The Commodore, a high-end restaurant with a dress code and mandatory reservations, was Eric's favorite. Not because he wanted to brag about his pockets or impress others, no, he never brought clients here, only friends and family. The honeycomb accent wall reminded him of his father's wine cellar, and the dark wood paneling calmed him. A black and white collage of photos papered an entire wall, and Eric never tired of seeing them. But it was the bright orange seats that were the best, reminding him of the days when Eric visited Yoshi at Main Street Realty with lunch. The slender guy had been a cheap lunch date.

The hostess greeted and seated them.

Eric hadn't planned on taking Kiko out to lunch, but when Amanda made a scene, he needed to escape, and having a friend who accepted his last-second reservation meant he and Kiko could enjoy some drama-free quiet. And Eric could finally spend some quality time with his long-lost best friend.

"This is fancy." Kiko unfolded a napkin and placed it on her lap.

"I should've asked your preference, but this place is exclusive, and we won't be bothered."

"I don't mind; I was just surprised at how…" she trailed off, searching for the right word. Romantic would be the word he'd use. "…formal it is," Kiko finished. "Very classy." She nervously picked at the corner of the menu. If all she wanted was to shuffle mail in the basement, her first day must've been intimidating.

"I'm sorry about all that back there. Amanda can be aggressive, which is why she's good at her job."

"Is she like that off the clock?" Kiko asked.

Eric chuckled. Right now he didn't have any nice words to use for Amanda. "She's definitely something else." But he didn't want to talk about her. "Can I ask you something personal?"

"Sure," Kiko said, dropping her hands from the menu and giving him her full attention. His heart skipped.

The waitress brought them iced waters, and Eric ordered a light appetizer of shucked oysters and lemon juice. "It's my treat, and I insist you pick anything you want." He hoped she read more into that.

Kiko smiled. He loved that smile. She leaned forward over the menu. "Baked brie, please."

The waitress scribbled on a pad of paper, gave a couple polite lines about their choices, and left.

"Of all the options, you chose cheese?" Eric teased.

"I've tried almost everything out there, but I draw the line at snails. I don't touch snails. Today, I was in the mood for something savory and safe."

Eric's brows lifted. A frequent traveler likely didn't have children. He never overheard a child or a spouse when he'd called late last night, but they could've been asleep. "You've traveled?"

"You could say that." A small smile played at her lips.

"I love travel stories." He loved any story he could get from her.

The humor left Kiko's face. She cast her eyes aside in conflict. After Roger had slain Yoshi in front of her and almost killed her next, perhaps she'd vanished to escape the pain—that Eric's comfort hadn't been enough, and his asking only rehashed it. "I'm sorry. I didn't mean to bring up—"

"It's okay," she said, waving away his worries. "I'm trying to figure out how to explain it. I've spent time drifting around, I guess you could say, trying to find something I was missing. I never spent much time in one place, and I want to stay put for a while, to put down roots and call a place home."

"I'm glad you chose this city." He wanted her to stay close.

Kiko's cheeks pinked.

The waitress delivered their appetizers, ran through the usual pleasantries, and left again.

Eric turned the dish. "Care to try an oyster? It's spritzed in lemon and nestled in brine. The salty and sour create an unforgettable explosion in your mouth."

Her tongue peeked out to lick her lower lip. He wanted to taste her, and a tingling rush of heat flooded through him. All these years he'd wanted Kiko, and here they were, alone together at the fanciest restaurant in town. On a date…maybe.

"I don't know if my stomach can do that right now."

"I'll show you." The soupy oysters floated inside the open shells on a bed of ice. He lifted one to his lips and slurped it in quick. The cold slippery saltiness filled his mouth, and he swallowed it whole. He groaned. "It's so delicious. Are you sure?"

"Yeah, I think it's best if I pass this time."

One of the best properties of oysters was their aphrodisiac nature, but with Kiko in front of him, Eric didn't need it. He wanted to show off his cultured tongue.

Kiko cut thin slices of the baked brie and lifted them to her lips. Desire roared through his system, and he closed his eyes, both relishing in his desire, and tampering it. Eric inhaled a deep breath, released it slowly, and opened his eyes.

Kiko stared at him with her head cocked to the side.

He chuckled.

"Are you okay?" she asked.

"It's the oysters. I wasn't exaggerating when I said they're amazing." Lunch would only last so long, and Eric wanted to know as much as he could about her. Since Kiko was never the boisterous type—the opposite of Amanda—he gently initiated. "I called your parents after you left. They assured me you were fine, but they didn't know where you went. I couldn't believe it, but then I remembered they skipped out on their own son-in-law's funeral." Eric was there. He'd never miss out on his best friend's funeral, and he comforted Kiko. She'd given him credit for her surviving the attack, but that strength was all on her. She just couldn't see it.

Kiko sighed, a topic she probably wanted to avoid, but the only way back into her life was to be part of it. "They're fine. Still married, still living in the same house, still happy I left." She chuckled, but it was a sound of sadness that made him ache for her. "Before I moved up here, I visited them. Told them I was between places—homeless, essentially—but they didn't even offer my old room back temporarily—not that I would've accepted. So, I keep my distance."

Eric brushed away a wretched visual of her in rags, sleeping in a car. He wanted to sweep her up into his arms, promise her she'd never feel neglected again, and pamper her in a life of luxury. It was the minimum she deserved. "They were always so cold. I get it, my Dad might've given me a job, but he's about as affectionate as a bunion."

Kiko chuckled.

"And I'm glad you're not homeless." Eric reached out and grasped her hand. A familiar feeling of heat and comfort rolled through him.

She withdrew, and the warmth was torn from him. Something about the slip of her wrist and the shift of her eyes told him she wasn't into him the way he was into her. Had they grown that far apart? Had he built her up into something she wasn't?

WHEN HIS HAND GRASPED hers, Kiko reluctantly retreated, a thick knot in her stomach.

"What's wrong?" Eric asked. Worry lined his brow.

"What about Amanda?" Kiko didn't want to be the cause of more fights between the couple.

"This isn't a business meeting, so it's none of her business."

Unsatisfied, Kiko said, "She's your wife, and I'm worried she's going to burst through that door and rage on me." His wife would have no reason to, since Kiko hadn't done anything, but she didn't blame her either. Eric's forwardness with her—his desire was like a neon blinking light—and Caroline's unusual behavior, led Kiko to believe Eric wasn't as straight-laced as she'd thought. Then again, he'd kissed her when he had a girlfriend. There were many lines Kiko was willing to cross, but cheating or interfering with a marriage was not one of them.

No matter how much rejecting him hurt.

Or maybe she'd gotten it all wrong. Maybe he was just a social butterfly, and in her endless lonely desperation, she was reading way too much into his actions.

Every time she had been in his arms it was never a proper embrace of two people who cared about each other. He had been dating someone or married, and she likewise. And with that thought, where was this mystery guy Chaos had promised her? Was spending time with Eric wasting her limited opportunity to find true happiness?

Eric studied her, and his lips pressed thin just like his father's did during the meeting. "How did you know she's my wife?"

Kiko had admitted to looking him up during their coffee—date—meeting, but that was before he was shot and Chaos gave her another chance. Navigating the world was so much harder when she had to face the consequences head on. "I kept an eye on you, wondering how you were doing and what you were up to, and a couple years ago, I found the newspaper announcement. She's not exactly subtle. I knew her name—Amanda Carter—but I couldn't recognize her from the grainy newspaper photo. The way she acted around you, it couldn't have been a coincidence."

A beaming grin spread his lips.

Kiko was embarrassed to admit how much she tracked him. She'd hoped he would remind her that he was married and that her deep interest in him was inappropriate, but the grin said otherwise. Eric reached across the table, palms up, inviting her to accept his grasp, and she was torn. "If that's all that stands between us, you have no reason to worry about her. In fact—"

Alarming high heels clattering on the tile floor interrupted his sentence, and Kiko craned her neck just as Eric's brows lifted in surprise.

Amanda Carter's rage was right there where Kiko expected it, but instead of targeting Kiko, she faced her husband, and Eric retracted his hands. The blonde flung her hands on her shapely hips. "I figured you'd show up here. What's the matter with you? You're out wooing your new employee, and we're still married. I shouldn't be surprised. You know, if you'd have shown me half the attention..." she trailed off when she noticed Kiko. "What?"

Kiko flinched at the sharp tone. Amanda's appearance here was both embarrassing and uncalled for. Away from the scrutiny of Eric's colleagues, Kiko dug down deep to stand up for the both of them. Besides, she was too old to put up with this kind of drama. "What are you doing here?"

"What am I doing here?" Amanda pressed a palm to her chest in mock offense. "I should ask you the same thing. He's my husband!"

Eric stood and lifted an arm. "Security!" Embarrassment, shame, and anger burned his handsome face bright red.

Kiko was none of those things. The knot in her stomach unraveled and whipped itself in circles until her insides turned to soup. The air was sucked out of the room, and she couldn't breathe. Kiko was not a homewrecker, and she was not interfering with this mess. Amanda was firmly in camp no-opposite-sex-friends, and as much as she despised the woman, Kiko had to respect her wishes.

"I need to go." Kiko stood on shaky limbs.

"Kiko, wait," Eric said.

Kiko rushed out of the restaurant with tears stinging her eyes. She was stupid for getting involved in his life. It was all her fault the perfectly dysfunctional power couple was going to fight. And while they could mend their issues, Kiko was still alone. She called a local cab and rode straight home while tears washed her face.

Chapter 13

WHAT ERIC WANTED TO do and what his wife made him do were two very different things. Rather than chase after Kiko, he'd escorted Amanda out of the building, disappointed in The Commodore's security response. And since lunch break was over, he'd dragged Amanda back to the office while plotting ways for her to have an accident all afternoon. He'd never go through with it, but a man could dream, right? His unusual good luck the other day made him dream of buying a lottery ticket to change his life, but in reality, it was already changing. He just needed to survive the process of separation.

Eric hit the speaker button for the incoming call while sorting his presentation paperwork for tomorrow, and as soon as he was finished, he was heading straight to Kiko's house for a massive round of apologies. He didn't blame her for not returning to the office after that disaster. "Talk to me."

"Eric, I've read through the divorce papers you signed, but we have a problem." It was Derek, his attorney downstairs.

"I don't want to hear the P-word, Derek. What's wrong?"

"Can you come to my office? We'll get this fixed in a minute."

"See you in two." Eric lifted the handset and dropped it back on the cradle. He read through every line before signing, but he didn't see any red flags. That was what he paid his attorney for.

Eric pressed a fresh line on his phone. "Caroline, hold my calls. I'm meeting with Derek."

"Yes, sir."

Eric caught the next available elevator and strolled into his attorney's office downstairs. The secretary waved him by with a nod and a smile. With a single knock against the open door's frame, Eric stepped inside Derek's classy office. Mahogany, leather, and black accents smelled like quality...and money. Blue Feather could use a facelift, but Eric's priorities for the company didn't allow such unnecessary spending, and as long as the company trended upward, his dad didn't argue. Eric wasn't cheap, as a meal at The Commodore proved, but he did value time. He wanted Blue Feather around for a long while, and Eric was the right numbers man for the job. He also wanted something else around for a long time, and he really needed to get out of here before he was too late.

"Have a seat. This won't take long," Derek said.

That was good news. Eric sunk into a squeaky leather chair across from the attorney's desk. "What's the issue?"

"To properly counsel you, we should go over them. Like here, line B, petitioner gives up the right to receive maintenance and understands that by giving up maintenance at this time, may never ask for maintenance," Derek read to him.

Eric leaned forward. Amanda was cunning, and that meant time was of the essence, which was why Eric had signed the papers already. "She waived free money. It's unlike her, but I'm not arguing."

Derek nodded and skimmed through the pages. "And here, division of real estate. She's requesting you keep the house and pay her half the equity value."

"That sounds like what I read."

"It looks to me like Amanda wants to take the cash and run. For being married two years, I'd say she's making out like a bandit, and as your counsel, I recommend you negotiate. But as far as the paperwork goes, it's fair."

Eric skimmed the pages again where Derek stopped his assessment. An angry finger stabbed the page. "Wait, she's getting half my cash and half the equity, but here, she also wants eighty percent of my next bonus. Cece's launch hasn't happened yet, and we don't even know how much it will be. How can she ask that?" How did he miss that?

"I'll get the paperwork drafted up for you." Derek dug in a desk drawer and set a notepad on the surface. He sighed. "I know you're a numbers guy, and I generally don't discourage my business, but I want you to be aware escalating this will cost a few hundred hours multiplied by my hourly rate. What's your usual bonus compared to that?"

Derek's fees would absolutely be higher than the bonus.

"Or you can sign and save yourself time and hassle. The real question is what's an amicable divorce worth to you?"

Eric was ready to move on with his life, and he could always make more money. "You called me down for a problem. Divorce is miserable, but I don't see a problem here."

"You missed a signature right here." Derek flipped pages, pointed at the blank line, and passed him the documents.

"Pen, please." Without hesitation, Eric signed away half his life and excised the worst part of him. The relief of being untangled from Amanda Carter gave him wings.

But she was still an anchor around his foot. He'd counted on that bonus to pay for her half of the equity. He'd have to give up the other half of his cash just to pay her off now, leaving him broke until his measly twenty percent bonus share came. And that share was needed to cover the legal fees.

In the end, he'd have a mortgaged house and an amazing job, and since he could always make more money, he'd be back to his old ways soon. A lottery ticket wasn't such a bad idea now. "You'll take care of it from here?" Eric asked.

Derek nodded.

"Thanks. Keep me posted." As a free man, Eric had somewhere to be.

ERIC HITCHED A RIDE in the company limo and told Stan to stop at the grocery store, because chocolates and flowers weren't enough. Stan insisted on helping Eric with whatever surprise planning he had in mind, but Eric wanted to do this. Unfortunately, it was the wrong time of year for what Eric needed, and short of baking from scratch himself, he had to settle for a frozen pie and a backup treat. Ready to surprise Kiko and apologize like his life depended on it, Eric launched himself out of the limo, and his feet ate up the porch stairs. A bright yellow square fluttered on her door. Curious, he lifted the sticky note and read it, half expecting it to be a goodbye to him.

The handwriting was messy. If he had to guess, definitely male, so it wasn't from her addressed to him. "My heart aches for how much I've missed you." Kiko had a secret admirer...or a husband. More likely an estranged husband. Eric's stomach twisted. Was this apologetic display a huge mistake? Before he could turn around, the door opened.

Kiko's red-rimmed eyes and grim features spotted the note in his hand, then the flowers, the chocolates, and the grocery bag.

With the unexpectedly cold response, Eric's heart pounded in his ears. He had to apologize, and he had to ask the one question that would change their futures. "Can I come in?"

Kiko glanced over his shoulders, stepped aside, and closed the door behind him.

"I'm so sorry for what Amanda did. That was uncalled for, inappropriate, unprofessional." Just like his ex-wife. The corners of his lips lifted. "It shouldn't have happened, and it won't happen again."

Kiko wrapped her arms around herself, bunching the material of an oversized sweater. "You shouldn't be here."

A chill ran through him. This was the question. He asked softly, "Are you expecting someone? A…husband or boyfriend?"

Kiko tilted her head at him. "No, no, it's not that. It's just, what's to stop her from banging on my door next?"

"It's simple. Sit with me, and I'll explain." Eric set the gifts on the dining table, heart soaring at her being single, and went straight to her oven. He turned it on, and then searched the kitchen drawers until he found utensils and plates.

"What are you doing?" she asked, still standing where he'd left her.

While the oven preheated, Eric set the flatware on the table and returned to her.

She backed up a step.

This was not at all how he saw this going, and his chest constricted. "I'm sorry you had to see that. If I could've shoved Amanda out the door, believe me, I would've. I'm going to have a word with The Commodore about their security response."

Eric expected a small smile, but he didn't get one. "I don't know what I ever saw in her, truthfully. I suppose I was lonely, and she was convenient. Have a seat. I insist."

Kiko picked up the bouquet and brought the flowers to her nose. "They need water before they dry out and wilt. Something so beautiful deserves a chance to shine."

Eric was not going to read into that. Repeat—not going to.

Kiko snipped the ends and placed the flowers in a tall drinking glass. They tipped off balance a few times before she got it just right. Next time, he'd get her a vase. Kiko set the table.

Eric flipped over the frozen pie. "Sixty minutes! Seriously." Eric turned off the oven. "Kiko, I'm going with the backup plan. It's not your favorite, but forgive me."

"There have been worse atrocities forgiven. It'll be fine," Kiko said, amused.

Eric put the frozen pumpkin pie into her freezer and slipped the backup treat out of the grocery bag. He carved up wedges of the cheesecake and licked his fingers, and Kiko watched him with a distant coldness he hated. He served a plate for her and then one for himself. "I brought your favorite pumpkin pie, but it's in the freezer for later. Until then, we have strawberry cheesecake. A worthy second place, I hope?"

Kiko lifted her fork, and a genuine smile reached her eyes. "You remember my favorite pie?"

Eric smiled warmly. "How could I forget?"

"This feels...I don't know," Kiko said, warming up to him but still hesitating to let him in. "Like a bigger apology than what a friend would do. I feel like...I should set stricter boundaries here, but I really want the cheesecake."

Eric chuckled, despite her use of the word 'friend' tearing his heart out. "Eat the cheesecake. I insist. You're right to feel like something is off here, because I feel it too, and I don't like it. This distance between us isn't natural."

The smile slipped away, and Kiko swallowed her bite. "Eric, things were different then. I've changed. I still want to be your friend, it's just…" she trailed off and looked at the door.

"I don't want to be your friend," he said. That got her attention. "Amanda served me, and our divorce papers were signed today." Eric lifted his hand and dangled his empty ring finger.

Kiko set down the fork and frowned. "Was this…my fault? Did I get between you two?"

The memory of her had. Kiko was all he could ever think about, but her appearance didn't change that. "This was a long time coming, I just couldn't see through the clouds, and now I'm better than I've been in years, honestly." Besides being broke, it was the truth.

"This changes things at the office. Amanda—" Kiko started.

"Don't worry about her. She will be dealt with. I would be honored if you came to work tomorrow."

"And your dad is okay with that?"

"My dad might make a snide remark here or there, but he's harmless."

Kiko nodded. "I'll be there."

Eric always hoped to find a match to his power-couple dream, something Dad had never found, something Eric thought he found in Amanda. Eric always believed Kiko was the one for him, and her bravery in showing face tomorrow, knowing

Amanda's ire, gave him soaring hope. Eager to get closer, Eric collected the plates. He brought them to the sink and filled the basin with soapy water, quickly finding his way around her kitchen.

Kiko's hand gently rested on his forearm. "Thank you."

He grinned at her. "You're welcome."

"No, I mean really thank you…for everything. The flowers, the candies. The note—"

Eric frowned. "You mean that yellow sticky note?" He pointed a soapy finger at the table where he'd stuck it.

"And the other one. I found it on my door."

Eric dried his hands off and turned to face her. "I'm more forward than that, as you can see. Those notes weren't from me."

Chapter 14

Kiko's eyes widened in...alarm? Surprise? Hope? Love? Fear? So many things rushed through her heart all at once, she didn't know which one to focus on. But gazing upon Eric's worried face made her heart bloom with heat.

Eric Woodson, single, sexy, amazingly kind—and did she mention single?—was the man for her. Chaos promised her three trips, and she'd spent one without knowing who her match was. The second was her failure to save Eric from Roger, and Chaos had asked if she was ready to 'try again'. Eric was Kiko's true happiness. Her true love. It seemed obvious now.

But Roger was safely three hours away, so who left her a note on her door? From what she could tell, this wasn't a woman's handwriting, and the only people she'd met since she moved in here...a few days ago... "It's probably for the previous tenant."

Eric smiled. "That makes sense."

Kiko and Eric, both single, both alone in her house. Her gaze shifted to his mouth, and Kiko's heart thundered in her chest. She remembered the moment she'd first made eye contact with him. There was an energy between them, something she couldn't ignore. She'd struggled to keep her eyes off him, so she grew vines around her heart to pad against the sharp edges of pain. She loved Yoshi, but after his death, her vulnerability wilted those padded vines. She and Eric shared memories and feelings, they'd watched movies and shared food. He was her best friend. She didn't have the strength to keep him out of her heart, but Eric had a girlfriend, and she had been offered the ultimate job.

Seeing no other option, she'd left.

Finding the newspaper clipping of his wedding to Amanda Carter wasn't the only time she'd checked up on him. Long before that, her heart had driven her to his door a few times, but what could she ever say to him? If she told the truth, she would've risked losing her only friend.

On the final visit, in the dark, across the street from his Milwaukee residence, she'd watched Eric laugh and dance with the beautiful blonde, now she knew was Amanda, and her heart had shattered. So she dedicated herself to the job, writing three hundred stories to escape her lonely thoughts.

Eric was the one. It just hadn't been the right time, and now everything was perfect. Eric had said he didn't want to be her friend. Kiko didn't want that either.

She wanted more.

As Eric gazed into her eyes, kissing him was the only thing she could do. With strawberry cheesecake on her tongue, Kiko lifted on her heels and pressed her lips to his. Eric eagerly curled himself around her, enveloping her in the safety of his arms, and decades of unrequited daydreams and wishes had finally filled Kiko's heart. Tears of happiness formed on her lids.

This was not the quick peck on the cheek Eric had given her all those years ago.

This was tender passion and desperation. The pain of being an invisible ghost fluttering through time evaporated. From the outside, she'd watched moments like this hundreds of times, but feeling it was something incomparable.

Eric lifted her off her feet, and she wrapped her legs around his waist as he easily carried her to the bedroom and rested her on the soft comforter. He gently caressed her face as if memorizing her features, and he swiped away her tears. "What's wrong?"

She remembered what the fun-loving grandpa said, 'If I don't have their trust, I have nothing.' Eric trusted her, but he didn't know her, and she couldn't tell him the truth—who she was, what she'd done, or where she'd been. She couldn't handle the look on his face if she tried. Kiko smiled. "Nothing. There's nothing wrong. Kiss me again."

Eric's touches trailed heat along her skin. His breath softly panted against her face. He leaned upright and shucked his suit coat in a flash, the fabric sailing across the room, and he unfastened the buttons of his shirt in a slow tease. All the while, he stared at her with sexy need, as if no one else in the world existed.

Heat rolled through her body in waves, throbbing in her head and pounding her clit with a wild desire to explore the unknown lands of Eric Woodson. Kiko climbed to her knees, and she peeled back his dress shirt and slipped it free from his shoulders. Her palms glided along his sculpted chest. For being a man of the desk these days, he sure did keep up with his gym routine. His work showed in the ridges of his abs, the rounded pecs, the taut navel. He was beautiful inside and out.

"Like what you see?" he whispered.

A pounding knock on the front door turned their heads.

Eric said with a frown, "That doesn't sound like a package delivery."

"Maybe it's the person leaving the notes," Kiko said.

"Then a polite conversation is in order." Shirtless, Eric headed for the front door.

Kiko climbed off the bed and rushed after him, wanting to see Eric in better lighting. But instead of focusing on the glorious view, she flinched in horror at the visitor—a broad, fluffy-haired Roger Meyer. Kiko covered her gaping mouth with her hand. How? When? More importantly, how?

Eric folded his arms over his bare chest and glared. "What are you doing here?"

Kiko figured out Eric was her true love, but Chaos gave her one last chance, so that meant something bad was going to happen. Kiko didn't know what or when, but now that Roger found her, the timer had been set. With the emergency responder in her pocket, she moved in front of Eric's glorious body. "It was you leaving those notes."

Roger's challenging stare shifted to Kiko, his designer sunglasses nestling on top of his fluffy hair. His wide eyes were framed with age lines, and he had shaved his beard. When she'd first met him, she thought he was handsome, and traditionally speaking, he was. But all she could see was the broken brain in his skull and his dead heart in his chest, and she wished her restraining order was actually useful.

"Woodson," Roger acknowledged Eric, and strolled past him as if he wasn't a threat at all. In an unwanted case of déjà vu, Roger strolled around her place, assessing it as if it were for sale.

Eric was half naked and empty-handed. Yoshi had told her how great Eric fought—Yoshi's only true match in kendo. But where Yoshi and Eric had speed and agility, Roger had bulk and strength, and history proved in a match between them Roger would be the victor. Eric was the one who needed saving, not her! Kiko had nothing but her emergency responder. Dashing out the wide open door sounded like a good idea, but if Roger was insulted or angered, he'd chase them down like a rabid dog. Eric had taught her to use distraction, and Kiko needed to keep Roger levelheaded until the right moment.

Kiko casually moved toward the kitchen, drawing Roger's attention away from Eric. The meaty monster's face was unreadable, and chills crawled to her marrow. She'd failed once to kill Roger with a steak knife, and she had nothing bigger. For once, she wished she had Yoshi's katana, not that she knew how to use it.

Eric did.

That was a useless thought. Focus. Calling the police would only anger him, and technically he hadn't done anything wrong yet, unless he carried his pistol. And angering an armed felon was not something she was willing to do.

Eric closed the door against the crisp spring evening and intercepted Roger like a bodyguard. No, he couldn't do that. He had no idea of the true danger.

Roger smirked. "Settle down, Woodson. No need to mark your territory."

Eric glared, tension pulling him like a tight string ready to snap. Kiko needed to redirect Roger. "You left those notes on my door, didn't you?"

Roger grinned at her. "I didn't realize I had competition again."

Roger never loved Kiko. He never wanted her or a committed relationship with her. He only wanted one thing, and that was something Kiko would never give him, something Yoshi died to protect.

Roger recited from memory, "'Been hiding in plain sight all these years. My heart aches for how much I've missed you.' The next one was going to read—meet me at Main Street Coffee for a surprise."

Kiko's breath hitched. Leaving Roger in the dust hours away wasn't good enough. "You wanted me to meet you in Milwaukee?"

"I didn't think you'd go so far from home."

"How did you find me?" Kiko asked, curious about how she'd screwed up.

Roger's gaze flicked to Eric as if checking for a threat, and his eyes fixed on the collage hanging on her wall. He turned and strutted toward it.

Kiko's breath released in a rush. She sent Eric a pleading stare that said, 'Don't make a move. He's probably carrying his pistol, and this is our last chance.' She had no idea if the message was received.

"I was there, man." Roger chuckled at the photos of their bowling night. "I don't remember it being so…happy. Eric and Yoshi both blocked me from you, Kiko, but all I wanted to do was apologize for coming on too strong." Roger laughed again, a sound that wasn't humor.

A chill snaked down Kiko's spine.

Roger spun on Eric with a snarl on his lips. "You and Yoshi treated me like an animal."

Kiko needed to figure out a way for her and Eric to escape before it was too late.

Chapter 15

W‍HILE R‍OGER'S MONOLOGUE DELVED deeper into dark memories, Eric watched and listened, not equipped at the moment to put an end to this. He wanted to embrace Kiko for her safety, but he knew, as well she, any affection between them would trigger his rage. The last time Roger had flipped, Eric consoled Yoshi's widow for months. He couldn't fathom what Roger was willing to do next. He wasn't the type to learn a lesson.

"I'm sorry if you felt that way, Roger. Eric and Yoshi were my friends, and they were worried for me. I was just trying to…" Kiko trailed off.

"Trying to what?" Roger prompted.

"Tell you I wasn't interested in you that way," she said carefully.

Roger towered over Kiko, but Eric stood sentry off her right shoulder, ready to strike if Roger made a move.

"And what about now?" Roger asked and squinted at Eric.

Kiko trembled. And while a mix of fear and anger burned in Eric's own gut, he contained himself to a silent menacing threat. In their dojo, Eric and Roger had been classed separately, so he'd never sparred with him. But from watching Roger in action, taking him on would do serious damage—to the few pieces of furniture in here, to Roger, and Eric admitted, to himself as well. Regardless, if he could keep Kiko safe, he'd never hesitate.

"Your messages are sweet, Rodg," Kiko said.

Roger's whole demeanor shifted from fired-up piston ready to charge to soft teddy bear. Eric could hardly believe his own eyes.

She added, "Can I think on it?"

Kiko was stalling, throwing him off his trajectory. Between her words and Eric's fists, they could get him to leave.

"Well, yeah. But is there anything I can do to...sway you?" Roger flashed his pearly whites, and Eric wanted to punch them loose.

"Just time. All I need is time." Kiko's lips pulled into a controlled smile.

"I've waited seven years. What's another day?" Roger asked.

For a flash of a moment, Eric pitied him. He understood the burning ache of waiting so long to be with Kiko. Eric was eternally grateful she'd chosen him.

"How about I call you, okay? I'll give you a call in a couple wee—"

Kiko stopped when Roger's face scrunched in disapproval. She quickly corrected, "Days. Just a couple of days."

Roger flipped up the collar of his shirt and tipped his sunglasses down onto the bridge of his nose.

Eric declined to inform him it was dark out.

Accepting her offer, Roger nodded and showed himself to the door. When his broad body hung half outside, he called back, "Just a couple days." His tone was light and pleasant, but Eric felt as if a timer on a detonator had just begun.

The door closed, and Kiko dashed over and flipped the deadbolt. Shaking hands fastened the sliding chain and turned the knob lock. She spun around, panting with fear, and the moment she saw Eric, she tackled him in a hug.

Eric squeezed her back, trying to soothe her trembles, and he closed his eyes in relief. "It's over for now," he said. Roger would return, but this time, he wouldn't take another delay for an answer.

"What am I going to tell him?" Kiko asked, voice shaky.

"Whatever you want to." Eric's hand rubbed her back while the other held her crushed to his chest.

"He won't take 'hell no' very well."

"I imagine not." Eric could call the police and tell them what—a man was going to come and make an unwanted advance? Speculative sexual harassment probably wasn't illegal. Roger should have a parole officer. Would he do anything? There was an easier alternative for both Roger and Amanda to cool off. "Let's get out of town for a while, a week."

Kiko's head tilted back. "Like a vacation?"

"My parents used to winter in Jamaica. Dad still owns a condo there," Eric said. "Good thing I didn't buy one too or Amanda would've taken that as well."

"A tropical vacation sounds amazing, but I just started a new job today," Kiko reminded him. "I don't have time off yet."

Eric smiled. Finally, an easy problem he could fix. He slipped his phone out of his pocket and lifted the antenna. "Caroline, message for Paul. Kiko and I are both taking a week's vacation starting now. Thank you." He closed his cell and said, "That's settled."

"You can do that?" The look of admiration on her eyes inflated his chest.

"My dad is the CEO. I can do whatever I want, for the most part."

"Well, my passport's expired. How about somewhere stateside?"

Traveling for business was a monthly bore. Sometimes

Amanda insisted on joining him just to go shopping, and every time a heavy weight settled upon his shoulders. But the idea of taking Kiko anywhere in the country, for fun, charged him with excitement. "Hmmm. It's April. Everything's half dead, damp, and brown. Where would you like to go?"

"Milwaukee."

Eric cringed. "Do you think half a million people in Roger's hometown is enough to hide in?" Eric had attended college at the University of Wisconsin Milwaukee and earned a black belt in kendo alongside Yoshi and Roger. Looking over his shoulder at every woman's face trying to find Kiko tore him up inside, but hope kept him there. He'd left because Blue Feather was located in Green Bay and Dad made him come help run the next family business. He didn't want to, but he'd started to lose hope.

"Roger's here now," Kiko said, "and I want to visit a couple of very special places."

If it meant that much to her, he would do it. "Done. Do you want to drive or fly?"

"It's only three and a half hours. We can drive."

Eric flipped open his cell again. "Stan, I need a ride tonight. Here's the address." Eric read off Kiko's address and hung up. "You've got twenty minutes to pack."

"Now?" Her eyes widened.

"I call and they do."

"Just like that?"

Eric was used to a lifestyle of people jumping when he said so and never asking for the price of anything. He did what he wanted, when he wanted. Of course, with the pending divorce, he needed to be careful with money for a couple months—after this vacation, a treat for her. Eric checked his watch. "Now you've got nineteen minutes to pack."

"What are you bringing?" Kiko asked, staring at his naked chest.

"You."

She chuckled. "We're leaving for a week, and you don't plan on taking any luggage?"

"I travel light. Getting out of here now is more important than extra clothes. Not that I'm saying you shouldn't pack, please do."

Kiko hesitated as if a spontaneous road trip was foreign to her. "What about your ID, personal items...cell phone charging cable?"

"I have my wallet, phone, and keys, and you're stalling." Eric patted his pockets to prove his preparedness.

"I just can't process leaving without taking anything. It feels more like fleeing than vacationing."

"You've got a point there. So, pack up for our fleeing, but I am going to grab my shirt." Eric collected his dress shirt off the floor of her bedroom and stuffed his arms back into his suit jacket.

Kiko followed and pulled a suitcase out from under her bed. While she packed, Eric went to the collage of photos he'd gifted her. They were smiling and having a great time until Roger showed up. He touched the glass as if pressing a comforting finger on Yoshi's shoulder. "I'll take care of her," he whispered.

The doorbell rang at Stan's arrival, and he was fully dressed in a suit and cap with white gloves. "Your ride has arrived, sir."

"We'll be out in a moment," Eric said.

"Yes, sir." Stan turned and walked down the steps to the waiting limo. The night air was a chilly reminder winter had just left. A cool breeze lifted the hair on his arms and the sidewalk was slick with condensation. He had the sudden urge to take Kiko by himself.

"Stan," Eric yelled over.

The limo driver returned to the foot of the stairs in a flash. "Yes, sir?"

"Take the night off. I'm driving."

"As you wish." Stan handed him the keys, turned, and slipped a phone out of his pocket to call for a ride home.

Eric closed the front door, and Kiko stepped out of her bedroom carrying two heavy bags.

He lifted them off her hands. "All set?"

"Just about." Kiko unplugged the coffee pot and toaster, checked the locks on her windows, and craned her neck around the house, pondering anything she missed. She turned the lights off on her way out the door. She needed a security system, or a more secure place to live. Another easy problem for Eric to solve.

"We can go now," she said, satisfied with her routine.

Eric brought her bags to the back seat.

"A limo?" Kiko asked. Her footsteps shuffled down the cement sidewalk.

Eric closed the rear passenger door. "Is there any other way to travel in style?" He opened the front passenger door and held her hand as she stepped inside.

"And I half expected a driver to be waiting."

Eric chuckled and closed the door. He slid into position behind the wheel, and his fingers found the controls and rolled the seat back half a foot. Stan was a short dude. "Nope, just us."

Eric rolled the limo away from the curb and merged onto the highway. It would be the middle of the night before they got there. He had one more call to make.

"Wilston Resort. Can I help you?" A familiar feminine voice rang in his ear.

"Sherise? This is Eric Woodson. I need the top level for a week."

"Hi, Eric." She purred in his ear. He smiled and shook his head, cheeks burning. "When are you checking in?"

"Tonight."

"And how many in your room?"

Eric glanced at Kiko and the realization he was booking a hotel room with her for a week dawned on him. His stomach swirled with nerves and excitement. "Two adults. No kids. Charge it to my card, please."

"Done and done. See you soon."

Eric hung up. Sherise's rough voice was always an obvious invitation, but Eric never acted upon it.

"You sound like a regular there," Kiko said.

"Blue Feather attends industry events there on the regular." His hand sought hers on her thigh, and their fingers interlaced. Eric drove half the night, stopping for gas and snacks, and resumed until they checked in. Roger couldn't find them here, but Eric wouldn't put it past him to try.

Chapter 16

Kiko was surprised but grateful for a quick getaway, and she couldn't wait to have Eric all to herself for a week. Kiko climbed out of the limo and stretched, legs stiff from the long ride. Eric carried her bags, despite her objections, and he led her to the front desk.

"Good evening, Eric," the hotel receptionist with curly blue hair and a nose ring greeted Eric with a familiarity and a fire in her eye.

"Hey, Sherise. Are we all set?" Eric was cool and nonchalant with her, oblivious to her unprofessional greeting.

Kiko had seen hundreds of matches through time, and Chaos never steered her wrong. She trusted Eric more than anything, so she waved away her unfounded jealousy.

"Top floor, suite two." As she held out the room key, Sherise's smile was top-notch customer service mixed with a hint of flirt.

Kiko couldn't blame the woman. Eric was definitely a man worth flirting with.

"Thank you." Eric bent and lifted Kiko's bags.

As a nomad for a century, it was weird to have someone do things for her. She didn't need help, and she didn't want to be treated as less than. "I can carry one or both. It's my stuff," Kiko said.

Eric scrutinized her. "Tell you what, we each take one, and I get to hold your hand."

Kiko smiled. "That's a deal I can live with."

Eric offered her a bag and took her hand, and she loved his easygoing flexibility. Her hand crackled with its own energy on the entire ride up. At the top floor, Eric led her to the right door as if he'd been here a million times. Inside was a mix of warm and modern with cozy cottage that worked. The kitchen had a commercial feel with dangling lights and bright stainless steel. Eric set her bag down and watched her.

Kiko moved into the living room in absolute amazement. The floor dipped down a couple steps, with the overstuffed couch and coffee table in the center and a large TV looming nearby. The living room exterior wall was solid glass, showing lights dotting the dark cityscape. She set her suitcase down and wrapped her arms around herself. Red and white pairs of lights crawled along the city streets below, and at the edge of the horizon, the moon shimmered over Lake Michigan. Kiko sighed.

"Nice view?" Eric said in her ear.

Kiko turned. "Beautiful."

"Do you want room service?"

"It's late. Everyone's asleep." Which sounded really good right about now.

"Not here. This room has service at any hour of the day."

Wined and dined like a princess. This was so out of her league, but a steaming plate of mashed potatoes, gravy, and a steak sounded perfect. Her stomach growled. But she didn't want to disturb people who should be sleeping. Kiko bit her lip. "That's okay."

Eric lifted the phone anyway. "Hi, Maurice. Give me two number sevens. Side of broccoli. Extra gravy. Thanks."

Kiko cocked a brow and laughed. "You can't be serious."

"I know the look of hunger when I see it. It's no trouble. The night shift is bored without something to do."

"You know them better than I do." Kiko didn't argue. She was starving and perhaps he was right.

While they waited, Kiko unpacked her things in the bedroom and carried her toiletries to the bathroom. Flicking on the lights, her eyes popped wide. She told herself the fixtures were brass because real gold would be crazy. She set her travel toothbrush holder on the sink's countertop and realized all the toiletries she'd brought, they'd already offered. As a time traveling matchmaker, Kiko had been an invisible nomad, so she'd always kept a low profile. This was definitely not low profile.

And Kiko wasn't completely sure those accents weren't gold.

When she left the bathroom, a stainless steel cart was parked next to the table. Eric had set both covered dishes on place mats across from each other and two glasses filled with wine. Eric settled the utensils rolled in cloth napkins on each side. Noticing her, he turned and flashed a smile. "Normally Maurice does this, but I thought you'd prefer the privacy. Have a seat."

Kiko sat where he gestured, and Eric settled across from her. When he went for his lid, Kiko lifted hers. Steaming steak, fluffy mashed potatoes with a lake of gravy, and broccoli. She didn't believe in coincidence. "Eric, this is…" she stopped, trying to control the emotion clogging her throat.

Eric smiled warmly. "I was stuck on a business trip during Thanksgiving 1987, and I regretted it every day of my life. I missed out on one last meal with you and Yoshi, so when I returned to town, I brought you a substitute, but it wasn't good enough. At the time, I didn't know you hated turkey, so I ordered you the steak and broccoli tonight, and if I remembered right—a trough of gravy."

Kiko blinked back tears. She had no idea he cared so much

about her or that he was such a romantic at heart. When she found her tongue, she said, "You remember that?"

"I promised you a Kiko-preferred celebration, so Happy proper Thanksgiving, eight years later."

"Thank you," she whispered.

"No thanks necessary. I always make good on my word, and it was my pleasure. Dig in before it gets cold." Eric lifted a fork and knife.

Kiko indulged her screaming stomach. The swimmy potatoes were perfect, and the steak was medium-rare, just as she liked it.

"Do you miss him?" Eric asked.

She swallowed and exhaled a deep breath. "I did. For many years I hurt, and I woke up with nightmares, but over time, as I indulged myself in distractions and put things into perspective, the pain lessened. The whole tragedy feels like a distant bad memory, but I feel like he's still around, you know?"

"You sound like you've aged decades."

Kiko chuckled awkwardly. "Feels that way."

"And yet you don't look a day older than the last time I saw you."

She shrugged to play it off. "Good genetics."

"You've got something here." Eric pointed to his lip to guide her.

Kiko stuck out her tongue to clean the spot. "Is it gone?"

"Nope. Here, let me get it." Eric leaned across the table, reaching for her face.

Kiko's heart thundered as his thumb softly swiped the corner of her mouth. Eric stared at her with a need that couldn't be satisfied with a table between them.

"I got it." He licked his thumb, and Kiko shivered.

Eric's cell phone rang. He swore and looked at the caller ID. On a sigh, he said, "It's the office, and it must be important at four in the morning. I need to take this. I'm sorry."

Kiko nodded her understanding. She wanted to explore every inch of Eric, but frankly, she was exhausted as hell and wanted nothing more than a cozy bed right now.

"Hello?" Eric answered.

Kiko couldn't make out the other voice.

"For sure? That's excellent. Yes, eighty-twenty like I agreed. Okay, fine. Look, I'm busy. We can talk about this another time." Eric slapped the phone shut and set it down, a mix of angry steam and bubbling excitement percolating through him.

"Everything okay?" It wasn't her business, but curiosity and drowsiness drove her to ask.

He swallowed a bite of steak and said, "That was Amanda. Why she's up at this hour, I'll never understand. Something about step aerobics. Anyway, Fred Carter put out feelers for stores and distribution centers. Cece's newest release has a quarter million preorders now."

Kiko's mind blanked. "What does that mean?"

"Besides never hearing the end of it from Amanda?" Eric grinned. "It means you joined the team at a great time. Expect a nice bonus before summer."

Kiko tilted her head. "I get a bonus and so far all I've done was show up to a drama-filled meeting?"

Eric chuckled, the excitement animating him. "The author's agent gets their standard cut, but Blue Feather gives employees a bonus with each successful launch. The amounts are higher for upper management, naturally, but you'll be included, and that was perfect luck."

Kiko didn't believe luck had anything to do with it.

Thanks, Chaos. Not for the money, but for Eric's happiness.

Chapter 17

Eric was alone in a hotel room with the only woman he'd ever truly wanted, and after their long night's journey to get here, a satisfying dinner, and a very welcome call from a very unwelcome person, he wanted to ravage Kiko between the sheets. But, he'd been awake for way too long, and he was running on fumes.

He yawned and collected their dishes and returned them to the cart. "I don't know about you, but I'm beat."

"I am too, but this luxury suite only has one bed."

Eric cocked a lazy grin. "I could fall asleep on anything right now, but I insist we share that expansive mattress. I promise I don't bite, unless you want me to."

Kiko chuckled.

"I don't want to disappoint you. I'm not sure I could right now even if you asked."

Kiko smiled. "I wouldn't ask that of you."

That wasn't a yes or a no, but more like a later. Eric liked that. She followed him into the bedroom, and he pressed the button by the nightstand. All the curtains rolled down, blacking out the breaking dawn. In the bathroom, he stripped out of his dress pants and shirt and covered up with a luxurious silk bathrobe. Kiko had her clothing in her arms, ready for her turn. "Bathroom's yours. I don't think I'll be awake the minute my head hits that pillow."

"Then I'll be quick so I can claim my half of the mattress territory."

Eric slipped between the sheets with a lazy smile on his face, and he shucked the robe. He fought to stay awake long enough to curl up next to her.

When Kiko stepped out, she wore cute pajamas—pink with unicorns, and she climbed into the other side of the bed.

Eric rolled onto his back, fighting his heavy eyelids. "Do you believe in unicorns?"

Kiko shifted on the bed, and her heat warmed the bare skin of his thighs and arms. "I believe there are elements around us we fail to see or understand, but they are real." Her voice softened as sleep pulled her down.

"Are you talking about ghosts?" For years he'd talked to Yoshi's ghost, but he never got an answer.

"Something like that. From my travels, I can resolutely declare these unicorns from my pajamas do not exist, but if you want to get technical, there are versions of unicorns around—narwhals, Indian rhinos, unicorn tangs, Texas unicorn mantis, goblin spiders, and the unicorn shrimp."

Eric chuckled, and there was a unicorn in bed with him. "How do you know all this?"

Her soft laugh vibrated across the sheets. "I read a lot, and I like animals. Unlike humans, when animals bite, at least it's expected. I like that predictability."

Eric made a note to clearly communicate his intention to bite. Intrigued, Eric drowsily asked, "What's your preferred genre?"

"I think it would be called time travel romance." Kiko sighed.

Eric smiled. All he'd known Kiko to read was college textbooks. "A dreamer of sappy fantasy."

"I'm not going to dignify that with a response."

"Hey, if you like cheese, I can get you cheese." Eric's arm snaked out and lifted the phone's handset. "I need cheese," he said into the empty receiver. "Lots of sappy…cheese."

Kiko swatted him on the shoulder, and he chuckled and dropped the handset, but her effort slid the sheets down. She asked, "You're not wearing a shirt?"

"I sleep naked."

Silence thickened the room's air.

"Is that okay with you?" he added.

"It's fine. I was just surprised." Kiko yawned, and Eric caught the yawn bug, too.

When he opened his eyes, the room was dark as night, the sheets warm as an oven baking cookies, and the air comfortably cool. The weight of Kiko's arm across his chest left a thick band of damp skin, but it wasn't covered in pink unicorns. Her arm was naked.

Alarmed, Eric reached over and pressed the button for the curtains to rise. He waited for light to shine upon the bed and reveal what had happened last night, because damn if they had sex and he didn't remember it.

A tangle of sheets and a comforter draped over their bodies. Eric lifted a corner of the material and checked her upper body. It was covered. He released a deep breath, and the hair on her head flitted in the breeze. Eric moved her arm off his chest, sat up, and slipped into the hotel's robe. When he returned from freshening up, Kiko and her pink unicorns lounged against the headboard, ankles crossed as if she'd had the most relaxing evening of her life.

"That was the best night's sleep I've had in years," she said, hopping out of bed.

"Well, we didn't actually sleep last night. It's two in the

afternoon. Room service?"

"Please."

Kiko freshened in the bathroom, while Eric dialed down for orange juice, coffee, and the whole breakfast buffet. The cart rolled into the room shortly thereafter and he tipped the man well. He appreciated the personal service the Wilston offered.

Kiko loaded up her plate just as high as he did, but she was much smaller than him. Where was she going to put it all? The corner of his lips lifted.

"So where's the first special place you want to go to?" Eric asked between bites of scrambled eggs. He unfolded the complimentary newspaper and skimmed the headlines. With no answer, Eric looked up.

Kiko squinted at him in a playful challenge.

"Bowling?" he guessed with an equally playful squint.

She grinned. "Without Roger this time."

"Done and done. I would be relieved to never see him again." The guy could rot in a cell for all Eric cared.

"Me, too. Do you think this vacation is enough distance to deter him?"

Eric wanted to reassure her they'd never come across him again, but he couldn't lie to her. After all the sneaking around his mother did, Eric couldn't stand liars. "After considering it, I wonder if it'll just tick him off more."

"That's what I'm afraid of." Her eyes sunk to her food.

"Hey," Eric covered her hand with his. "I won't let anything happen to you." And he truly meant it.

At the shop downstairs, Eric's cell phone rang while Kiko bought a disposable camera. The caller ID displayed Amanda's name. He gritted his teeth and canceled the call. Every time he started to enjoy his time away with Kiko, his ex-wife interrupted, almost like she planned to keep herself in his thoughts. Frustratingly, it worked. A moment later, his phone beeped with a voicemail.

Sliding the phone back into his pocket, Eric drove them to the old bowling alley, which was already busy with leagues. Memories flooded his brain while he watched people rolling balls down the alley and cheering, while upgraded animated turkeys danced on screens overhead. Beer cups splashed in celebration. A fast grin cracked his face. They stepped up to the counter and rented shoes.

"Do you want the bumpers?" he asked.

Kiko smirked, and it fired up his competitive engine. "The gutter ball queen is dead."

"Oh, looking for a challenge, are we?"

"Just keep your shoes on, fella. I've been practicing."

Eric collected their shoes and paid for the lane. "So you're planning on scoring over ninety?"

"I'll be scoring plenty."

Eric hoped so, and he didn't mean the game. They both chose their balls and set them into the return. Kiko dug out her disposable camera and motioned for him to join her.

Eric eagerly sat next to her and she wrapped her arm around his waist, sending sparks from the point of contact straight to his cock. She snapped a few photos and smiled. Shaking off his nerves, he hugged her shoulders, and they made faces for the camera and laughed. She kept snapping away.

"I wish Yoshi could be here," he said and then thought, as much as that was true, how would it change what he had now?

Kiko didn't directly answer. "Let's save a few shots for another day."

Eric liked the sound of that. "You name the place, and I'll be there."

A glint shined in her eyes. "Let's play."

"Sure, short stuff. Show me what you're made of."

"I'm not that short."

"Not when you wear heels, sweetheart."

"You'll regret calling me sweetheart, too." Kiko winked, collected her ball, and curved her wrist, sending it rumbling down the lane toward the pins. Strike.

Eric's brows lifted. No longer the shy girl, she was confident and skilled. This new Kiko excited him in ways he feared would be his undoing, but he loved it.

KIKO SPENT DECADES HONING skills in all things interesting, including sports requiring only concentration and accuracy—darts, billiards, bowling, and yes, beer pong. Sports requiring coordination still embarrassed her. She would never shoot a 3-pointer on the basketball court.

But bowling she could finally do.

Strike after strike earned her a turkey. Eric kept pace, and with only one frame left to roll, they were only two pins apart in score. The excitement of the game, the friendly competition, the happy memories overlapping, all pounded through her veins in a carefree excitement she hadn't experienced since she was much, much younger. A happy sigh escaped her lips before she swallowed down a red plastic cup of beer.

Eric's phone rang again, and he frowned at it.

"Something wrong?" Kiko asked.

"Amanda's pestering me again. The last call was about a mountain of preorders. I wonder what news she has now."

"Maybe you should answer it."

Eric stared at the phone, debating. Kiko didn't believe he liked his soon-to-be ex-wife very much, but that was understandable.

"I suppose." He flipped open his phone, and the call instantly answered. "Hello?"

Kiko couldn't hear Amanda's side of the conversation, whether she wanted to or not. All around them pins crashed, people shouted in excitement, and bowling balls made sucking and thumping noises when they returned.

"I'm on vacation." Eric paused. "A prelaunch celebration? Yeah, she's here." Eric glanced at Kiko with wide eyes. "What are you talking about? I signed the papers. We're done." He flipped the phone closed with more force than necessary.

"I guess it wasn't good news."

"She's having regrets. Just give me a minute, okay?" He opened his phone again and dialed.

Oh, that was bad news. People married for a reason, and just because their bond was broken now, didn't mean it was irreparable. She hoped Eric wouldn't reconcile, and suddenly she felt dirty interfering with their marriage.

Had she been wrong about who her happily-ever-after was?

Kiko's stomach swirled with the unsettled beer. She no longer felt guilty about hijacking Eric's time away from his girlfriend after Yoshi's death, but there was a disappointing pattern emerging.

"Derek? Amanda's flying off the hook. I don't care what it costs. Get this thing over ASAP. Bribe the judge for an earlier hearing if you must. Yes, I'm aware of your rate. Yes, I know the financial disclosure statements I signed. Don't worry about it. I'll buy you a six-pack. Thank you." Eric sighed with frustration.

Kiko was hopeful but didn't press. It wasn't her business after all.

"Only a month ago I thought my marriage was fine," Eric said, staring at his closed phone. "Not awesome, but you know, going through the motions. We shared a big house, the suburbanite McMansion symbol of success. I worked, she worked. But when we were home, we stayed separate. She left to go out with friends and shopped frequently. I admit when I was home, I was still working most of the time. Maybe my subconscious was avoiding her all this time. I didn't see a point to picking up a hobby when there was work to be done. Even kendo and bowling fell by the wayside."

"That's terrible." Not only the loss of his favorite hobbies, but also the coldness of his marriage.

He chuckled. "I see that now. And then one day, she hands me papers, requesting a divorce. At first, I was blown away, but it didn't take much self-reflection before I got over it."

"At least you have your whole life ahead of you," Kiko said, assuming she didn't screw up saving him one last time.

Eric's smoldering eyes turned to her. Heat roared through her body, and she wasn't going to waste the time she had. Kiko glanced at his lips. "You remember that kiss in my house after Yoshi died?"

Eric shifted his weight in the seat next to her, facing her properly. "Every day."

Kiko sucked in a breath. She had no idea what to say to that.

He continued, "I thought about that kiss every day for years. I wondered if I'd made a mistake, because you disappeared right after. I couldn't help but think it was my fault, that I chased you away." Eric rubbed the back of his neck with his hand. "Ironically, I went there to tell you how I felt, but shame and guilt over that kiss made me leave."

"Because of your girlfriend?" Kiko asked.

Eric smiled sadly, "We broke up that day. I felt guilty over Yoshi. I always felt like he was watching me and watching over you. I know it sounds wild, but I pictured him raging at me."

Kiko's heart stopped in her chest. He hadn't cheated. If what he said was true, her doubts were entirely unfounded. "You didn't chase me away. I took a job, and I couldn't return for a while."

"And what was that?"

Kiko needed an excuse fast. The journals popped into her head. "Writing."

"Those adventure stories?"

"Time travel romance," she said with a cringe. She was well-aware of the stigma around romance.

Eric shook his head with a grin.

"What?" she demanded.

"I would've pegged you for scientific journals, psychology studies, or The Effects of Fast Food on Emerging Children's Brains. Stuff like that. But hey, write what you like to read, right?"

"Are you saying I don't have passion?"

Eric leaned back with surprised interest. "You have far more passion than I recall."

"That's just a nice way of saying—look, you're not a nerd anymore."

"If you want to take it that way."

"Hey!" Kiko took mock offense.

"I happen to like nerds," Eric said. His eyes roamed her face. "A traveling writer, huh? I happen to know a guy who publishes…"

She laughed and her cheeks heated ahead of her confession. "I did travel all the time, but I wanted to see you. When I had a break between…stories, I stopped by your house. You seemed so happy, I didn't want to interfere, dredging up the past. I thought it was best if I didn't contact you after that. The kiss was no mistake—"

Her words were cut off as Eric's eager lips fell upon hers. His hands cupped her cheeks and moved to the back of her head and nape of her neck. He didn't let go, he didn't let up, and she didn't want him to. His perfect lips shifted, and the throbbing need to be with him returned.

Why hadn't she pulled back the sheets to see him last night!

She was too tired then, but she definitely wasn't now. Heat roared through her body, pulsing in rhythm to her heart.

Kiko's hands slipped into the thick strands of blond hair and grasped his back, pleading with him to get closer. Muscles undulated under her fingertips, and a small moan escaped her lips. Eric groaned in his restrained pleasure.

"Get a room, you two." A voice carried over the din of the bowling alley, and Kiko and Eric pulled apart. His forehead rested on hers, and he panted against her face. After a moment, they both cracked smiles.

"Busted," she whispered.

"We weren't being discreet."

"True. How about we roll the last frame and get out of here?"

"You're on."

Eric bowled a strike, of course. Kiko debated whether she should throw the game for him or not. The sparkle in his eye told her he loved the competition.

She rolled a strike, too.

Chapter 18

Kiko needed to finish what she'd come here for last time. Eric wrapped his arms around her shoulders as he guided her through the cemetery. A cool spring breeze swirled around her. The clouds above closed in, and the mossy greenish-brown grass underfoot was soggy. Kiko shivered, and she stopped at Yoshi's headstone. A bouquet of purple flowers rested in the holder, petals gently fluttering. Kiko's eyes watered. She didn't know anyone who'd bring him a bouquet, except maybe his adoptive parents, but that wasn't likely. Yoshi had been the black sheep of the family, even moreso than her.

"Who brought the flowers?" she asked the all-seeing breeze.

"I did," Eric said. Kiko faced him in utter astonishment, and he continued, "I bring him flowers every month, except during the restricted winter season."

Kiko blinked back tears, and the breeze quickly dried them. "That's so thoughtful. Thank you."

"It's not only for him that I come."

Kiko sniffled softly. "What do you mean?"

"For seven years, I've tried to find you, and I have people, but no one ever succeeded. You've been a ghost, but I always believed you'd come to visit Yoshi, no matter where in the world you were. I fly down here every month hoping I'll see you here."

Kiko's gaze switched to Yoshi's stone and back to Eric's soft eyes. His words washed the loneliness right from her heart. To be wanted, to feel like she mattered and belonged, was the best feeling she'd ever had. She felt terrible for never reaching out. "I'm sorry for not calling or visiting. I really am."

"You're here now, and that's all that matters." Eric's smoldering gaze heated. "Fate has a way of playing games, doesn't she?"

Kiko's lips spread into a smile. Chaos, not Fate, but that was a conversation for another day. "Can I have a moment alone with Yoshi?"

"Take your time." Eric patted her on the shoulder and turned to wait at the limo.

Kiko folded down, sitting on her heels, and picked loose debris off his grave. "Yoshi, it's been seven years for you, and a hundred for me, but I haven't forgot. I could never forget my first love." Kiko smiled through her tears. "Many years I spent wondering, wishing, and waiting for the purpose of all the pain and suffering in life. Where was I headed, and when would I find peace? Life isn't about rushing to the end—it's about the journey. You were one chapter of many, one amazing chapter. But you destroyed my ability to finish school." She chuckled and tossed a twig aside.

"I forgive you. I was given a gift of helping people that four more college classes couldn't have replaced. And now I'm here for a selfish reason." Kiko paused to collect her thoughts, hoping Yoshi could truly hear her. "There's a part of my heart that will always be yours, but to fill the void you've left behind, I need to move on. I want to move on. But I need a sign telling me you're okay with that." Her voice trembled at the end. It was silly to ask the breeze to answer a loaded question on behalf of the deceased. Simply getting the words out into the open lifted a weight off her shoulders.

The breeze kicked up, and the flowers left by Eric shifted just slightly forward as if giving a single nod of approval. Chaos better not be playing games, Kiko thought. She waited, but nothing else happened. She believed Yoshi himself was telling her to live her life.

Kiko's eyes watered again, and she swiped the tears with the back of her hand. Her feet tingled, on the verge of falling asleep, so she stood and stretched. Kiko stepped around his grave and set the bouquet back into an upright position. They were beautiful, thoughtful, loving, and...from Eric, his best friend. Kiko sniffled and wiped her eyes again.

Satisfied she didn't look like a drowning rat, Kiko returned to the limo where Eric had the engine running and heat filling the cabin.

She climbed in beside him. "Did you need a minute with him?" she asked.

"Yoshi and I are good."

Kiko wanted to ask him something. Since he believed he felt Yoshi looking over him, her question wouldn't be dismissed or laughed at. "Does he ever answer you?"

Eric turned his thoughtful green eyes her way. A shimmer seated at his lower lids, and he laced his fingers with hers. "Once."

ERIC AND KIKO STEPPED out of the limo at the Milwaukee County Zoo, a favorite spot of his as a child. He wanted to end their day on a happy note, and he knew Kiko loved animals. Eric passed over a credit card for their tickets.

The ticket booth attendant in her striped uniform returned it. "I'm sorry, it's been declined."

Eric frowned. That never happened before. He slipped a different one out of his wallet.

"Nope," she repeated.

Kiko's hand stilled his wrist. "I can get this."

"You sure?" Embarrassment crept up on his cheeks. Probably a technical glitch, but still. Nothing made a man feel more like a failure then when a finance guy couldn't keep his finances straight, and now the line of people behind them knew it. Thankfully, they were strangers.

"It's no problem, really," Kiko insisted, and passed her card over.

Eric stepped away from the ticket booth and called the number on the back of his card, fuming under the skin for being made a fool. After pressing various numbers for what felt like an eternity, he finally reached a human. "My card isn't working. Can you tell me what's going on?"

The female voice replied, "Your account was closed."

"What? Why?" Eric kicked a small stone.

"A request to close the account was received yesterday, and we closed the account today."

"I didn't close my account. Who did this?"

Keys of a computer keyboard clicked in his ear. "Your joint cardholder."

"Amanda," he growled. Eric strangled the phone for a few

seconds and gritted his teeth. Derek couldn't fix his problem fast enough. He exhaled a deep breath. "Can you reinstate it?"

"Sorry, but no. You can apply for a new account—"

Eric slapped the lid shut on his phone and stuffed the antenna back down. He swung his fist through the air, wanting to smash the phone on the pavement, but he refrained. After blowing out a dark groan, he punched in the numbers for his attorney's office. "Derek, I need damage control. How much longer until Amanda is severed from my life?"

"I've got a whole team working on it. A hearing with Judge Anderson is tomorrow."

"Good," Eric said.

"What happened?"

"Amanda canceled my credit cards. I don't know what else she's done."

"We're on it. I can't promise your accounts will be functioning, but we can send a Cease and Desist to her actions."

"Do it." Eric hung up.

"Everything okay?" Kiko asked, concern creasing her brow.

"My ex is destroying my life."

Kiko laced her fingers through his. "Is she though?"

Her radiant smile and genuine concern softened him. In that moment he realized with her by his side he could lose everything and be okay. "You're right. She's just making it more difficult. Soon it will all be over."

"Come on. I've got tickets, and we have hundreds of animals to see. Plus, a giant doughy pretzel is calling my name."

Eric smiled and brushed aside the infuriating thoughts of his not-soon-enough-to-be ex-wife. "Which animal is your favorite?" Eric asked to make light conversation.

"I like cats."

"Like lions, tigers, and leopards?" Eric's hand found hers, and they strolled leisurely inside the zoo.

"No, just house cats."

"That sounds boring. Not that you're boring. It's just…I expected something more…exotic, a unicorn tang or something."

Kiko laughed. "House cats are the most entertaining little things. Knocking stuff around, spooking themselves until they run into walls, dragging around random objects like they're prizes. And they warm your lap and don't require long walks through deep snow and blizzards."

"Yeah, good ol' Wisconsin. Ever have a cat?"

"My parents didn't allow pets, and as an adult, I've never been in one place long enough." Her response was melancholy, as if all her wonderful writing while traveling was too isolating.

"If you hated it so much, why didn't you quit?"

They stopped at the elephants and watched the caretakers hosing down their enclosure. She said, "I didn't hate it, but quitting wasn't an option."

"Recruited to write romance novels?"

Kiko flinched. "It was more like a calling." The questioning tone left him wondering what she was hiding, but he nodded, and they watched lions napping on sunny boulders.

"Hungry? Let's get some chow." Kiko brought him to a food stand, but he had no access to money, and it pained him to allow Kiko to pay for everything. Judging by the interior of her house, she was in no position to buy either. How did his life of limos, luxury, and no limits turn to thoughts of how he was going to buy lunch or cover the gas to get home?

"Kiko, you really don't need to..." He touched her forearm, not wanting her to fork out cash on his behalf.

"Don't worry about it." Kiko passed him a bowl of nachos and a cup of cheese.

He hadn't eaten anything like this since he was a kid. They sat on a nearby bench. She rubbed the salt off her pretzel and tore off bite-size hunks, dipping them in cheese and popping them in her mouth. Her eyes rolled with pleasure, and Eric enjoyed the exaggerated tease.

"I haven't had this in so long. You've got to try it." She tore off another bite and dipped it.

Eric held his hand up. "I don't think so." His stomach wasn't acclimated to this level of junk food.

"It's good," she insisted.

He reluctantly opened his mouth, and she placed the bite inside. Seizing the opportunity, he instantly closed his lips and licked her fingers. Her lips curved in a knowing smile, and lust roared through his body.

"What do you think?" she asked with a whispered gasp.

"I think the results need to be duplicated before a determination can be made."

Her cheeks turned pink, and Eric grinned while chewing. She slipped the disposable camera out of her pocket, and they used the rest of the roll making faces, laughing, and posing in front of the animals.

It was the best day of his life.

Chapter 19

Kiko couldn't believe when she'd met Eric at the Gap, the instant crush was something real. Her head swam with excitement, and she bit her lower lip to hide her smile for the long ride home. After all this time, they were finally together. But that lovely buzz vanished the moment Eric swerved the limo to a stop in front of her house. A yellow square hung at eye-level on the front door. Eric squeezed her fingers—he noticed it too.

"Stay here," he said, shifting into park.

Kiko gripped his forearm to stop him. "You know what he's capable of. Don't go." With one chance left at Chaos's game, she wasn't taking unnecessary risks. Kiko dialed the local non-emergency police number. "I need a police escort into my home, please."

Minutes later, a comfortingly beefy officer arrived.

Kiko and Eric stepped out to greet him.

"I'm Officer Bob Van Rip. Come with me."

Kiko urged Eric to follow, so they'd both be protected, and he stayed by her side. The officer remained alert—head bobbing, searching for anyone lurking, and all the while, his hand remained at his utility belt.

The front door was locked. After Kiko unlocked the door for the officer, she removed the note.

"I'll have a look around. You two wait here." The officer slipped inside and turned on the light, announcing his presence.

Eric glanced around from the safety of the porch. "I expected our trip wasn't long enough for him to cool down. It's not safe for you to stay here. Pack up whatever you need for another week or two."

The officer returned to the door. "There's no one here."

Kiko went inside and Eric followed. She glanced around for signs Roger had lurked around, but nothing appeared to be disturbed. She had already packed enough for a week's vacation. What else did she need to postpone her return? Kiko collected a few toiletries from the bathroom, and with her arms full of hair products and period supplies—yay for resuming a normal life span—the officer escorted them back to the limo.

"Everything okay here?" Officer Van Rip asked, hands near his hips.

"Yes, thank you for coming." Kiko slipped into the passenger seat, and the officer returned to his car and pulled away.

Curious about what Eric had in mind, Kiko asked him, "Where are we going this time?" Not that she'd mind another week of luxury alone with him.

"My place. Roger doesn't know where I live," Eric said, putting the key in the ignition.

"Is Amanda still there?" She hated to ask the obvious, but she'd rather get a hotel than share breathing space with her.

"She left. You don't have to worry about that. What did the note say?"

"'Two hours left'," Kiko recited.

"I wonder how long it had been there."

Kiko swallowed a thick lump in her throat. "Good thing we had an escort." Her eyes scanned the area while Eric buckled up.

"And I'm glad I sent Stan back to the office." Eric floored the gas pedal, and all eight cylinders roared under the hood.

"Who's Stan?" Kiko asked, relaxing as the vehicle moved away.

"He's the limo driver for Blue Feather, among other things." Through several turns and stops, Eric kept alert until his gaze settled like a working dog on a duck. Glaring out the rearview mirror, his hands squeezed the wheel. "We have a tail."

A hard lump formed in her stomach, and Kiko craned her neck to find what he saw. "Are you sure?"

"Blue sedan, three back in the left lane."

It was there. Cars changed lanes, sped, slowed, and still it kept pace. Kiko slumped lower in the seat, hoping Roger hadn't seen her.

"He won't get you. Don't worry." Eric frowned, keeping vigilant watch behind them. Perspiration beaded on his forehead.

Kiko wanted to snuggle in his arms and squeeze her eyes shut against the return of the monster—who was now less patient and more angry.

Eric turned left properly with turn signal and all, and the blue sedan copied, two cars back. Her pulse roared in her ears, while helplessness drove her to the brink of screaming. Eric rolled through a yellow light, but the sedan ran the red. Kiko peeked over the headrest, and the car was one behind and one lane over. She made out Roger's features through the tinted glass. His face pinched in a raging snarl.

Kiko's stomach twisted. "He's getting closer."

Eric turned twice more, but Roger stayed tight. "It'll be fine. Another mile and one more turn."

Roger changed lanes and now nestled right behind them. Traffic was thick enough that it didn't raise eyebrows. Kiko's breath became uneven.

"Come on, asshole." Eric glared at him through the mirror.

"Do you have balls to follow me the whole way? I'd love to brake-check the bastard, but I don't want to stress Stan any more than I have to. The man jumps hoops for me."

"Can he swoop in with the cops? I renewed my protection order a few years back, and he's in violation of the terms by being this close."

"We don't need Stan." Eric made the final turn, and Kiko sighed in relief as they pulled into the parking lot for the Green Bay police department.

"He'd be stupid to follow us here." Eric stopped at the front, right next to the handicapped parking. "Let's go inside. We can file a complaint for harassment. With the notes, probably stalking as well."

They slammed their car doors shut just as the blue sedan curved into the lot and stopped right behind the limo, blocking their exit. Kiko ran to the doors and Eric followed closely at a jog, keeping an eye out behind them.

Once inside, Kiko's nerves trembled her hands. The more distance she could put between them the better.

Eric grasped her hand, steadying her, and led the way to the desk. "We need to file a report."

The soggy balding man with glasses too small for his face tilted his thick neck, and as the front door opened behind them, they all turned. Kiko gasped and Eric maneuvered himself to block Roger's reach to her.

Roger's pinched anger had vanished. He was just the normal sweet-talking manipulative man she remembered. He leaned casually against the counter, absolutely unfazed by their location, and that lump sunk down low. "Chad! How are things going around here, man?" Roger made a show of looking at everything in the room, and he feigned a gasp at Eric and her. "Well now. Look what the cat dragged in."

"Hi, Rodg," the pudgy officer named Chad said. "What are you up to tonight?"

"Funny thing, I was planning on having a chat with Kiko here, but she doesn't want to talk."

"Imagine that," Chad said, disinterested.

"Dearest Uncle Chad," Roger said with a mocking tone. "This man here tried to run me off the road. I think he's had too much to drink."

Chad perked up. His bushy white brows rose in understanding, and Kiko wanted to vomit.

"Is that so?" Chad pressed a button on an intercom device behind the desk. "Bob, I think we got a live one."

"Roger," the disembodied voice of presumably Bob said. Bob? It couldn't be the same...

"Yeah, Roger's here too," Chad replied to the silent device.

A side door swung open, and all the heads in the suffocating lobby turned to watch the beefy officer approach with his hands on his hips in an attempt to be intimidating. At once, any comfort Kiko had found in him was gone. Officer Bob Van Rip's demeanor was different as he sized them up. "You two again?" But when his gaze met Roger's, his features softened. "Hey, Rodg," Officer Van Rip said.

Shit.

"How's it going?" Roger asked.

"Not bad. This one here is the imbiber?" His thumb gestured toward Eric.

"I didn't drink anything," Eric declared. "You were just with us. Roger left threatening notes on her door. You saw it, and he tailed us here."

Officer Van Rip and Chad exchanged glances.

"All right," Officer Van Rip said on a sigh. "Come with me."

Kiko froze in disbelief while Eric was yanked to the back room by the arm, and she was alone with Roger. How could this be happening?

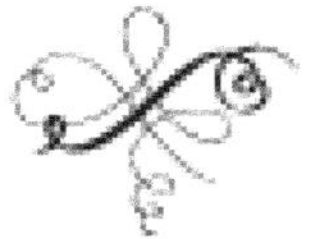

ERIC WAS FORCEFULLY ESCORTED to a holding cell by the man who'd just helped them, who also happened to be twice his size and packing heat. "You can't do this. I have my rights." The barred door noisily slid shut behind him, and it clanked as the locks engaged.

Bob rested his hands on the bars. "Cool off, man."

"I want my phone call."

"It'll only be a little while," Bob said with boredom on his tongue.

"I didn't drink anything. I didn't run Roger off the road. He was chasing us. Did you smell any alcohol on me?"

"Plead the fifth." Bob's shoes clopped on the tile floor as he walked away.

What in the absolute hell?

Eric pressed his head against the bars to see down the hall. There was no one in either direction. He sighed and plopped onto the minuscule plain bench. The white concrete blocks sent a chill up his spine. He'd been surrounded by walls like these twice before, but he had been guilty then. Not his proudest moments.

Eric ran his hand through his hair, helpless. Roger had badges on his side. That explained why he only served seven years for murder. Eric always knew Roger was bad news, he just didn't realize how bad.

He leaned back until his head thumped against the concrete. A pressure spot on his butt cheek reminded him he still had his phone. With a spark of excitement and a sneer on his lips, he slipped the phone out of his pocket, but it rang the second he opened the cover, forcing the call to be accepted. "Hello?" he asked, not seeing who called.

"Hi, sugar lips. Where are you?"

Eric gritted his teeth against the last person he ever wanted to talk to. "I don't have time for this right now, Amanda."

"Oh, you never have time for me. Listen, I thought I'd do you a solid—"

"I don't need any favors from you..." Eric trailed off, glanced around his holding cell, and groaned.

"Well, I thought we could make an exchange," she added.

"You already took half my money, half my house, most of my bonus, and then canceled all my credit cards. What else could you possibly want, because I know it's not the house." The only cash he had coming in was the tiny remaining portion of his bonus and that was for his legal fees.

She chuckled in his ear, and he shivered from the revolting noise. "I have a piece of information of great use to you."

"That's unlikely."

A noise feigning offense permeated his eardrum. He gritted his teeth. "I can't believe you'd assume that. Listen, I've been doing some digging, and I found something about Kiko that you need to know."

Curiosity had him say, "Go on."

He heard the smile in her voice. "You need to ask her about The Wounded Soldier."

Eric frowned. That was a low-brow sports bar in Greenleaf. "Why?"

She hissed a snake-like chuckle. "You never were one for listening. I said, you need to ask her."

"What do you want for it?" Eric stood and paced the confining cell.

"The rest of your bonus from Cece's launch."

His steps paused. "Not a chance."

"You already got your information. I want the bonus."

"I didn't agree to that before you willingly gave it, which wasn't anything at all."

"Oh, well. I suppose you'll be needing it more than me anyway."

"What's that supposed to mean?" Eric's eye twitched. He restrained himself from hurling his phone against the concrete wall.

Her voice was like acid in his ear. "You'll see. Toodles."

Eric slapped his phone shut, dropping the call. He flipped it open and speed dialed his attorney. "Derek, I'm in a holding cell downtown. They have nothing on me. Get me out of here."

"I'll be down there as soon as possible. Hang tight."

Eric closed his phone and resumed pacing, unable to stay still. While Roger, surrounded by family and friends, had Kiko out there, and conniving Amanda dropped a hint about Kiko just to ruffle his feathers, Eric was trapped like a bear in a cage. He was familiar with the rough and tumble sports bar, because he'd overheard Ted and Barry from the mail room talking about a fight that killed a guy there. Why was Kiko involved with a place like that? Eric was curious, but he couldn't trust his ex-wife. Kiko was here with him, and that was all that mattered. If only Derek could spring him from these iron bars, he'd lay out Roger, and even if he took a few nasty hits himself, he looked forward to it.

Chapter 20

Kiko had underestimated Roger's resourcefulness and determination. That was a mistake. And the one place she thought she'd be safe, wasn't. Roger's meaty hand touched Kiko's arm, and she recoiled away from him.

"Don't touch me," she said and then pleaded with Chad, "Officer, help me! I have a restraining order against him."

Officer Chad ignored her request.

"Come on, babe. I'm only asking for a chance to talk."

"That's it—just talk?" Suspicion narrowed her eyes.

"I swear." Roger lifted his palms in surrender.

She wanted to punch him in his million-dollar fake smile. "And you'll have them release Eric?"

His levity faltered for a moment, and he straightened his back, crossing his thick arms over his chest. Kiko's heart skipped a few beats and her head swam. They couldn't keep him locked up, could they?

"Yeah," Roger mumbled.

She didn't believe him. "Swear it."

Roger sighed. "I swear I'll have him released."

"Fine. Now what do you want?"

"Come with me." He grasped her upper arm and pulled.

Kiko ripped out of his grip again. "I'm not going anywhere with you. Talk here."

"I apologized so many times to you all those years ago, and I tried to find you, but it was like you vanished, man. Then one day you just popped up on my radar. Doesn't matter." His hand touched her shoulder. Kiko fought to stay still while he kept talking. "You and I—we were meant to be. That day I met you in at Yoshi's desk, it clicked for me. There's never been anyone else but you since."

Considering his lack of options in prison, that didn't mean anything. Kiko didn't want to entertain the conversation, but she needed Eric released. "What about Jessica?"

Roger frowned. "Who?"

"Your girlfriend. You had a girlfriend when we met, and for many weeks after."

His face lit up as he finally remembered. "Oh, yeah. Jess. She did a number on me. She dumped me because I wasn't over you, and I still ain't."

Kiko resisted a scowl. "I don't know how else to tell you that a knife in your gut, years of avoidance, and a renewed restraining order don't already say, but I'm not interested in you. There's nothing between us, and there never will be." Kiko stepped back and addressed the pudgy officer, "Excuse me, Officer Chad, can you release Eric now? I fulfilled Roger's terms."

"We ain't done yet," Roger said before Officer Chad lifted his chin.

"What else do you want from me?" Kiko's voice threatened to tremble, but she held herself in check. She refused to allow Roger to see the control he had.

"I want you."

"Want me what?" She didn't like the sound of that, and playing dumb was safer than outright disgust.

Roger moved in closer, attempting his sweet smile again. "I've served my time, and I've changed. I'm not the same stuffy rich womanizer you knew."

But the last time she said no to him at the coffee shop, he shot Eric in a jealous rage. He hadn't changed at all, but she kept her cool because Roger was holding all the cards. "Keeping Eric hostage so I'll talk to you doesn't show you changed."

"Will you give me a chance to prove it?"

Desperation to free Eric and escape forced her to agree. "Sure. Prove it. Now let Eric go."

Roger lit up like a kid in an arcade with a bag full of quarters. Bright lights reflected in his eyes, lips spread wide and gleaming. He clapped his hands in excitement. "You won't regret this. You'll see."

Kiko crossed her arms and frowned, ready to make a scene.

"What?" he asked.

"Eric."

"Oh, I don't think so," Roger said.

"You promised to let him go if I talked to you."

"Our 'talk' isn't over until you're mine."

Kiko was sick of playing his game. She swallowed her pride and said, "Letting Eric and I go will do wonders to prove you've changed."

Roger scratched at his chin to make an obvious show of considering her request. She wanted to kick him in the balls, but she didn't want a witnessed assault inside a police station. "You're being sneaky. That's one of many things I like about you—smart as hell. Plus, you haven't aged a day. You're the most beautiful woman I've ever seen."

Roger was delusional. "That's not true and you know it."

"Don't be so modest."

A man in a suit, carrying a briefcase and a pack of papers, pushed his way inside like he owned the place. He shoved them in Chad's face, and the pudgy officer sprung to attention. He pressed a button on the intercom. "Bob, release the suspect in cell A."

"Roger," the voice on the box replied.

"What does Bob want?" Roger asked.

Kiko rolled her eyes and turned to face the mysterious suit helping Eric. "Who are you?" she asked.

"Who I am is of no consequence—" The back door opened, cutting off the man's words.

The sight of Eric, distraught and disheveled, stopped her heart. She wanted so desperately to rush into his arms, but that would only anger Roger more. Kiko fought back the yearning as Eric slowly returned to her side. She discreetly reached for his hand.

The suit raised his eyebrows. "Well, I guess I should introduce myself. I'm Derek O'Connell, Eric Woodson's attorney."

"Good work, Derek."

"That's what you pay me for." Derek turned back to Chad, "Now I trust there will be no further incident with my client."

Chad nodded.

"Good." Derek left as swiftly as he arrived, and Roger's face twisted with rage.

"Roger," Kiko interrupted. "You promised to let us go."

He paced the lobby in front of Chad's desk, and Chad finally spoke up. "Rodg, I can't let you hold them any longer. You saw the shark. Game's up."

Roger dug his fingers into his hair and tugged. His breathing was strained and erratic. Kiko reached for Eric's hand.

"Let's go," Eric whispered in her ear and tugged her toward the door.

Once clear of the door, they both jogged to the limo, slipped inside, and locked the doors.

Eric swore. "That guy is insane. Let's go to my house. Roger won't be following us now." Eric fired up the limo, pulled the shifter into drive, and steered them away—over curbs since Roger had parked them in.

She knew Roger wouldn't leave them alone, but since Roger didn't know where Eric lived, his house was better than hers. She never wanted to be away from Eric again, but this wasn't over yet.

ERIC CARRIED HER BELONGINGS inside, locked the door behind them with his key fob, and set the security code. The layers of security he had made her feel safe for a change, but Eric's home also made her squirm a little. One, it was his and Amanda's marital home, which was icky, but two, while the outside was pretty, the inside was...expensive. Despite all the zeros in her bank and investment accounts, Kiko never lived a life of luxury.

"I don't have a guest room made up," Eric said. "Look around, and don't be shy. My house is your house."

Kiko nodded and Eric took the steps two at a time.

Overhead, a chandelier hung, softly illuminating the foyer, and a split grand staircase hugged the walls. A round table between the two staircases had a fern and group of candles on it. The house was clean, large, bright, and...cold. Kiko hugged herself. She strolled around, searching for photographs, but she didn't find any hanging. There were none on the round table with the plant, either.

As she passed by a door to a side room, a voomp sound from an igniting fire turned her head. Was the fire on a timer? Kiko stepped into the dimly lit library and sunk into the cozy couch in front of the licking flames. She held out her hands to warm them. This was more her style.

"So now you think you can just move right in?" a snarky female voice said, and Kiko recognized it with dread.

Amanda Carter strolled out of her hiding spot in the corner, hips swaying with confidence. Towering over Kiko, Amanda brushed her mane of blonde hair over her shoulder and parked her rear on a chair near the couch. "Who do you think you are trying to steal my husband and move into my house?"

"Uh, you're getting divorced," Kiko said.

Amanda chuckled with a condescending tone. "Oh, honey, you know nothing. I've forgiven many misdeeds by my husband. This is just one more. He'll crush you, just like all the others. It's what we do. Both of us." Her arms lifted around her. "How do you think we bought a place like this? It wasn't helping sick children at the hospital or volunteering at soup kitchens. There are two kinds of people in the world—Kiko, is it?—and you're either on top or trampled. If you don't get away from Eric, you'll be under my shoe. I shouldn't have to explain how much the spikey end hurts."

Kiko swallowed a lump, and her tongue stuck in her throat.

Amanda stood and sauntered out of the library toward the front door. When Kiko heard it close, she blew out a breath.

She'd stood up to Roger, who intended to kill her once, but for some reason, Amanda was scarier. She wasn't as obvious or simple to predict. The power-hungry type were willing to do and say anything to get their way, and they were crafty about it. The question was, how much of what she'd said was true? She hated to think Eric had been corrupted by Amanda.

"Kiko!" Eric shouted with an edge of panic. His feet thundered down the stairs, and he dashed across the foyer to the front door.

"In here," she said numbly.

He raced inside and dropped to his knees by her lap. Firelight flickered across the worried lines on his face. His hands sought hers. "I thought you left. Are you okay?"

Kiko stared at the fire. "Amanda was in here, and she said some terrible things."

He frowned. "Don't believe any of it. The woman is insane."

The truth was, to get rich or stay rich meant a person had to have questionable morals—her own extraordinary circumstances beside the point. The trust she'd so blindly given was shaken, and she glared at Eric as if he were a stranger.

"Whatever she said, it's a lie," Eric said, nearly in a panic. "She's all bark and no bite, I promise."

Kiko was finally afraid—of the truth. "She said she forgave your misdeeds. What did she mean?"

"Your guess is as good as mine. The woman is unstable, and I only learned this after she served me with divorce papers and took most of my estate with her. She cannot be trusted. Kiko, please, don't let her fill your head with nonsense."

Kiko bristled. "You know I don't fall for lies and bullshit. Don't insult me like that. I'm asking because—"

"You believe her," he interrupted coldly, standing up.

"Honestly, some of it made sense."

Eric paced the room. A hand slid through his hair. "I've been nothing but honest with you, Kiko, but I admit, I was arrested for assault."

"What?" Kiko asked, shocked.

Eric continued, ignoring her surprise. "The frat guys deserved it for hazing a bunch of freshmen that went way beyond tricks and games. My ass got tossed in the drunk tank to sleep it off. Sensei was pissed because I threw all my discipline out the window, but I made it up to him, though. I can't believe that's what she means, since it happened long before her. Kiko," He kneeled before her. "I can't lose you again. I'll tell you anything you want to know, and I never lie. Give me a chance to clear up anything she made you doubt."

"Frat guys?" Kiko emphasized the plural.

Eric sent her a prideful smile. "Three against one, and I was half in the bag. They were in worse shape than me afterward."

"That wasn't what she'd said at all, and I'm not angry about that." Kiko knew he would fly off the handle when she told him the accusation, but she wanted the truth, and right now, throwing shade felt good after being humiliated and treated like pond scum by his ex-wife. "You and her, as a team, destroy people for your own success."

"Excuse me?" Eric placed his hands on his hips, eyes burning hotter than the fire crackling next to them.

"That's what she said."

"I may not be as innocent as a baby bunny, but I didn't destroy anyone for my job. My dad bought the company and handed me my job at Blue Feather after I graduated college. I assure you, no one was harmed in my career. Amanda's a different story." Eric sat on the couch next to her. "Rumors, of course. But office gossip was she spiked another candidate's drink before their competitive presentations, and naturally, Amanda won. Another time she supposedly—rumors, mind you, and I've never bothered to believe them, but now... She hired someone to slash another co-worker's tires, preventing them from showing on time to a big client meeting."

Kiko believed it all. "Why does she still have a job if it's your dad's company?"

"That's what I asked him. Ultimately, her father is on the board of directors. They, collectively, can overrule anything by the CEO. So far, Fred Carter has cemented Amanda's position in the eyes of the board. And...Dad says she looks nice."

Kiko cringed. "That's disgusting, but it explains the big head."

"Come again?"

"When someone has power, a person tends to let it go to their head, and without consequences, they show their true colors. I've seen it many times."

The corner of Eric's mouth lifted. "I never thought of it that way before. She was always so confident. That's what drew me to her in the first place."

Kiko recalled the threat of Amanda's speech, and she realized Eric wasn't her equal in the power-grab; he was a victim. "Now you're getting trampled too."

"What?"

"She's systematically taking everything from you. She told me that you're either on top or trampled, and she warned me that I'm next if I don't leave."

Eric's eyes glowed with primal rage. "That's what this

was—she's trying to split us up. I promise you, she won't touch a hair on your head. I'll burn down the world to keep you safe."

Kiko's heart thundered in her chest. "Might want to start with changing the security code."

Chapter 21

Eric zoned off while Caroline droned on at the conference table. Her shirt was unbuttoned too low to be considered decent. She wore her short hair loose and wild around her head, as if she'd woken up that way, and her nibbling on a pencil was grating on the ears. But Eric was too busy trying to dissect what Kiko had figured out last night to focus on his secretary. Amanda wanted the divorce, so why did she threaten Kiko? And why did Amanda want to destroy him? He couldn't help but wonder if his entire marriage was a sham. Doubt, fear, and surprise warred in his mind. Confusion showed up late to the party with a bottle of wine in hand—after drinking half of it.

"Eric, what should this line say?" Caroline said forcefully.

"What?"

"Here is subsection 4b. It lists the chain of command for complaints. Nowhere in the handbook does it address expenditures. So, I can add it in."

Eric checked the paperwork she'd brought, and frustration gritted his teeth. "The policy needs to be amended in the management handbook, Caroline, not the employee handbook," Eric said.

Caroline feigned shock. "Well, I guess meeting adjourned, and I'll reschedule us to meet again when I have the correct passage for amendment."

"Caroline," Eric said with impatience, not wanting to rehash this pointless meeting. "Use the strikethrough for the line to be corrected. Then add in the following—are you writing this down?" Caroline lifted a pen. "Departmental expenditures are bound by the initial estimates and cannot be exceeded, unless explicit permission in writing is received from two or more relevant departmental managers. Amendment date April 30, 1995. Got all that? Then forward the memo to me for signing."

"Yes, sir." She scribbled furiously.

Eric stood, ready to be done with this.

Caroline said nervously, "Eric?"

"What is it, Caroline?" Eric said with boredom and impatience on his tongue.

"I was wondering"—she giggled. She actually giggled—"for a long time now. If you'd like to catch lunch with me sometime. Like...today?"

Getting a simple task completed shouldn't be this much effort. "Email the memo to me. I already told you we don't have to meet for me to sign it."

"That's not what I meant." Her doe eyes pleaded understanding.

He should've seen it coming with all her flirting, which amplified once the divorce rumors spread. He quickly thought of an excuse to shut her down for good. "Caroline, I appreciate the offer, but I don't date within the office, and I have plans."

Caroline frowned. "What about Amanda?"

"That's when I made the rule."

This secretary, clearly unhappy with his rejection, folded her arms across her ample chest. "Then how do you explain Kiko?"

"I...uh," Eric faltered. "We're not dating." Eric didn't know what they were officially, but he made a note to keep his relations with her strickly professional in the office.

Caroline's easy smile returned as if the challenge was still on. "I see. The offer's open anytime. You know where to find me."

Eric excused himself from the short meeting, and after erasing that painful interaction with Caroline, excitement bloomed in his chest. Light on his toes, he strolled down the hall toward Kiko's office. Barry pushed a cart full of mail his way, and Eric sidled against the wall for him to pass.

"Hey, bossman. There's an open bowling tournament at The Wounded Soldier next weekend. I heard you like to roll," Barry said, his deft hands shifting and flipping mail.

"I do. I didn't know The Wounded Soldier had lanes."

"Yep. Balls, beer, and big screens. It's too late to join as a team but come check it out, and maybe you'll be impressed enough to join ours."

Eric thought Kiko would love to kick his ass again, and he wanted her to. "Count me in."

"Awesome." Barry grinned and handed Eric an envelope.

Eric tucked it under his arm, and continued to Kiko's office. He rapped his knuckles against her door and opened it before she answered.

Kiko slammed shut a red journal and covered it with her arms.

"Working hard or hardly working?" Eric teased. Kiko blushed and fussed with her office supplies. He added, "Don't worry about it." He closed her door behind him and sat across from her. "What are you working on?"

"Those figures you requested are ready. Do you want me to print them?" Kiko asked.

"No. I mean that." He pointed at her red journal.

"Oh, it's nothing."

Eric lifted an eyebrow to challenge the response, and she shyly handed it over, cheeks flushing bright pink. Curious, he opened the cover and paged through it. All handwritten in a delicate cursive. The beauty of her calligraphy wasn't lost on him. He read the first line out loud, "'Your rock smashes my scissors, April McCall said dryly from losing this round of her favorite argument-breaking game of rock, paper, scissors.' You can tell a lot about a book by its first and last line. I like this one. The character is playful and happy to lose. What kind of girl wants to lose? I'm interested, and let's see. The last line—'She laughed, throbbing in all the right places but still ready for more.'" Eric cleared his throat and heat rose up his neck and face. He wished it was Kiko who throbbed for him. "Enticing. I like it. Is this your novel?"

"One of them," she replied, pink rushing up her cheeks. "I was doing another editing pass."

Eric smiled. "If it's okay with you, I'd like to give this a thorough read-through."

Kiko nodded. "Okay, sure, but I have marks in there from edits I need to make."

"I'm not going to judge, trust me." Eric stood and gestured with his head. "Let's go."

"Is there a meeting I failed to mark down?" Kiko fumbled with papers on her desk, clearly concerned about screwing up the job. There was nothing she could do that would warrant Eric letting her go.

"Lunch time."

"Oh." Kiko stilled.

Eric held out his hand. Kiko took it, and heat roared through his body, strengthening his limbs, and giving him an invincibility he thought only possible in fiction. On their way out to a waiting limo, Caroline sent him dirty looks, but Eric ignored his secretary.

Eric wouldn't bring Kiko anywhere Amanda was familiar with. "Where would you like to grab lunch?"

"Dine and Dash. It's a cute café—a cross between fast food and home cooked."

"Sounds perfectly like something Amanda would hate," Eric said.

"What? Why does that matter?"

"I don't want her to interrupt us this time."

"Me neither."

And she didn't. Perhaps all his worries earlier were unfounded, and Eric fully enjoyed himself with the best date he could've asked for.

Chapter 22

After work, Kiko stripped down to her pajamas and sipped a cup of hot chocolate by Eric's fireplace. He'd changed the security code to the house and given it to her, so now she could relax and not worry about Amanda making an unwanted appearance again. After lunch, he had been busy in his office while she pretended to work. Honestly, why had he hired her? She had almost nothing to do, so she started another novel, this one her own, because after all the practice she'd had over the last century, she was pretty good at it.

Kiko didn't bother unpacking anything but some personal items. She wasn't really moving in with Eric. This was more of an extended vacation, so she kept her clothes in suitcases except for her suits, which hung on hangers. Kiko sipped again watching the fire crackle.

Eric's feet thundered down the stairs. "Kiko?"

"In here." Kiko set her drink down on a coaster and stood.

Eric panted as he paused at the doorway to the library, a look in his eye she didn't recognize.

"What is it?" She closed the distance to him.

"This." He shook her red journal. "You wrote this?"

"You know I did. Why?"

"I finished reading it."

"Already?" It had only been a few hours.

"I couldn't put it down. Your story felt so real, as if you experienced it personally, and I want them all. I'm not an agent, but I can guarantee no one will fight for you more than me. I'll get you set up with marketing, and we can assemble a budget for you. You'll be invited to the meetings, of course."

"Wait," Kiko said, reeling from his excitement. "You want to publish my books?"

"Absolutely. These are going to be huge. How many others are there?" Eric's eyes glistened.

The real answer wasn't too unbelievable, was it? "Three hundred," Kiko said softly and smiled to herself.

Eric's face twisted with disbelief. "You have three hundred of these stories written?"

"I do."

Eric beamed with stars in his eyes, as if he were imagining a huge paycheck, a winning lottery ticket, a free car, or any number of unexpected and wonderful pieces of news. She was happy to see him so radiant. She'd expected to rub elbows for years before getting a chance at publishing. Having a personal contact in the right place was simply luck. Eric was her cheerleader, announcing to the world she'd made a difference to the lives of many, that she mattered, that she belonged. No one would know her tales were actually nonfiction, but that was inconsequential.

"I'm going to call an emergency meeting with my team. I'm going to assemble the biggest crew of editors and cover designers ever. Three hundred? You are incredible. I can't believe—yes, you know what, yes I can. Kiko, I've always known you're amazing."

Her cheeks heated with the praise. She bit her lower lip to fight the smile from splitting her face.

"How did you write three hundred books in seven years?"

Shit. She hadn't thought of how that would be possible. She actually wrote only a few per year over the course of the last hundred years, which was a totally normal pace. Dictation might've been believable, but she wanted to give him a sliver of truth. "Magic?" she answered with a small chuckle.

His radiant smile swelled her chest.

"I like the sound of magic, and I'll let you know ASAP tomorrow what's happening next. You are my client now, and I'm getting you a contract. Whatever you want, I'll get it for you, because you're mine."

The sound of those words rolled through her ears and heated her heart—not the contract, not the implicit promises of riches she didn't need, but the words 'because you're mine'.

In Eric's excitement, he lifted her up into her arms, and he spun them. His laugh was contagious, and she loved the feeling of him wanting her. He lowered Kiko back to her feet, and with the fireplace crackling behind them, Eric's lips found hers, and her knees gave out. Eric supported her weight while his mouth explored hers. Kiko's body exploded with the lust she'd harbored for him all this time. As if reading her mind, Eric scooped her off her feet into his arms and carried her upstairs.

"King size this way," he explained between panting breaths.

He gently set her on her feet, and Eric meticulously unbuttoned his shirt, as if unwrapping a luscious candy bar needing to be savored, and taut skin under firm muscles peeked through, begging to be licked. Kiko couldn't wait. She'd waited far too long already. She ripped off her pants and dove at him, knocking him back onto the mattress. Eric smiled at her enthusiasm. Straddling his hips, her hands went for his belt buckle.

Eric leaned upright, capturing his lips with hers, and he eagerly freed her shirt and unclasped her bra. A hard dick grew beneath her. Eric pulled her down close to him, and he flipped them with her underneath his firm body. Kiko's fingers explored the ridges of his chest while Eric shucked his pants, and boxer briefs strained with his need for her. "I've been waiting for years to eat you out. If you need to scream, feel free."

Kiko's throbbing made her hips move in anticipation. His head dipped low, and he pulled her underwear free. He inspected her first, learning the lay of her land, and he dove in, eagerly licking and gliding along her with his nose and chin. Kiko rocked against him, helping him as her pleasure grew rapidly with each stroke, faster than the previous. She panted. "Oh, yeah. Don't stop. Don't you stop, Eric. That's it. Oh, yes. Fuck me."

With his mouth busy, Eric only growled.

Kiko's body tensed as she crashed over. She cried out as the waves rolled through her. It was fucking amazing, but she wanted more.

Eric wiped his face on his sheets and climbed back over her. "You have the most beautiful cries when you come. I want to hear it again." His hard dick effortlessly slid in, stretching her and filling her.

Kiko arched her back and cried out again—not in orgasm, but in the most amazing feeling of being wanted by someone as amazing as Eric Woodson.

"That's it. Now I'm going to fuck you until you scream again. You will know nothing but the pleasure I give you." Eric moved, thrusting into her slowly at first and gaining speed and grinding against her. She bounced with his effort. The bed shook, slapping the wall, and something fell off the end table. She would let the world crumble just to stay with him.

Eric's body stiffened, and he grunted with his own release. He throbbed inside her, filling her up completely. His panting slowed, and he lowered himself to his elbows. Little kisses dotted between his smiles and the gaze of absolute warmth in his eyes—the same look he'd given her earlier. Now she recognized it as admiration.

"What's that look?" Kiko asked, teasing. His dick still held firm inside her.

"I'm happy."

So was she.

ERIC'S MOTHER ABANDONED HIM for the pool boy, and his father was colder than an arctic wasteland. His best friend was murdered, and with all the scheming bullshit with his ex-wife, he'd believed life existed to give him a hard time, until last night. For the first time in his life, the frayed threads of his life were knitting back together.

And she curled up naked next to him in the sheets.

Kiko's long hair tickled his chest, and he had nowhere else he wanted to be. But, with a collection of amazing books waiting to be published, and his soon-to-be flat-broke status, Eric had to get to work. He leaned over and kissed her forehead. They had been up late, and if she needed the extra half hour, he'd let her sleep.

When he stepped out of the shower, she was rolling out of bed and stretching. "You should've woken me up, we could've saved water."

Eric stalked over and planted a juicy kiss on her lips and a playful smack on her naked ass. "Rain check. Come on down for breakfast when you're ready."

"Did you cook?" Kiko asked with surprise.

"I dial a mean food delivery service."

"Give them a good tip, and they'll probably be nicer," Kiko said.

Eric laughed.

When Kiko came downstairs a short while later in a blouse and a black suit, Eric's jaw dropped. Her hair was tied up in a bun at the nape of her neck, and she carried a red journal in her hand. Her single fingertip lifted his chin up to close his mouth.

"Catching flies."

"I'm catching all kinds of things." A sparkle shined in his eyes while he stared her down. "But for now, we have biscuits and gravy and breakfast sandwiches."

"Pass the sausage, will you?" Kiko asked, marveling at the delivery spread. "Where's all this from?"

"A quaint hole-in-the-wall. One of my personal hidden favorites—The Foot Long," Eric said.

Kiko chuckled. "Sounds exotic."

"I can show you something else that's a foot long." Eric wagged his brows.

"You wish."

Eric scoffed. "I didn't hear any complaints last night."

"For a numbers guy, Mr. Spreadsheets, you might want to measure twice." Kiko grinned.

Eric grabbed her and pulled her into his arms, letting his firm cock press against her leg. "Sounds like someone's memory needs refreshing."

"I'll never forget last night." Kiko blushed, and Eric's heart hammered in his chest. The urge to take her lips and strip her naked right here was powerful. "But since we have to go to work, your measurements will have to take a rain check." She slipped out of his arms with a wink.

Eric groaned. She was simply amazing, and he still couldn't believe his luck. "The idea pains me, but maybe I should buy a lottery ticket." Eric served himself a plate, while Kiko made her selections. He bit into a breakfast sandwich.

"Nah," Kiko said. "The odds are terrible. Buy a winning lottery ticket instead."

Eric laughed, and they ate quickly while playing games with their feet and eyes, laughing at silent jokes, making cross-eye faces, and having a staring contest. She was completely perfect for him. Eric paused mid-chew.

"What's wrong?" Kiko asked.

He blinked away the thought lingering at the corner of his heart and smiled. "Nothing. Let's go. We're going to be late, and we have exciting things to do today."

They cleaned up, and Eric brought them to work in the limo, pulse roaring in his ears. His thumbs drummed the steering wheel, and Kiko's hand rested on his lap. Her simple touch soothed his anxious hands. At Blue Feather's floor, Eric said, "Be in my office in an hour."

Kiko nodded.

Eric unlocked his office door and logged into his computer. From the shared drive, Eric pulled up the standard contract and filled in the blanks with the usual offer from Blue Feather Publishing. He couldn't give her special treatment without the whole office coming down on his head for hypocrisy.

He printed and stapled the document and opened a new client file. He researched the projected sales based on her genre, and his eyes widened at the very successful category her books would be filed under. Kiko stepped into his office, and Eric sat up straight, excited to personally sign her as a client.

"Have a seat. This is the standard contract for all new clients. With your signature, you'll be represented by Blue Feather, and I'll personally be your agent. The usual advance is broken into three payments spread over key completion dates of the contract. After each book earns out, you'll receive a biannual royalty payment in the amount of seven percent." His voice trailed off at the end, hoping she wasn't disappointed with the offer.

Kiko read through it thoroughly which surprised and impressed him.

"What do you think?" he asked when she finished.

"I think it's biased against authors."

Eric's hopes sunk. He didn't want to lose her to another agent, because he wanted to spend as much time as possible with her. "You wouldn't be wrong," he answered. "The business is designed to package your product for sale while shaping it to maximize the audience size and profits. You'll lose creative freedom, and the pay is peanuts."

Kiko's eyes widened. "Why are you telling me this?"

"I want to be honest with you. So, I'm also going to tell you to sign anyway." She quirked a brow at him, and he added, "For you, I'll make it worth it."

She pulled a pen out of her hair bun.

While she signed, Eric focused on his breathing, reminding himself this was only a professional commitment, but his muscles were taut with excitement. She set the pen down. "I'm yours now."

Eric loved the sound of those words. He brought over a pair of flutes and a bottle of champagne from his office mini fridge. The cork popped with a bang, and he filled both glasses while Kiko watched him with amusement on her lips.

"To new beginnings, to a future full of possibilities, and to new relationships," he said, toasting her directly.

They clinked glasses and sipped.

"What the hell is going on in here? Sounds like a drive-by shooting." And she was back. Always interfering.

Annoyance clipped his dry words. "Yes, Amanda, drive-bys are really troublesome on the fifth floor. Of all people, you should be plenty familiar with the sound of champagne opening."

Amanda's eye caught on Kiko. "Oh, I see. Well, what's the bubbly for?"

"I signed a new client. Put together a marketing package for a time travel romance," Eric said proudly.

"Her? This girl from your past pops up out of the blue, and you hand her a job and a publishing contract. Are you milking the company for as much cash as you can? She must have some magic—"

"Stop," Eric interrupted, his face twisting in anger. The last thought on his mind was money. "She has real talent."

"I bet." Amanda glared at Kiko with an unsettling mix of hatred and jealousy.

"Look, I don't care if you believe me or not," Eric said. "I know you don't read any of our clients' books. All you need to worry about is getting her in front of the eyes of every English-speaking romance reader."

"I want eighty-twenty on this one," Amanda said.

Eric growled. "I don't give a shit about the bonus. You can have it all if you leave our personal business out of it."

Amanda's anger dissipated. "Just like that?"

Even if he demanded his equal share, as the usual split was among management, he would never argue over it in front of Kiko like she was nothing more than a dollar bill. Eric didn't care about the bonus at all. As her agent, the commission would be enough, but even that he'd give up just to be by her side. As long as he had his day job to pay the bills, nothing else mattered. Although he still hoped Amanda was quitting.

"Just like that," he repeated.

"I'm on it." Amanda turned and left the room with a grin on her face. If all that accomplished was getting her to work as a team, so be it.

"Sorry about that," Eric said.

"All I can say is I'm really judging some of your life choices right now," Kiko said.

"Hey! When she and I met, Amanda was driven, confident, and smart. The other traits didn't surface until after the nuptials." Eric lifted a brow at her, silently asking if she had hidden traits.

"If you're insinuating you'd like to be informed of my Mr. Hyde side, I can assure you, I'm all Dr. Jekyll. What you see is what you get."

"And by calling yourself Dr. Jekyll, can I hope you're not battling a dark side in that brilliant mind of yours?"

Kiko approached him with a saucy grin. "Everything in my head right now is downright dirty. Take what you will from that." Her hand gripped his ass tight.

Eric groaned.

Chapter 23

Kiko didn't care about the money—she was a multi-millionaire after all. But she was thrilled her books were going to be in the hands of people all over the country, so thousands could experience the stories she'd lived through. Feeling like she existed mattered more than money. The look on Eric's face when she'd signed was worth more than all of it.

In her office, Eric tasked her with digging up sales estimates based on similar books' sales histories. Some numbers were astronomical and some disappointing. How could she figure where her books would land? There was a reason it was called an estimate. Kiko downloaded data into spreadsheets with hyperlinks to the original data for future cross-reference.

A knock on her office door had her smiling. She loved when Eric interrupted her, which was generally four times a day, one of which was lunch.

"Come on in," she called.

The door opened, and Barry pushed in a mail cart, but it wasn't baskets of envelopes in front of him.

"What's this?" Kiko stood as Ted strolled in next with another cart full of red roses, as if someone bought the whole florist's shop. The two men unloaded their carts, filling every flat surface in her office.

"You've got a secret admirer," Barry said, handing her a card. "Yeah, I looked. So sue me."

"Beauty is only the beginning." Kiko flipped the card over. "No one signed it."

"Kinda strange if you ask me," Ted said.

"No one asked you," Barry replied. "I think it's sweet. Someone who really wants to make an impression without the kudos."

They finished unloading all the bouquets and pushed the carts back out. "Must be an awesome guy to buy that many. I'd be broke," Barry said.

"Maybe we should pool our funds to afford one extravagant show like this," his cohort said.

"First you have to find the right girl. Then how are we supposed to convince her to be shared?"

"Good point, Barry."

Kiko stood in their wake, amazed and embarrassed at the slightly creepy show of affection displayed at her new job. With Amanda's vitriol and the obvious looks of disdain from Caroline, Kiko guessed Eric would've stayed under the radar with gifts. So why had he sprung for this extravagance here and not at home? She wasn't upset, but certain others could see this as creating a hostile work environment, and Kiko certainly didn't want to give the boss a reason to fire her. Well, her boss's boss. Did Eric really send these? The cryptic message wasn't his style. What was she going to do with them all?

In the meantime, Kiko sat down and crunched numbers for the rest of the afternoon, distracted by the scent-free roses surrounding her. The light from the small window glistened against a couple bouquets, turning their deep red into a brighter, cheerful shade—the color of Valentine's Day, seductive lipstick, and love. Sprigs of white baby's breath dotted the red, a common flower combination. Was there a message in the flowers for her?

Kiko hadn't thought of remarrying or starting a family. She had no reason to contemplate it for the last hundred years. She'd believed after Yoshi was killed, her only chance at a family had been taken from her. But now she had Eric. Did she have Eric? They sort of lived together, they carpooled together, he'd given her a job and a contract representing her work, and he'd treated her to a vacation and daily lunches.

They needed to have a chat.

A knock on her open door turned her head. This time, Eric

arrived at the end of the day for their daily carpool home. The look on his face told her he didn't send the flowers. A knot twisted in her stomach.

"I came to see what I've been getting credit for. Wow. This is impressive." He walked around the room, counting bouquets as he crossed. "Kiko, I hope you realize I didn't send these."

"I had a feeling."

Eric wouldn't risk her job over flowers. She handed him the card, and he read it. "I don't like the sound of this."

"Roger," they both said in unison. Kiko would've chuckled at their matched assumption if the implication wasn't so frightening.

"How did he find out I'm here?" she asked. "And how did he find my house so quickly after I moved in?"

"I don't know, but with law enforcement friends, anything's possible."

"I've never had a run-in with the police. My escort request wasn't written, and my new address isn't on the restraining order paperwork." But she'd gotten a ticket for an expired registration. Was that a record he had access to?

"I don't think it's the cops," Eric said. "He's great at tailing. If he's got the free time, he can do anything." Chills crawled down Kiko's spine. Eric continued, "We're not going to take your Bronco. He knows that vehicle, and we can't take the limo anymore..." Eric trailed off, thinking.

"I'll get us a car," Kiko offered.

"If you buy one, he can get his hands on the registration address."

"I'll rent one."

"That's like two hundred bucks a week."

He'd flip if he found out how much it cost in her present year. Kiko shrugged. "I can do it. It's only until this blows over, or until I can convince him to leave me alone." And by blowing over, she meant Roger getting killed at The Wounded Soldier, assuming she hadn't changed the future by accident.

"Rental it is. Need a ride over?" Eric asked.

"I'll call a cab," Kiko said. "Then I'll pick you up."

"I don't like that. I don't want you out there alone with him roaming free, hunting for you."

"Is there another company vehicle besides the limo?"

A devious smile spread Eric's lips.

"What?" she asked, not liking where this was going.

"I have an idea. Wait here, give me twenty minutes."

"Okay."

"Promise me you'll wait here."

"I promise." Kiko chuckled, loving how worried he was for her.

Eric swiftly left with his cell phone to his ear. She didn't know what tricks Eric had in mind, but she wanted to find out. Kiko sat at her desk and focused on her screen. Her eyes glazed over at the numbers, wondering what exciting idea Eric was unfolding. Twenty minutes later on the dot, Eric strolled back in her office holding a pair of helmets.

"Oh, I don't think so," Kiko said. "Where did you get a motorcycle that quick?"

"Come on, pack up."

"Can you ride?" Kiko didn't want to doubt him, mister limos-in-waiting, but she did.

"Of course. It's my bike. I had Stan deliver."

Kiko's imagery of Eric on a bike both roared her engines and scared the crap out of her. "What if Roger finds us? If he gets close enough in his sedan, I don't want to be meat soup."

"He won't."

"Promise?"

His lazy smile crashed down on her lips. Kiko's body curved into his, and her hand pressed him tight against her.

"I promise nothing bad will happen to you."

"And you, too." Kiko couldn't explain that if she failed to save him one final time, Eric's fate was an early and extremely untimely death. The explanation of her previous seven years and Chaos's philosophy would have to wait.

"Me?" Eric asked, amused.

"Bikes are dangerous. I don't know what I'd do without you." And that was the truth.

"I'll be fine. Let's go."

Kiko hoped it was true. The wind blew her hair, and the free open road zipped inches from her feet, a feeling like none other. And the best part—well, two really—pressing her body against Eric's back and the vibration of the motor between her legs. But they made it home safely.

Chapter 24

Roger had always been...a large personality. The notes were a bit much, and the guy couldn't take a hint, but the excessive display of roses was concerning. Eric directed Ted and Barry to dispose of the flowers before Kiko returned to her office the next day. They expressed regret for not having a young lady to regift them to. Meanwhile, Eric was terribly distracted knowing Kiko was only a few doors down from him. Many times a day he wanted to check her office, just to reassure himself she was still here.

A woman entered his office, and Eric looked up, excitedly hoping to see Kiko. It wasn't. Kiko kept things professional, which he respected.

But his secretary had no reason to stroll on in. A simple call would suffice. "Caroline," he addressed her curtly.

"Your dad wants to see you right now in conference room C."

Eric had nothing scheduled, and the interruption annoyed him. "Regarding what?"

"He didn't say."

Eric pressed his lips together and collected a pen and searched for clean note paper. A skirted butt landed on the edge of his desk. He almost snapped at Amanda out of habit, but it wasn't her this time. "What is the meaning of this, Caroline?"

"I was wondering if you'd like to take me up on my lunch offer today."

"No." Eric moved around the desk.

Caroline's quick fingers snagged his tie and held him in place. Surprised, Eric stopped.

"Listen to me," she whispered, pulling him close. "Someone is after you, and they won't quit. I'm not supposed to say anything—not even that much, but I can tell you more if you meet me for lunch."

That sounded like Dad's cryptic warning. Eric had to find out what Caroline knew. "Fine. Meet me at The Foot Long, noon sharp."

She smiled and released his tie, taking an extra second to smooth out the material she wrinkled.

Eric brushed past her, seething at the secret hostilities at his own job. He swung into the conference room, and Dad sat at his usual spot at the head of the table. Eric closed the door behind them.

Dad sighed. "Son, I warned you, and now I have no choice."

Eric's stomach flipped itself over. He didn't like those words. "What's going on?"

"I didn't know what they did until it was too late, but Fred and Amanda have removed you from Cece's bonus."

"They can't do that. We had an agreement for eighty-twenty in the divorce settlement." Although she'd demanded the remaining twenty for information about Kiko, he'd denied her.

"She says you verbally discussed changes to the bonus," Dad said solemnly. "And her father heartily agreed with the change."

Eric had been alone in the holding cell, so he had no proof. "Management shares the bonus. The only agreement in writing is my and Amanda's split. How can you let them take it from me? Why don't you get rid of them?"

"Keep your voice down and sit." Eric did and Dad continued, "Now, you know how I run things here, but there's only so much power in my hands. The board—"

"Don't give me 'the board' bullshit. This is your company," Eric interrupted.

"It was." Dad sighed with nostalgia on his tongue. "They've taken control away from me. The Carters have two votes to my one before any issue is brought to the table."

"Then why can't you convince the others to see your side?"

"They don't agree with my viewpoints."

"Then why don't you add me to the board? A pair of Woodsons would even out the balance." There had to be some solution. This couldn't be happening.

Dad's eyebrows lifted in surprise and sunk in defeat. "It's too late. If you would've accepted when I first offered—never mind. We can't change the past no matter how much I wish I could. New members must be voted in, and Amanda and Fred won't let you in now. Like I said, something is going on around here, and I don't like it. I was hoping you'd tell me more, but it seems you're in the dark as much as I am. Now get out of this room before anyone gets suspicious."

"Caroline gave me a warning a few minutes ago, and we're having lunch to talk more in depth about it. What does she know?"

"I wasn't aware Caroline knew anything."

Frowning, Eric picked up his documents and swiftly moved down the hall, ignoring Caroline's flirty wave to catch his attention. He returned to his office, shut the door, and dropped into his chair. He'd counted on that remaining sliver of bonus to float him after the divorce and cover Derek's fees. Surviving on his paychecks alone meant indentured servitude for decades. A bonus for Kiko's book wasn't on the horizon for about a year yet, although he'd agreed to give the whole thing to Amanda just to get her off his back. That wasn't such a great idea now. Eric was going to need to refinance his mortgage with the divorce, and hopefully he'd get a better rate to lower the payments.

Eric lifted the phone and called his attorney's office. "Patch me through to Derek, please."

"Derek here."

"Please tell me you have something good to share with the class."

"Well, I do. Judge Anderson rubber-stamped your divorce papers. It's done, effective this morning. If you haven't already, you'll want to open new credit accounts."

"Great," Eric said without enthusiasm. "I'm thrilled to be divorced. What's this business about Amanda taking my whole bonus? Did her attorney send over an amendment?"

"Nope, still says eighty-twenty in the documents. Why?"

"Somehow, they managed to revoke my bonus entirely."

"The divorce is final, so there's nothing more for me to do here. You'll have to deal with them and the contract between you."

"Thanks." Fire burned in Eric's veins at her blatant theft. "Do you have the bill ready?"

"My secretary will email it over shortly," Derek said.

"I hate to ask this, but is there any chance I can get on a payment plan?"

"I'll see what I can do."

Eric hung up, feeling dejected and embarrassed. After resting his head on his desk for a few pitying moments, he went online to apply for a new credit card. Derek was right, he should've done it already. After filling out forms for ten minutes, he pressed the 'submit application' button, and a blue circle swirled on his screen. And swirled and swirled.

He read the response quietly to himself. "A letter will be arriving in the mail with the company's determination and next steps, if appropriate. If you feel there's been a mistake, please dial 1-800-555...Dammit!"

After being raised in a position of privilege, payment plans and credit card denials were a foreign concept. At lunch, he'd get to the bottom of the bullshit in the company, and afterward, he'd call for that credit card.

He could fix this.

There was hope.

KIKO STROLLED DOWN THE carpeted aisles on the hunt for the

mysterious vending machine lobby. She hadn't seen it yet, but the rumors made her believe it was quite impressive. Kiko rounded on an open nook with a bank of windows drenching the room in natural sunlight. Around the perimeter was a selection of vending machines that rivaled a unionized factory full of starving hard-working adults with above-average appetites.

"Whoa," Kiko said, dazzled by the options. She bumped into a fellow snack-seeker. "Oh, sorry."

"Hey, no big deal," A lithe man with large glasses and a thatch of curly brown hair chuckled. He had the look of a man who spent his youth running for his life or getting beat up. "Hi, I, uh, helped deliver your roses, and then removed them. Nice to finally meet you officially." He struck out a hand. "I'm Ted, short for Theodore, not Edward. It's a common mistake, but I take no offense."

"Kiko." She shook and smiled. Eric must've requested the flowers to be removed. "Nice to meet you, Ted, short for Theodore."

"What's the flavor you're after?" he asked. "In this corner is primarily salty. Against that wall is sweet. Over here is savory, but if you're interested in a meal on par with high school cafeterias, we have white bread sandwiches with questionable innards. My favorite in this glass jungle is"—he paused to tap on the glass of his preferred machine—"gummy worms. See with bears, you feel guilty about biting their heads off, but with worms—no heads to worry about. And the dual color is just so…" Ted trailed off and made eye contact with Kiko. "…pretty."

"Sure," Kiko said. She had to smile at his passionate snack choice. "I'll try some worms, too."

"Excellent."

Kiko dropped in her quarters in a flash and pressed the buttons. A metal coil released her bag of colored sugar, and Ted handed her a pinch of quarters. "I'd like to buy your snack, if that's all right with you."

Kiko's cheeks heated. "Um, thank you."

Ted smiled and waved. "I have to head back. Enjoy the treat." He was cute in a nerdy sort of way and just as sweet as his snack choice.

Kiko slipped the quarters into her pocket and realized he was the only person nice to her besides Eric. So far, here at the office, she'd received only snark and vitriol. Kiko appreciated the kindness so much her chest constricted. Had she made a friend? She swallowed the lump in her throat. "See you later."

Down the hall, Amanda careened into her from an adjacent hallway.

"Oops, didn't see you there," Amanda said. "Oh! Kiko, I've been looking for you."

"Me?"

"Yeah, let's chat."

Kiko went to her own office with a worm hanging from her lips and a different kind of worm following her. What could Amanda want from her? Any marketing decisions impacting the finance department had to be approved by Eric. She slid behind her desk and set down the bag of gummy worms. Amanda closed the office door.

"How are things going around here? Settling in well?" Amanda asked.

"So far, I think so."

"Gummy worms? Those are gross."

Kiko smiled because Amanda was wrong.

The unpredictable woman continued, "Anyway, I love to just chit chat, but I came here for a reason. Eric had a bad morning."

"Oh?" Kiko hadn't heard.

Amanda pressed her lips together. "A meeting went very sideways, if you know what I mean."

Kiko didn't but she listened.

"And I noticed you're chummy with him. You like him, don't you? Everyone does, so don't deny it."

Kiko's cheeks heated despite the condescending tone.

"Well, if you want to get on his good side, one of his favorite restaurants is The Foot Long. I don't know why. The food is just…" Amanda exaggerated her disgust. "Anyway, if you picked him up the number five for lunch, I know it would lift him out of his funk."

Kiko considered the idea. She was right about The Foot Long. Of course, Amanda would know that, she was his wife. The refreshing word being 'was'. Kiko smiled. "That sounds like a great idea."

"I think you two are cute together, and you don't need to worry about me and him. We had our issues, and we ended up going our separate ways. It's over. Have a great lunch. Toodles!" Amanda wriggled her fingers in the air, and Kiko lifted a hand uncertain if she should copy the movements or not. Amanda disappeared before she decided, and Kiko checked her watch. Picking up lunch for both of them was a great idea. So why had Amanda mentioned it?

Was it possible the woman wanted Eric to be happy? Perhaps she was seeing someone else and wanted him to move on out of guilt. Kiko didn't know, but she slung her purse over her shoulder and Stan was at the curb holding the limo.

"Where to, Miss Kiko?"

"Uh, I think I'll catch a cab. It's okay, really."

"I'm here to bring people where they need to go, and since you work for Blue Feather, that includes you, too. Come along now. A cab will only take longer."

"I shouldn't." Kiko checked up and down the sidewalk and didn't see a blue sedan or a blond psycho. "There's someone I'm trying to avoid, and he's seen this vehicle and knows I work here."

Stan left the door open and stepped up to her. His kind, aged face calmed her a little. "Miss Kiko, while under my services, no one will ever touch you." Stan flipped open his tux jacket and displayed a concealed pistol. "It's licensed, and I'm trained. This is a very generic limo, but if it makes you feel safer, I can swap it for a different vehicle."

In reality, knowing Eric trusted Stan helped, and Kiko didn't have lunchtime flexibility like Eric did. Every moment she delayed was another moment she risked getting back late and losing her job, where she liked working with Eric, and she'd just made her first friend.

"I'm convinced." She chuckled and let Stan help her into the vehicle.

"Where to, Miss Kiko?" He glanced at her through the rearview mirror.

"Oh, The Foot Long. Thanks."

Stan's brows lifted, and he brought her there without a word.

Amanda had told her the number five was Eric's favorite, and Kiko couldn't see a reason why she'd lie about that. If Amanda was wrong, Kiko would eat whatever the number five was—unless it was snails—but this place didn't seem like the type. Three burly men, appearing fresh off the construction site with denim overalls, thick work boots, and long-sleeved T-shirts, arrived moments ahead of her. They waved her ahead of them.

"You were all here first," Kiko said, insisting.

"Thanks lady," the first one said. "We're starving."

She smiled at them, and their large bulk took up the entire entrance. The line inside was long up to the counter where orders were taken and received. The menu was handwritten on a board above the cashier. Kiko squinted to read it while leaning side to side to see around the men. Hopeless, she waited until she was within 20/20 range. The walls were rustic with exposed plaster. In Wisconsin, that would be disastrous in winter, but since the diner was sandwiched between other businesses, it wasn't so critical. The hardwood floors underfoot were dinged and scuffed and scratched. With the number of customers in this place and the way Eric talked about it, you'd think they'd have the funds to fix it up. Or maybe it was meant to appeal to the demographic here.

Kiko craned her neck around and found mostly filthy men, the meat and potatoes kind, where working meant sunrise was the alarm clock and nightfall was for passing out. Eric didn't seem the type to fit in here. He was the clean guy—the one where hard work meant sitting in an office all day, speaking on conference calls, and exercise came in the form of a gym. She was surprised at his preference for this place.

The corners of her lips lifted thinking of him. He was sexy in all the right ways, and irresistible when he made that face just before he ate her out. Eric was one word—perfect. And all she could picture was his warm smile that crinkled the corners of his eyes, his thick shock of sandy hair, and his shadowed jaw she ached to caress. But when he shaved, which she learned was twice weekly, she wanted to kiss him. The need to feel his lips on hers drove her mad when they were together and more so when they were apart. Perhaps a kiss would greet her when she brought him lunch.

Chapter 25

Caroline—sweet, flirty, doe-eyed Caroline—didn't seem the type to choose a rough-and-tumble spot for lunch, but he didn't know her all that well. Or had she chosen it because it was known to be Eric's favorite? Either way, Eric eagerly ordered a burger and fries while Caroline picked a plate of nacho fries, and she led him to a booth near the front glass panes.

Eric dug into his burger hungrily while Caroline poked at her fries, back straight, legs crossed. She leaned her exposed cleavage toward him with each bite. Yeah, he noticed, and no, he wasn't interested. He only wanted Kiko. She was it for him, and no one and nothing could get between them.

Caroline's leg kept touching his, but he shifted away from her. Again and again she kept touching and rubbing his leg.

"Is there a space issue on your end of the booth?" Eric asked.

"I'm just cold." She smiled sheepishly.

"We can switch seats. The windows are drafty." Eric munched half the fries and returned to his burger. The front door opened and closed as a pair of customers entered, holding hands and gazing at the menu.

Caroline frowned. The second a new thought entered her mind, she smiled again. The woman was utterly transparent. "Mother's Day is coming up. Would you like me to buy a present for your mom? I only need the address to send it on your behalf."

Eric blanched and stopped chewing. He hadn't seen or heard from his mom in a long time, and that was only a quick visit. She'd left Dad years ago, and Eric was still angry at her for it. "No. I don't have any need for a Mother's Day present."

"Why not?"

Eric's mind shut down. He didn't want to discuss his private life with her.

"It's okay. You don't have to tell me."

Eric sighed and slurped down his chilled bottle of water.

"But, you know, if there's anything I can do to fix it..." Caroline said in a teasing voice.

"No."

"Father's Day is next month," she added.

"My dad doesn't need anything."

"I'm sure there's something I could think of." A sly smile shifted her lips, and it made Eric uneasy. A fry, broken in half and dangling precariously from the end dropped into her cleavage.

"Oh, oops." Her surprise was fake, angering Eric even more. She leaned forward and made a show of digging it out with her fingers. "Silly me."

"Caroline, if you want to bang my dad for career advancement, that's between you and him. I want nothing to do with it."

Caroline gasped. "I would never."

Eric didn't believe her. She flirted very obviously all the time. "You seem interested in me and my dad, and I want to make it clear that I'm—"

"Eric, that's unnecessary," she interrupted. "And I haven't done anything wrong."

"Right," he said curtly.

Her leg found his again and slid along his pants.

"Drop it, Caroline."

"I'm just cold." She picked at her fries, dabbing them in the cheese lazily as if she intended to drag out her meal.

Eric inhaled the last two bites of his burger and licked his fingers. "What's the information you agreed to disclose?" Eric said, patience dangerously thin. "You haven't told me anything about Blue Feather."

Surprise lifted one eyebrow, and Eric blew out a breath. This had better not have been all a ruse.

"That's fair. Scoot over." Caroline slipped out of the booth across from him and forced him to move over. She leaned in close. Her breasts pressed up against his arm as she twisted closer.

He tilted his ear toward to her mouth, and his hands gripped his knees, pulse roaring with the anticipation of discovering the name of the threat hanging over his head. "It's me," she whispered.

"What?" Eric leaned back.

Her fingers pressed his jaw, turning his head to meet her gaze. He searched her features and found nothing but sneakiness. He was in such shock, trying to reconcile everything he'd seen and heard with his innocent, doe-eyed, flirty secretary, that he missed her hand grabbing the back of his neck and forcing him into a kiss. She'd lied to him. He hated liars.

His eyes squeezed shut in defense. Her lips were wrong—sticky with lipstick and the flavor of cheap cheese. Her tongue begged for entrance, but he denied her. Fingers raked through his hair. Reeling from the surprise attack, a beautiful feminine gasp pulled him back to his senses. He shoved Caroline back and sought the source of the sound.

Kiko, with a crushing look of horror on her face. She stepped back slowly, mouth gaped open, and turned to dash back out the door.

Eric pushed at Caroline, trying to give chase. The woman smirked and wouldn't move. In desperation, he slipped under the table, forced his eyes to look straight ahead and not at the disgust of what lurked beneath a restaurant table, and shuffled on his haunches out from Caroline's legs. She still tried to stop him.

"Hey, where are you going? I didn't tell you the information yet."

Eric stood after battling her high heels and turned to her. "Keep it."

Screw Caroline and Amanda. He ran off after Kiko, feeling like a complete jackass. One stupid mistake and he risked Kiko's trust. Fixing this was the most important thing right now.

KIKO DASHED THE SHORT distance back to the limo, where Stan opened the door as if expecting her return. The Foot Long was definitely a hole-in-the-wall as Eric described, and as she'd found out, more than just the décor sucked. Eric had been swapping spit with his secretary. Caroline's hands had been all over his suit and in his hair, messing it up—just how it looked when Eric rolled out of bed in the morning. A knife—as figurative as expected, as literal as possible—twisted in her belly. Kiko struggled to pull in a breath. Her hands trembled, and her chest fought the vice gripping her. Sparks blurred her vision.

Stan cranked over the engine, and tears filled her eyes. The smart man drove without asking her anything. A few miles later, she composed herself, and Stan noticed right away. "Where to, Miss Kiko?"

She hadn't thought about it. She only wanted to escape the crushing pain. "I don't know."

Eric was a great catch, and Caroline had her eye on him—she was very obvious. But Kiko lived with Eric. He was her best friend, wasn't he? Kiko hadn't considered labels before, and they were long overdue for that conversation. What was she? A girlfriend, a casual fling, a convenient twist in his sheets, a long-lost goal to conquer, a bonus?

Stan stopped at the curb to Eric's house.

As her door was opened for her, Kiko smeared her face as dry as she could manage, and she climbed out with the assistance of Stan's gloved hand. "Can I have a moment, Miss Kiko?"

Unable to speak, she nodded.

"I've known Eric Woodson since he was a boy. He has a reputation among women, and I've driven many of them myself, but in all my thirty years of driving for the Woodsons, the way he looks at you is unparalleled. Whatever you saw back at The Foot Long wasn't what you think it is."

Kiko nodded again to appease Stan. No matter what the reasonable explanation was, it still hurt. "Can you wait for me?" Kiko sniffled. "I'll only be a minute."

"I'd love to, Miss Kiko, but I have another pick up."

"Thank you for the ride."

Stan waved an informal salute, and Kiko walked up to the house, disengaged the security system, and shut the door behind her. In a hurry, she was upstairs in Eric's room, and she grabbed her meager clothing off the racks and out of the drawers. Her small pile of vacation clothes didn't take long to pack, and she headed out the front door, hoping beyond hope she returned before Stan left, but he was gone.

Another car sat at the curb—a familiar blue sedan. The blood drained from her face.

Roger stepped out of the driver's seat with an apologetic smile—she was becoming too familiar with that—and holding a bag of gummy worms.

What the hell?

"I heard you need a ride. My car isn't a horse and my clothes aren't shiny, but I hope you'll take my offer anyway." He'd promised he was a new Roger. This was definitely unexpected, and not in a good way. A—how the hell had he found her? And B—how did he know about her gummy worm snack?

Kiko dropped her bags in shock, and Roger dashed to retrieve them before she could.

Kiko took a step back. "How did you know I needed a ride?"

Roger shrugged noncommittally and stuffed her bags into the trunk of his sedan. "I have friends in many places."

Kiko narrowed her eyes at him. He'd murdered her husband, and previously murdered Eric. Roger had cop family allowing him to play dirty, and he'd been stalking her. She'd seen the dangers from all her years of matching couples through time, and with that experience on her side, she'd never fall for his lies. How could she get away from him?

"That's so thoughtful of you, Rodg. But I just remembered I forgot something inside. Can you give me a few minutes?" Kiko hooked her thumb toward the front door and stepped backward.

"I can wait." Roger slammed the trunk shut and leaned against his sedan, crossing his legs at the ankles. "Don't be too long."

Kiko walked up the sidewalk with stiffness in her legs. She rummaged through the keys to find the right one, wishing she could stealthily see what Roger was doing.

She pinched the brass key between shaking fingers and

unlocked the door. Kiko flung herself through the doorway and locked the door behind her. In a second, she turned off the security alarm but didn't reset it—she wasn't staying, but in case Roger followed her inside, she needed time before he figured out she'd left. She blew out a breath and leaned against the door.

Kiko dialed the local cab company and instructed them to pick her up on the block behind Eric's house. While waiting, she checked the front window, and Roger still leaned against his car, checking his watch. Knowing her time was running out, Kiko dashed out the back door, through the trimmed backyard, and into the woods dividing the properties.

Leaves smacked her face, underbrush scratched her legs, and her ankles twisted with her heels on uneven ground. She had to be careful of her footing or she'd be stuck here, lamed. Sunlight flickered through the pine boughs while she bolted straight ahead, almost hitting a wooden privacy fence. Kiko followed the pickets until she reached another trimmed lawn and dashed to the sidewalk of the next block. No car.

The cab wasn't here.

ERIC RUSHED OUT THE front door of The Foot Long, guilt churning his stomach like curdled milk. He was an idiot for getting duped by Caroline. Frankly, he was shocked by her cunning. And now, he'd hurt the only person who mattered.

"Kiko!" he called after her. He spun, breath panting. Where did she disappear to? Her Bronco hadn't been at Blue Feather, so she would've gotten a ride over here. Eric dialed Stan. The phone rang and rang.

"Stan, pick up," Eric growled into the flip phone. Stan had never ignored his request before.

Eric flipped the phone shut and fought himself from smashing it against the brick building. He opened it again and dialed the local cab service. He paced the sidewalk for a whole city block, restless with his thoughts consuming him.

Caroline stepped out of the diner and waited for his return pace. "Can we talk?" she asked.

"You had your chance." He kept walking right passed her.

"Can I catch a ride with you?" she called to his back.

Eric ignored her. Like hell he would share a cab with the woman who destroyed his life. Eric chuckled. She could be best friends with Amanda—two peas in a pod.

A cab pulled to the curb and honked. Eric jumped inside. "Go," he commanded.

"What about that there lady?" the driver asked, hesitating. "She seems upset you're ditching her." The older driver wore a tweed golf hat with reddish gray hairs curling out from under it. He looked like the average Joe at a dive bar—hardworking but a little too chatty.

"I don't know her. Go."

"Alrighty then." The cabbie floored the car, and they zipped away from the curb.

Caroline stood with her hands on her hips, her face a mixture of anger and surprise.

"So where we going?" the cabbie asked.

Eric gave his address. After seeing Kiko's face, there was no chance she went back to the office.

"Hang on to your britches. I'll have you there in a jiffy."

Cabbie wasn't lying. Eric grasped the oh-shit handle, so he didn't fall over on the curve. There was a reason he rode with Stan, but in a pinch, this guy was becoming his number two man.

In no time at all, the cabbie screeched to a halt in front of his estate—once the symbol of success, but now the anchor around his neck—a sham, a fake, a façade to a life that didn't exist anymore. Eric tossed his last few bills at the cabbie. "Thanks, friend," Eric said. "Great driving by the way. Got a card?"

"I'm not fancy enough for a card. But the name's Richard Johnston. No one knows that name but my boss, so ask for Quickie Dick, and I'll be where you need me in a jiffy."

Eric smiled and tapped on the door. "Sounds good. Drive safe." It sounded like the right thing to say, although counterintuitive.

Quickie Dick nodded with a friendly smile. "I'll hang out in case you need another ride soon."

"Whatever floats your boat, but I'm not on the clock," Eric said.

"Understood."

Eric rushed inside. His steps weren't as firm as they usually were. His hands weren't as steady either. He unlocked his door and fresh panic entered his mind. What if she wasn't here? The idea gave him palpitations.

Eric stepped inside and found the security system was deactivated, as expected, and he relaxed. He closed the door behind him and then wanted to slap his forehead for forgetting an apology gift. Even a single head of broccoli would've been better than being empty-handed.

"Kiko?" he called out to the expanse of foyer. Nothing was out of place, no boxes stacked, no suitcases piled. His steps echoed against the tile floor. He climbed the stairs, taking two at a time, and jogged into his bedroom.

She wasn't here.

Eric opened the closet, and her clothes and suitcases were gone. The drawers were emptied. She couldn't be that far ahead of him. How could she disappear so quickly? Eric spun and called her cell phone, panic surging in his chest. It rang and rang and eventually the voicemail picked up. He disconnected the call. "Dammit, Kiko. Where are you?"

Eric rushed back out the door, and Quickie Dick had waited. How did he know? That was a thought for another time.

Eric rattled off Kiko's home address and in a flash, they were swerving through streets to Kiko's small rental. No notes on the door, and the Bronco was still here. Eric knocked, but he received no answer. He pounded, and still nothing. Eric went inside and turned in place. She wasn't here, and it didn't look like she'd been here at all. The possibility that she could vanish for another seven years sent him reeling on his feet. He inhaled a deep breath and another. And then fisted his hair.

Please don't disappear on me again, he silently begged.

He dropped onto her bed and tears coated his eyes. He screwed up big time.

ANKLE SORE FROM HER dash through the neighborhood, Kiko's cab pulled into her driveway. Dread crawled under her skin. Roger was likely very upset again, and now he knew where she lived, and he had the perfect excuse—he had her suitcases.

"Wait for me?" Kiko asked.

The cabbie nodded.

Taking a deep breath, she stepped inside and rushed to twist the deadbolt, hook the chain, and turn the knob lock. She closed her curtains and flicked on the light. It didn't feel like home anymore, and she couldn't stay here. Kiko went to her bedroom and packed what little remained of her in-season clothes. She'd get her toiletries from a hotel. Kiko checked the front window before exiting, just in case Roger appeared or the cabbie left, but the gracious cabbie stayed.

Kiko locked up behind her and took a ride to a hotel. She tipped him well and checked in to a room on the third floor. While she cranked on the hot water for a bath, images of Eric with Caroline flashed through her mind. Wrenching pain twisted her insides, and Kiko wished she had booze. It was more likely to be granted than a wish for normalcy.

A lifetime ago, she'd thought she had everything, but then it was all ripped from her. A hundred years of floating through time she never mattered to anyone, and she wished for a real life of her own and a second chance at love and a family. For a moment, a painfully short moment of her hundred and twenty years on this planet, she'd once again had it all—a home of her own, a job with friends, and Eric, who was sweet and thoughtful and the perfect lover. She remembered Eric's desperate kiss on her lips, his teasing at breakfast, and his makeshift Thanksgiving dinner at their hotel. He'd brought Yoshi fresh flowers for his grave. Everything was perfect.

And then she lost it all again.

Her home wasn't safe.

Most of her co-workers hated her for existing.

And the most horrific thought, she'd learned Eric wasn't so perfect after all.

Why Caroline? Why bother with that woman if Eric wanted Kiko? The whole thought didn't make sense, but there was one thing Kiko learned over the years. Love wasn't rational. Clearly Eric was having a grand old time with Caroline, while Kiko stewed over her irrational heart and Eric making a fool of her.

She dipped her toes into the steaming pool of liquid relaxation and sunk down to the rumble of the water, steam heating her lungs and bubbles growing at the surface. Kiko scooped a handful and blew them off her hands. Suds flew across the tub and she scooped more—anything to keep her mind busy.

Why was everything ripped from her again? Anger spiked at Eric and more so at Chaos.

The bastard went back on his deal.

Chapter 26

Kiko rubbed the sleep from her puffy, bloodshot eyes. She'd barely caught a wink, but she dressed in her skirt suit anyway, unable to be left alone with her thoughts any longer. She looked forward to seeing her new friend, gummy worm Ted, but most of all, she needed to see Eric, even though he'd crushed her. A sliver of hope told her Eric would be there with a non-creepy single bouquet of flowers, a big fat apology, and a logical explanation. She slipped her emergency responder into her pocket, never going anywhere without it.

She'd had awkward days at her job long ago when she'd worked at the Gap. Various customers did unimaginable things in the dressing rooms, and she, being lowest on the totem pole, was tasked with cleaning it. Some of the garments she'd found…she shuddered at the memory. But this was a different kind of awkward. This was personal and a foreign territory for her.

Kiko unwrapped a Pop-Tart and stuffed it into the toaster. The hot pastry warmed her insides. It had been far too long since she last had one, but for some reason, today it didn't taste the same.

Under the hotel's porte-cochère, the morning was muggy and warm—a typical May in Wisconsin. Songbirds whistled their musical conversations and popcorn clouds drifted on a slight breeze. A beautiful day, except to her. She opened her phone and dialed a cab—no reason to bother Stan. After her blubbery mess yesterday, she didn't want to face him. She waited far enough from the sliding doors to not activate them, and a cab pulled up for her quicker than expected. She climbed into the back seat.

"'Ello, kid. Where to then?" the friendly driver asked, wearing an outdated golf hat over reddish gray curly hair.

"Hi. Blue Feather Publishing, downtown."

"Ah, I know the one. Hang on to your britches. There's a handle just above the window if you need it."

Kiko smiled. She'd experienced many things in her hundred years of travels, but never a warning about a cabbie's driving. After the first couple turns, Kiko found her hands gripping the armrest and the overhead handle before the next turn.

Faster than possible, the cabbie screeched the car to a halt in front of Blue Feather, shoving Kiko forward in her seat, despite bracing herself. "Uh, thanks." She pulled cash out of her wallet and passed it to the driver.

"Any time, kid. The name's Quickie Dick. If you ever need to be somewhere in a jiffy, I'm the man for you."

"That's your name?"

His eyes crinkled in the rearview mirror with a smile. "Yes, siree."

Kiko fought a smile pulling at her lips and ducked out of the cab. "Have a great day."

He winked at her and spun off. Kiko stared after him for a few moments, smiling and shaking her head. What a strange man. She craned her neck up at the towering building, squared her shoulders, and entered, while hope and fear swirled her insides.

She discreetly searched for familiar faces, hoping to catch an expression giving her a warning about possible grapevine gossip, especially about Eric and Caroline. Kiko hit the elevator button. The ride up was plump with the humming of the pulleys shifting and lifting, which stopped short on the second floor. The doors opened and gummy worm Ted pushed in a cart next to her. Kiko smiled at the friendly face.

"Hi, there," he said.

"You were right about the gummy worms. Delicious."

"I'm glad you like them." Ted pressed the button to the floor above hers, and when the doors closed, he asked, "Saturday night Barry and I are going bowling, and I heard you're into it.

They have a bar and great food, too. Would you like to come?"

Bowling with work buddies sounded like fun. "Sure, where is it?"

Ted's face lit up—a youthfulness and excitement that made Kiko smile again. "Don't worry about it. We'll pick you up. Seven sharp."

The elevator door opened, and Kiko stepped off, light on her toes. It felt embarrassingly great to be included. With fresh confidence, Kiko strolled down to her office and logged into the system. She checked her work calendar and found a meeting scheduled with Paul Woodson. Her eyes popped. What did he want with her?

Kiko scrambled to set her purse down and collect paper and a pen for notes. She checked her watch, and she had two minutes to get her buns down to conference room B. On her way, Kiko noted Caroline wasn't at her desk, and smugly smiled that Kiko had the courage to show up when the other woman didn't.

In the conference room, Kiko stopped short as if trapped in wet concrete. Paul, Amanda, and Caroline sat around the table. This had bad news written all over it.

"Good morning. Thanks for coming on time." Paul invited her to take a seat, and Kiko stiffly dropped into a chair. Amanda had a smug smirk on her face while Caroline avoided eye contact entirely. Paul added, "Caroline is taking the minutes. Amanda and I have some paperwork for you."

Kiko regained her sense of breathing. Paperwork. She could handle that. "What's this in regard to?"

Amanda slid a stapled pile of papers toward her. "We need your signatures on the noted lines, and then I can move forward with contacting wholesale distributors."

The office door opened, and Kiko spun, hoping for Eric, but no. She didn't recognize the medium-built man in a suit with streaks of gray in his hair. He addressed Amanda, "I heard what's going on here. This isn't your department. The acquisitions editor, me, handles incoming clients. Not you." He turned to Paul. "Sir, why are you allowing the marketing director to take over my role? Is there something I should be aware of?"

Paul cleared his throat. "This special circumstance is only for one client. Your job is secure, but don't ever barge into one of my meetings again, Shawn."

"Understood. Sorry, sir." Shawn ducked out of the room with his tail between his legs.

Paul gestured to the contract, and Kiko skimmed it, confused. She re-read the first few paragraphs. "This is a waiver form and a contract, but I already signed a contract."

"That's correct," Paul said. "But it has come to our attention that your needs will be better met with this contract."

Between notes, Caroline stared her down. Amanda watched her with a twisted lip, while Paul appeared friendly and genuine. She didn't trust the former two, but as owner of the company, sitting CEO, and Eric's dad, she trusted him. But, she was smart enough to cover her own ass. "I think I should talk this over with Eric first," Kiko said.

"That's not necessary, dear," Amanda replied with an irritating condescending tone.

"As Eric is my representation, I feel it's necessary to discuss changes with him," Kiko countered.

Amanda cleared her throat.

Paul sighed. "Kiko, no one here is trying to pull a fast one. We all have your best interests in mind. After all, what's good for you is good for us. This change is an improvement that will benefit both parties."

"I'm not comfortable with this."

Amanda grunted in frustration. "Eric knows, okay? This was his idea, but he was too ashamed of the subpar contract he had you sign that he couldn't show his face today."

Kiko knew right away Amanda was full of it. Eric would never be too ashamed to face her about an industry standard contract. This had to be about Caroline.

"Then I'll need to read over all the terms first," Kiko said, advocating for herself now that Eric wasn't 'taking good care of her' like he'd promised.

"Go ahead," Amanda said. "When you're satisfied and done signing, give them to Caroline to make copies."

Kiko's face pinched at having to rely on Caroline for anything.

Paul cut in. "It's standard. I get the contracts from Caroline. Nothing to be alarmed about."

Kiko stood and collected her papers and the new contract. "Then they'll be no problem if I take my time reading these through."

"Well," Amanda said. "Don't take more than a day. We have to get feelers out to the wholesalers ahead of the holiday reading season or we'll miss out on a lot of sales."

"Okay." Kiko returned to her office. She closed the door behind her and dropped the papers on the surface. A higher priority was checking her work email. She wanted to keep up with messages and announcements, but really, she wanted to see if there was anything from Eric.

She'd received one message last night from his personal email.

That wasn't a good sign.

'Kiko, we need to talk,' it read.

No kidding. About him pressing faces with Caroline? About how it was his idea to have his dad and ex-wife rework her contract? Kiko sighed under the crushing weight of Eric's rejection. She read every word of the new contract. It was identical to Eric's, except they gave her an extra one percent in royalties. Since Eric didn't want to represent her for whatever reason, Kiko signed.

Chapter 27

FOR THE FIRST TIME since he was a teenager, Eric called in sick to work. Dad would have his hide later, but for now Eric needed a chance to plan. He didn't sleep a moment last night, worrying about Kiko—she'd vacated his house, and hers was empty as well. She hadn't responded to his email. He'd kept it light, hoping he wouldn't write the wrong thing and hurt her worse than he had. His calls had gone to voicemail. Although he hated to imagine the possibility, he'd called Roger. As expected, Roger was furious and made several threats, which meant he didn't have Kiko.

Eric's secretary was nothing to him, and the woman wouldn't leave him alone. It was his fault he hadn't stopped Caroline sooner or had her transferred away to remove the interoffice risk, since the woman couldn't take a hint.

Dammit.

Eric's head was a bag full of cats, incapable of rest, incapable of logical thought. He shuffled to the coffee pot and pressed a button. While coffee beans percolated through the kitchen, he stuffed his legs into jeans and pulled a T-shirt over his head. Cold feet were alleviated with flip-flops. The foam slapped his feet while he crossed over to the steaming pot of brain function.

He leaned against the counter and checked his phone for missed calls. None. Not even Amanda, who lately called all the time just to get under his skin.

Eric poured a mugful and sipped. With a caffeine jolt powering his muscles, he decided to fix up his bedroom—make the bed, straighten his side of the closet, and pick up dirty laundry.

A tidy house wasn't good enough for her. No, he needed something more extravagant in case he brought Kiko back, even if he had to wait another seven years. The idea hit him square in the head. He'd reprint the best images from when he, Yoshi, and Kiko bowled together in their college days, blow them up as large as the pixels could handle, and mount them around the foyer. The one of Eric and Kiko together he would mount above the headboard of his bed. Eric chugged the cooling drink and dialed for Stan's assistance.

"That's a brilliant idea, sir. Will you be coming to work after?"

Eric considered. Now feeling lively and refreshed, he had no reason to skip work. Losing pay was a bad idea anyway. "Yeah, give me a lift."

"I'll arrive in ten minutes."

"Thank you, Stan." Eric hung up with a smile on his face. He set his empty mug down and a flip-flop slapped his foot. Oh, shit. He had ten minutes to get presentable.

Eric rushed upstairs and changed into a suit as usual. He cleaned up in the bathroom and jogged down the steps as Stan rang the doorbell.

"What size images did you want?" Stan asked.

"Eighteen by twenty or larger is best. Hang them here and here." Eric gestured at the walls.

Stan assessed the space. "Yes, sir. No problem. For now, your ride awaits. Would you, perhaps, care to stop for a gift?"

Eric followed his personal—what was he? Stan had worked for the family since he was a kid, but Stan's services seemed to fulfill more than just a gopher and driver role. Stan opened the back door, and Eric ducked inside.

A gift? Why would he need a gift...unless...

Stan peered through the rearview mirror. "I think a certain someone would like a little cheering up."

Eric's breath caught in his throat. "Kiko is at Blue Feather? Now?"

"Yes, sir."

She'd showed up, while he wallowed. He was an idiot, but a giddy idiot knowing he wouldn't have to wait seven years to apologize and explain. "Bring me to the closest grocer's and then right to work. Step on it."

Stan gave Quickie Dick a run for his money.

Eric rushed inside the building, carrying a proper vase filled with a heady mix of tropical flowers that reminded him of her scent, and a strawberry cheesecake. While chanting for the elevator doors to open faster, his legs twitched with impatience. Eric jabbed the door close button, and he watched the numbers flip painfully slow as if the universe mocked him for his screw up.

Freed from the metal box, Eric swiftly tore down the hall, intentionally intimidating people to prevent being stopped. His palms were sweating against the glass vase as he approached Kiko's closed door. He knocked politely, hands trembling.

"Come in," her voice called through the door, and Eric lips formed a smile of relief.

He opened her door, and Kiko clicked away at her keyboard, scrunching her nose and squinting at the screen. His heart skipped one too many beats, and his legs felt loose. When her eyes met his, she gasped, but her face turned cold, and she crossed her arms.

"Ready to save face?" she asked.

"Can I come in?"

"You already are." Her icy tone pierced his chest.

"Right. These are for you." He passed her the flowers, and she set them on the corner of her desk without a second glance. "And if you're hungry I brought dessert."

"I'm not hungry."

Eric set the bag down on a shelf, closed the door, and sat across from her desk. Her frown never wavered, and her eyes just followed him.

"Look, I know what it looked like at The Foot Long, but I can assure you, Caroline means nothing to me."

"What you do in your free time is none of my business."

"I want it to be your business. I'm so sorry."

"I don't want to hear it. If I was a conquest from your past, congratulations for making another mark on your extensive list of triumphs. Now that our contract is terminated, we have no relationship except you're my boss, so I expect professionalism."

Eric tensed, his pulse roaring in his ears. He expected her to be angry, and it was justified, but to have him cut from her life? They had many things to unpack, if only she'd give him the chance. "What happened to our contract?"

SHE WASN'T GOING TO forgive him for the Caroline incident, but Eric's genuine confusion perplexed her. "I was told you wanted our contract terminated," Kiko said, trying to sort the facts.

"Who told you this?"

"Caroline, Amanda, and Paul were at the meeting this morning, and it very much looked like Amanda was running the show with Paul as backup."

Eric stood and raked a hand through his hair. "Amanda again. Such a thorn in my ass. Of course she would. Is she ever going to stop? Kiko, I don't know what's going on around here, but I didn't cancel our contract."

Paul Woodson and Amanda had lied to her. She didn't know whether to be angry, insulted, or embarrassed about it, but a little thread of guilt wove its way under her skin. "I signed an annulment waiver for us and a new contract with them. They offered me an extra one percent in royalties."

Eric's face darkened, and her veins hummed with a familiar flight response. "So, a few extra bucks is all it takes?"

It wasn't the contract he was angry about. It was the personal slight. The need to defend herself grew. "They assured me you wanted out of our deal, so what other choice did I have?"

Eric leaned against the backrest of the chair. "Caroline tricked me into going to The Foot Long. She had information about what was going on around here. Instead, she made a move—the one you regrettably saw—and now they manipulated you into canceling our contract."

The words hung in the air like a stifling tarp threatening to suffocate them. His explanation made sense, but in that moment when her heart had been ripped from her chest, logic flew out the window. Now she understood why so many of her matches made so many dumb moves. It was easier to judge on the outside looking in.

"I don't like this," Eric said. "Not one bit. Dad won't—or can't—tell me anything. I don't know if he's in on it. Caroline—what a waste of space. And Amanda...?" Eric stepped around her desk and held out a hand. "I've made many mistakes in my life."

Kiko accepted, and he lifted her to her feet, warmth blossoming in her chest.

"But there is only one thing in my life I regret more, and that was not finding you seven years ago."

Tears bathed her cheeks—a mix of regret, guilt, and happiness.

Eric's hands cupped her face and his thumbs brushed the tears aside. "I'm so sorry for dragging you into this mess. You could be safe at home, writing your heart out, while I rake in the big bucks for you. Instead, you're stuck in the middle of this drama. Despite it all, you're here, facing it head on with a strength I always knew you had. I love you, Kiko."

Fresh tears popped into her eyes. She wanted him to keep going, and he did.

"I've loved you since that first night we went bowling with Yoshi. I kept my distance out of respect for my best friend. I did everything I could to help you grieve, and I gave you time. I love you so much, Kiko. I would never break our contract. I would never do anything to hurt you. I'm so very sorry for the horror you saw, but I only have eyes for you."

Eric's soft green eyes bore into hers with vulnerability. It had been a century since she'd last heard those words. Heat flooded her chest. For the first time, she felt a lightness, a feeling of completeness that made her whole again.

Eric laced his fingers with hers and squeezed. "Say something," he pleaded.

There was only one thing to say. "I love you, too, Mr. Spreadsheets. I think I always knew too."

Eric beamed. He lifted her into a broad hug with a comforting squeeze. Kiko closed her eyes and filled herself with his warmth, protection, and familiar clean scent. She smiled and pressed her face against his chest.

The knob rattled with a second's warning before the office door opened, and Eric and Kiko sprung apart. She turned and wiped her face as best she could. Caroline stood with documents in her hand, and her face twisted in disgust. "Here's your copy of the contract." Caroline tossed the papers onto the floor and closed the door on her way out.

Kiko and Eric exchanged looks, and Kiko smiled slyly with an idea. "The contract composed of the main sheet and two carbon copies. Caroline just dumped off the pink copy. If we can get our hands on the original and the yellow copy, I'll send them to the shredder."

"There's still the waiver, and I can get that from Derek's office."

"Mission Impossible: Rogue Documents." Kiko's eyes crinkled with a devious smile.

"You are such a nerd sometimes. I love that about you."

Kiko laughed. At least she didn't slip up this time. She'd referenced the modern movie series, while he thought she'd referenced the TV series from the 1980s. One day she planned to tell him the truth about her missing seven years. Hopefully he believed her, and she didn't lose the best thing in her life.

"Before the day is over, we'll meet back here for the shredding ceremony, and I have strawberry cheesecake to celebrate," Eric said.

"Game on." A lightness filled the room, and Kiko was ecstatic that her best friend was at her side. Never again would she doubt Eric's loyalties.

Chapter 28

Mission impossible? Not a chance. Eric confidently rode the elevator down, pushed through the glass doors, and strolled toward his attorney's office. With Eric's regular appearances, the secretary simply nodded to him while she was on the phone. After getting out of sight, Eric ducked around and headed for the records room. He'd watched Derek sort his important files back here, so he had an idea of where to find the waiver form—in a small room with rows of metal filing cabinets lit by harsh fluorescent lights.

Tags on the fronts told him the alphabetical order. His first try was to search the W cabinet for his contract termination document. Negative. Lots of divorce paperwork, though. Next he searched the T cabinet for Kiko Takai's waiver. Bingo. The waiver form wasn't missing any tear-offs behind the original. He folded the pages and tucked them into his suit jacket pocket.

Eric closed the drawer and turned around to find Amanda leaning against the frame. In an accusatory tone, she asked, "What are you doing in here?"

Heat tore up his face. "I should ask you the same."

Amanda chuckled. "I brought your attorney a thank you gift for being so speedy in our divorce."

"How thoughtful of you," Eric said, deadpan.

Amanda sauntered over to him, hips swaying. She grasped his tie and caressed the wool. Her two first fingers formed tiny legs, and she walked them over his chest. "What's your excuse for being here?"

Eric struck out a hand and batted her away. "I don't need one." Eric smoothed his tie. "Now if you don't mind, I'm busy."

"Of course, you are. Always so busy. Why not take a few minutes and slow down, explore, taste...touch?" Amanda's hands slipped up to the back of his neck, and he knew where she was going. He disengaged her hands in a flash and dipped out of the room.

"Been there, done that. Toodles," he finished with a mocking salutation.

Amanda crossed her arms and steamed. Eric was glad to extricate himself from the situation before she tried to take it too far. He rode the elevator back up to Blue Feather's main floor and found Kiko's office empty.

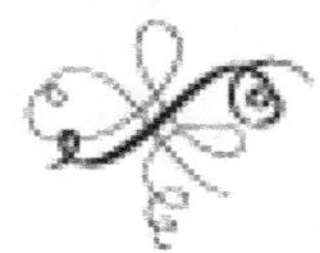

Kɪᴋᴏ ʙᴇᴇʟɪɴᴇᴅ ᴛᴏ Cᴀʀᴏʟɪɴᴇ's desk where the secretary would be making and filing the copies. With the pink copy just dropped off, the others must still be around. The small woman with doe eyes and a pixie cut was perched behind her desk sorting papers. A spark of resentment coursed through Kiko.

"Caroline," Kiko interrupted sweetly. "Seems I made a mistake on the new contract. Can you give me the pages again? I'll fix my error."

The secretary lifted a suspicious brow at her.

"I promise to return all the documents in their original form, and you can continue copying and forwarding them as Mr. Woodson requires."

"Sure thing." Caroline dug in a drawer and handed her the yellow copy. "You'll have to see Paul for the original."

Kiko gulped. Over the years, few people intimidated her. Many scared her. Only one had accomplished both—Chaos. But after Paul's deception, he was quickly becoming a runner up, and now she didn't know who to trust.

Kiko knocked on his office door with flutters in her belly. She didn't want to interrupt her boss's boss, but it needed to be done.

"What is it?" his distracted voice called over.

Kiko opened the door slowly and found Paul covering the mouthpiece of his phone. "Oh, sorry. I didn't mean to—"

"You've already interrupted, just finish what you need to say."

"I need the original copy of my new contract. I made a mistake on it."

Paul absently shuffled papers on his desk and spoke into the phone. "I agree, that cover isn't good enough. Find Brian and get him to clean it up."

Kiko's cheeks were on fire while she waited.

Paul held out the papers and turned his head back to his work. Kiko snapped the pages from him and escaped his office in a flash. Like a spy stealing secrets, she floated in success while she walked down the hall to her office. Inside, she closed the door and sat down. Her eyes roamed the documents to confirm they were the right ones. Paul had given her the termination form and the new contract she'd signed. Kiko's mouth dropped open while her door swung wide with Eric's return.

"What is it?" he asked her.

"Those conniving assholes." Kiko wanted to use a much

more colorful string of descriptions for them—the parties responsible, but she refrained in the supposedly-professional environment.

"What?" Eric tilted his head as Kiko turned the documents. He scanned the papers. "I don't see anything."

"They not only told me you didn't want to rep me anymore, they also had me sign a new contract for more royalties. But here, after the fact, they changed the seven percent down to six." Kiko pointed.

"Goddamn liars. I hate liars. Well, looks like it's not a pay cut switching back to me after all." Eric snapped a photo with his flip phone and collected the other copies. He skimmed them too. "They changed them all. I knew they would stoop low, but even I thought they had limits."

Kiko didn't miss the quip about liars. Brushing it aside, she took all three copies and fed them to her shredder. After the loud grinding stopped, Kiko asked, "Did you get the waiver?"

Eric passed it to her, and it met the shredder, too. Score one point for Team Eric and Kiko.

"We did it," Kiko said, standing.

Eric embraced her again. "Welcome back to my team. Next time, don't sign anything without me."

"Advice committed to heart." She chuckled.

Traffic in the hallway gained volume and Kiko glanced at the clock. The day was nearing its end. "Time to head out."

"Let's punch out and celebrate our victory," Eric said. "I'll take the cheesecake to go, and I have a surprise for you."

"On one condition," Kiko said. "My treat." She knew Eric was broke, and she didn't want him to worry about paying her way.

"If you insist." Eric collected the cheesecake.

She did.

Chapter 29

Kiko wasn't sure what the surprise was, but Eric wouldn't spoil it. She'd explained she needed to check out of her hotel room first, and she promised to meet him at his house.

"No leaving your phone off this time," Eric insisted.

"I won't," Kiko said.

Stan dropped Eric off at his house and unloaded Kiko under the hotel porte-cochère. Kiko headed up to her room, changed out of her suit and into jeans and a T-shirt, zipped the duffel closed and checked out. She didn't take more than ten minutes, and Kiko actually expected Stan to be waiting. Instead, she wished it was Stan waiting. Her back stiffened. "Hi, Roger."

"Hey, pretty lady. You, uh, left me hanging."

"It was an emergency. I'm sorry I didn't get back to you. How is it you always know where I am?" Being nice was her best bet, as much as it made her want to vomit.

Roger chuckled. "I have my ways."

Yeah, cops for family, Kiko thought. She shivered and lied.

"Well, I have a ride on the way. Is there something you need?"

"I just stopped by to take you out—bowling and a movie—remember?"

She'd play along, stalling, knowing a true nice-guy Roger didn't exist. "I don't remember specifying the date. I already have plans tonight."

Roger stepped forward, and Kiko backed up a step. The simple dance flashed her back to Roger cornering her in her kitchen with murder on his hands and ravenous lust in his eyes. Roger took another prowling step forward, and Kiko stepped back again. Her heart pounded in her chest, and her breaths became shallow. Kiko squeezed her eyes closed, wishing Stan would return right now.

"So what makes these plans so important you want to toss ours aside?" Roger asked, menace on his voice.

Kiko searched for an escape, a defense, something. She couldn't outrun him nor give him the slip again. The police were useless. She didn't want to put the hotel receptionist in danger either. Eric, please, she silently begged. Please come or even call—or something. Think, think, think.

Roger was easily manipulated. Kiko smiled. "How about some popcorn and a movie in my hotel room?"

Roger stopped and considered. "What do you have to watch?"

Kiko's hands trembled, but her breathing stabilized. The big dumb brute could be outwitted easily. "Whatever's on the listings, or there's a Blockbuster a couple blocks over. By staying in, you can pause the movie for a bathroom break, and there's something to be said for privacy."

"Yeah, I dig it. 'Clerks' released on VHS, and we can get some candy at Blockbuster, too. This could be fun," Roger said.

"Is there anything else you'd like to see? A double show perhaps?" Kiko teased. She had no intention of watching a movie with Roger, but she was buying time to make a plan.

"Maybe, I don't know what else is out there."

Ugh. "Okay, well, you meet me in the car, and I'll be right back out."

He chuckled deep and low, and the blood drained from Kiko's head. "I'm not the simple dude you think I am. We've played our games and now I'm done. I can't even pretend to be the nice guy anymore. I want you Kiko. That'll never change, and before that sun sets today, I will have you."

Kiko's feet froze in place. She refused to believe what Roger's pie hole just uttered. His lips curved into a snarl, and he stalked forward. Kiko dropped her bag and ran inside the hotel. Footsteps thundered behind her, and a meaty growl hissed in her ears. She panted, arms pumping, feet navigating the turn down the hallway.

A large hand landed on her shoulder, and with a vicelike grip, Roger yanked her back. Kiko sailed to the floor, and her head bashed against the low-pile carpet. Her vision sparkled, and her stomach flipped—the sensations of being pulled through time enveloped her.

"No," she mumbled. "No, Chaos," she begged. Kiko hadn't saved Eric yet, and this was her last try. "No!" Kiko sat up and rubbed her head. Chaos stopped, but that was warning enough.

Roger grabbed the back of her shirt collar and dragged her down the hall. Her hands flew to her neckline to stop the fabric from choking her. Both of Kiko's phones were in her purse, discarded in the lobby.

She thrashed her legs, trying for purchase against anything—the drywall, trim, or doorways. He kept on dragging, and her pants slid down her butt, exposing her flesh to carpeting. Kiko tilted to save herself rug burns, but Roger fought her with minimal grunts. "Fighting only makes it more fun. Keep it up, chick."

The Roger monster was back in full swing. Last time he'd run a sword through Yoshi, and she'd sheathed a steak knife in Roger's gut. She wouldn't get that lucky twice as Roger dragged her into a broom closet. Kiko grasped a mop handle, but that was like tapping a wall with a toothpick.

Roger kicked her knees out from under her, and she crashed to the small floor. Time was running out, and her only chance was reason. "Roger, Eric is on his way here. If I'm not in the lobby, he's going to come for me."

His face twisted into a smiling snarl. "Good. I hope that punk shows up. More fun for me." Roger fought to remove her jeans, while she kicked and thrashed to keep him away. He chuckled in her ear as if she told a mildly amusing joke.

Kiko was stupid—a fool—for letting Roger anywhere near her. She knew what he could do, what he'd done. Tears sprung to her eyes. Roger's hand gripped her wrist and squeezed. Kiko cried out.

"Oh, yeah. Cry and scream for me. Throw my name in there a few times, would'ya?" Roger groaned in pleasure. "Speak. Say my name," he demanded.

Kiko desperately held in a whimper to give him the least amount of pleasure possible. A crack echoed through the small space before her nerves recognized the pain on her cheek. A sob broke through her resolve, and Roger laughed.

Another bang sounded inside the little closet, but Kiko was numb to it.

ERIC ADJUSTED THE LIGHTING in the foyer to maximize the impact of the portraits Stan had so generously printed and hung for him. Her smiling face would be the first thing he saw waking up in the morning and coming home from work, and the last thing he saw leaving for work and going to bed. Satisfied with the lighting, Eric turned on the ice maker and laid bottles of wine inside the fridge. He set the cheesecake next to them.

In the living room, he turned on soft instrumental music. Kiko should've been here by now. Now that she was Blue Feather, Stan would always give her a ride with a single call. Eric called Stan. He hadn't seen Kiko since he dropped her off.

Eric called her next, worry growing by the second. While the phone rang, Eric rushed to his garage.

"Kiko, pick up, dammit."

No answer.

Kiko wouldn't ditch him after both of them admitted their love for the other, and Kiko wasn't a liar, never had been, so he knew her words were true. A line from his Dad came to mind: 'Don't dismiss fear as a weakness. It's intuition. Pay attention to it. Your gut just might save your life.' Eric didn't worry about himself.

Eric rolled his cherry red Ducati out of the garage and turned it over. He cranked on the handle grip, purring the engine, and zipped down the road with only Kiko on his mind. When he turned into the hotel parking lot, he saw the blue sedan, and anger ripped through his veins. The Ducati rolled under the porte-cochère, and he took off on foot inside the lobby. He feared the worst when he found her discarded bags, and no one manned the front desk.

He ran down the hall and shouted, "Kiko!"

Muffled screams, grunts, and groans came from a room nearby. Eric's stomach flipped over, and he swallowed several deep breaths to brace himself for what he was about to see. He charged into the door, bashing it open, fists tensed into steel balls, anger furrowing his brow.

"Get away from her!" he boomed. Eric grabbed the larger man and tossed him into the hallway. Roger dropped and rolled. Kiko laid on the floor, shaking. Her jeans were unfastened, shirt torn, and her hair was a matted mess. Her eyes were wild with fear, paralyzed like a child cowering from a parent's angry hand. It crushed him, but Eric only thought about getting her away. He lifted her to her feet and shushed her hair in comfort. "Go. Get out of here. I'll handle this."

Roger regained his footing. A hand landed on Eric's shoulder. "Now!" Eric shouted.

Kiko stumbled back a few steps, shaking her head in the negative. Of all times to ignore his wishes...

The asshole's long arms and iron grip forced Eric to face him, but Eric ducked under the expected swing of his fist. Eric had watched Roger's style at the dojo. He was brawn, but slow. Eric leaned back and pulled a fist into Roger's left flank, knocking the wind out of him. With a moment bought, Eric jogged over to Kiko.

"Not so fast, Woodson. She's mine," Roger called.

Eric pushed his phone into her hand. "Call Stan. Get a ride out of here."

Roger growled. "Last warning, punk."

Eric turned to face the crazed man. "She's not yours. Kiko chooses who she wants. Now leave us alone," Eric demanded, knowing his words were useless.

Roger's face curled into a devious smile. "Or what? You'll call the cops? Go ahead. My uncle will take care of any report you make."

"Rodg, I'm not going to warn you again," Eric said darkly.

Roger shrugged. "You don't have to." The meaty fist flew, but it was slow enough Eric dodged it and returned another of his own.

Grunts exploded from lips, thumps echoed from fists, and panting breaths accompanied sweat. Roger was skilled, but like hell Eric was going out the same way his best friend did.

Kiko whimpered behind him, and a sudden surge of power took over his fists. His arms hammered into his opponent's abdomen left and right, left and right, until he couldn't feel his knuckles anymore.

Roger finally dropped to the carpet.

Eric's fists continued on his face. A tugging at his arm registered, and Eric stopped.

"It's over. Eric, stop. He's done," Kiko said.

Eric's breaths came and went as if he'd just run a marathon, and his arms tingled with exhaustion as he towered over the shifting form of Roger on the floor. Roger's face quickly swelled, purple and red, and his hands covered his belly where Eric tenderized him. Eric's knuckles were swollen and bleeding. He flexed his fingers, and fresh blood seeped up, but he didn't feel it.

"Let's get out of here before he comes around," Eric said.

Kiko and Eric rushed down the hall, and she scooped up her purse and bag on their way through the lobby. The last thing Eric remembered was Kiko running terrified next to him, then a bold sting on the back of his knee. Confusion twisted his face and blackness took him down.

KIKO SCREAMED.

Roger had somehow caught up to them and kicked Eric on the back of the knee. His skull hitting the tile knocked him out. The effort had taken Roger down, but not for long. There was no time to waste. Kiko dialed Stan.

The driver picked up, and Kiko spilled her plea, "I need help. Eric is hurt, and Roger is coming around. Hurry!"

"Give me five."

Kiko hung up. Eric's lips moved, and Kiko curled up next to his face to hear. They moved again, but no sound came out. Tears came to her eyes at the similar situation she'd already witnessed. Last time they were at a coffee shop, and he'd never regained consciousness. Roger wanted Eric dead. She didn't have five minutes.

Kiko stepped behind Eric's head, and with her hands under his arms, she pulled. His upper body lifted off the floor, and his head sagged back, but he didn't move an inch.

Kiko huffed with the strain. Tears washed down her cheeks. What could she do? Roger shifted, attempting to get back up.

He groaned with each movement.

She had seconds. A minute at most.

Looking around the lobby, she wished for Yoshi's katana—a perfectly ironic ending, but it was in police evidence. What else did she have? A chair, a large potted fern…

Even if she had access to the employee lunchroom, Kiko didn't have the guts to use a knife against him again. Last time she'd gotten lucky in knicking an artery. If she missed this time, she'd be dead, and those odds weren't good enough.

Out of options, Kiko lifted a lobby chair and struck Roger in the back of the head as hard as she could. He flopped down, but he recovered quickly. His meaty hand snatched the chair leg and wrenched it from her grip. He threw it over his shoulder, and a wooden leg snapped as it hit a wall. The loose length of wood tumbled nearby.

Kiko stepped back toward it as Roger climbed to his feet and stood slightly hunched. At least it was possible he could feel pain. "Face it, you're mine, Kiko."

"I'll never be yours." Kiko hefted the broken length of wood.

Roger chuckled. When he prowled close enough, she used the jagged edge to stab him in the abdomen where Eric had already softened him. Roger folded. She pulled it back and flipped it over her shoulder, baseball style, and slammed him against the ear with it. He tumbled over, and Kiko ran for Eric.

Her love groaned and sat up, pressing his hands to his head. "What happened?"

"No time. We have to go."

While she led him out the sliding lobby doors, Eric leaned on her. Stan pulled up, and the handy man rushed over to help. Stan eased Eric into the backseat.

Roger limped to the sliding doors, and stopped, hand pressed against his bleeding head wound. "This isn't over."

Of course not.

Kiko jumped in the limo after Eric.

Stan thankfully pulled away before bothering to ask where they wanted to go, and Roger's angry face shrunk in the background. Kiko eased against the backrest, and Eric flopped over with his head in her lap. She combed and smoothed his hair. Eric's hand found her thigh, holding on for comfort as much as stability from Stan's rough corners.

"Hospital or home?" Stan asked at last.

"Home," Eric answered.

Yes, home. Kiko smiled. They'd escaped alive this time, and now Eric needed rest. He didn't take much damage from the fight, but he knocked himself in the head pretty good. Roger's last words hung in her mind. She didn't doubt he actually intended to kill her. The cops wouldn't believe her even if Roger didn't have them in his back pocket. Even though Roger knew where Eric lived now, Eric had a great security system at his house. For tonight, she wouldn't dwell on it.

Stan helped her bring Eric inside.

"If there's anything else you need, don't—" Stan started.

"Hesitate to call," Kiko finished.

Stan smiled. "Precisely. Good night, Kiko. Give Eric my best when he's alert."

"Thank you."

Stan closed the door, and Kiko engaged the alarm before returning to Eric on the couch by the fireplace. Soft orange light flickered around the dim room. Satisfied he was awake, Kiko collected an ice pack, glass of water, and some ibuprofen. "Here, take these. It'll help."

Eric swallowed the pills and flopped back on the couch with a groan.

"I'll call in for you tomorrow. You're in no shape to be working." Kiko sat next to him and inspected his damaged hand. "This looks bad."

"What does?"

"Your knuckles are a mess."

"Mostly old damage. If I'm not gushing, I'll live."

"Let me bandage it up anyway."

Eric groaned with a hand on his head.

Kiko dug in the bathroom for whatever wound care was available. She sat next to his hip, rested his hand in her lap, and cleaned the wound with hydrogen peroxide. "They're not gushing."

"Did he hurt you?" he asked groggily.

She layered gauze padding and wrapped it with bandage tape. "I'm fine."

"I promised I wouldn't let anything happen to you, and I meant it," Eric said.

Kiko's cheeks heated with a blush, and she tore off the end of the tape. "Roger tried to have his way with me. If you didn't show up, he would've." Kiko shivered at the unwanted image. "So, thank you for saving me. How that monster can walk the streets a free man, I'll never understand."

"I remember kicking the shit out of him, and then...nothing. Did I win?"

Kiko chuckled. "Roger took a cheap shot—nailed your knee, and the floor sucker punched you."

"Ah, I thought I recognized the swirling vision and raging headache. One of these days I'm going to exact revenge on the tile. That shit's sneaky. So much for our celebration." He chuckled, turning his green eyes to her. His soft smile flickered under the firelight.

Kiko caressed his jaw with her thumb and cocked a smile at him. "We're both alive, away from Roger, and we have our jobs. Plus, we saved our contract. We can always share a bottle of wine, amazing cheesecake, and lots of sex another night."

"Lots of sex, eh?" Eric perked up.

Kiko chuckled. "Hang on there, big boy, not tonight. I don't want you to end up with more brain damage."

"Well, now that just sounds kinky."

Kiko laid on the couch next to him, nestled under his chin. Her fingers swirled on his arm, playing with his shirt sleeve, caressing his skin. She leaned up and kissed him. Eric pressed her tight, and she finally felt at home.

Chapter 30

DESPITE WHAT OTHERS WOULD see and assume about him, Eric had never been what he considered on top of the world. Real life, behind closed doors, wasn't that perfect. He had to tolerate his ex-wife at work, his finances were destroyed, his house was an anchor around his neck instead of the symbol of success most believed it to be, and Kiko had a psychotic stalker. Eric's shit was a mess. But that morning, even with a raging headache, he felt on top of the world.

"You're right—train wreck," Eric groaned and lifted his weary form off the couch. But at the sight before him, he instantly felt better.

Kiko was naked.

What did he do to earn that?

"Lay down," Kiko insisted, pushing him back onto the cushions. "I'll get you something for it."

Eric grinned at the view and grimaced in pain as he flopped over with her touch. His naked woman walked out of the room, giving him the best morning TV ever. He was back to grinning.

"Oh, my god," Kiko said from the foyer.

Eric fuzzily remembered his gift Stan had hung. They hadn't seen it last night. Eric pulled himself upright and shuffled carefully over to where a naked Kiko stood, hand over her gaped mouth.

"Do you like them?" Knowing she'd love them, it was a rhetorical question. Eric grinned with pride and heat swelled through his chest. It swelled elsewhere as he gazed upon her smooth skin and curves of her body.

"You made my favorite pictures bigger. Of course I do." Kiko gently pulled his lips to hers for a slow sensual kiss that brought Eric to his knees. He was more than on top of the world; he was invincible.

She released him, smiling. "These are amazing. How did you get them so big and clear? I didn't think the megapixels were high enough back in the '90s."

That was a strange way of wording the current tech limitations, but Eric shrugged. "Magic."

"Really?" Kiko asked with a hint of sarcasm.

"Yep. Stan is very magical."

Kiko laughed, and Eric groaned with his pounding head.

"Back to the library." Kiko deposited him on the couch and

returned moments later with another glass of water and more pain killers.

"I like you playing nurse. Can we stay naked all day?" Eric asked.

"Sure, but turn the heat up, would you? These floors are ice cold."

"I can give you all the heat you need, but give me those first." Eric swallowed the pills. "Could use a vodka chaser."

Kiko took the glass from him and collected his hand in her fingers, turning it over, inspecting it. "There's no bleed through. I'll unwrap your knuckles and clean them. Back to bed, big fella."

"I like when you call me that. It's better than Mr. Spreadsheets."

Kiko narrowed her eyes and pressed him down onto the cushions. "But only one of those is appropriate for work."

"Unfortunately." Eric's smile was drowned out by a frown of pain.

"Hold still," she insisted.

"I can't make promises that all of me will hold still." Eric wagged his brows.

Kiko chuckled, but it was clear she was trying not to. "This is serious. I'm still on the fence about you going to the hospital. Can you move all your fingers?"

"Yes."

"I don't want you to tell me. Show me."

Eric swallowed his smile and kept his hand perfectly still. "Ok, here it goes."

Kiko watched his fingers intently, but he didn't move them on purpose. "Did you try yet?"

"Yep." He fought a laugh.

"Shit." Worry filled her brow. "We're going now. You could've torn tendons or something. Get dressed." Kiko leaned over, collecting clothes off the floor.

Eric sat up with a wince. His wounded hand gripped her upper arm firmly. "I'm just playing with you." He wriggled his fingers in front of her face.

She tossed the armful of clothes at him. "Jerk."

Eric laughed and pulled her back onto the couch. "I've heard worse than that."

She landed on top of his bare chest, and despite his playfulness, he didn't have the strength to do anything but snuggle now. She was the one, the only one for him, and there was nothing he'd ever deny her. And that meant he needed to tell her the full truth of who he was—his less-than-forgiving past. "Hell, I've been arrested before."

"Yeah, I was there."

"No," Eric's levity dropped away. "Before then."

"The frat guys who deserved it. You told me."

Eric shook his head. Kiko didn't press, waiting for him to continue. "When I was a teen, at that impressionable age, my mom was miserable—she drank, she smoked, she shopped. We had everything you could ask for, but she hated it. One day she skipped town with the pool boy. At the time, I'd believed she wasn't cut out for family life running a Fortune 500 company—the long hours, primarily. Dad was never home. I started working with him at sixteen here and there, so with work and school and time at the dojo, I was only home for sleeping. Even then, some days I didn't come home, I'd sleep in the office."

Kiko held his eye contact, patiently listening. He loved the respect she showed him.

"When Dad bought Blue Feather, Mom was the secretary, trying to be supportive, but she'd decided with Dad's hours doubling over the years, she needed to be home to coordinate all the domestic duties, so she quit. I'd harbored resentment, because Mom couldn't cut it. I think that's one reason—the main reason—why I clung to Amanda. I knew she could handle the high-powered life because she fought in the race too. I liked the competitive edge and having my interests align with hers. And our departments required us to frequently get together, so we had more time to spend than typical couples did."

Kiko gently squeezed his good hand and smiled softly.

"After I got married, Mom showed up to visit, and everything I knew came crashing down that day. She told me the truth." Eric shook his head, the guilt still eating him.

"I had shunned her because she left with the pool boy, when in fact Dad cheated on her and kicked her out. Mom and I talked for hours that day, and after I confronted Dad, I put him in the hospital and I spent that night in jail."

"I don't know what to say," Kiko said softly. "That's terrible."

Eric's hopes sunk. She didn't agree with his actions, and he couldn't blame her disappointment. Understanding was all he hoped for. Even Amanda scolded him for being an idiot when she bailed him out. His wife wasn't around when it happened—girls' weekend. So many missed flags... Eric shook his head to clear away that stain on his life.

"Your poor Mom," Kiko said. "What happened after the hospital incident?"

"Dad told everyone he was taking a vacation for two weeks. My hands healed. His face healed. Then Caroline met him at the office extra early to apply some makeup to cover what time hadn't. I have a misdemeanor battery."

"Wow." Kiko rubbed her thumb along his hand.

"Yep, and I deserved it. He was unrecognizable after I was through with him. I apologized, he apologized, and I told him to apologize to Mom. Reluctantly he did, and then he and I continued to work together, the same cordial coolness we'd always had."

"What happened to your mom?"

Eric smiled. "She married the pool boy."

Kiko laughed. "I love happy endings."

"Me too. And that's why I hate liars. Since we're clearing the air, there's still something I want to know about you."

"Oh?" Kiko stiffened.

"Where have you really been for those seven years?"

KIKO KNEW ERIC HATED liars, and Kiko had committed the worst crime—a sneaky lie by omission. The truth was hard to swallow, even for those matches experiencing it firsthand, and even they struggled to believe. If she told him the truth, best case scenario Eric wouldn't believe her. Worst case? He'd assume she was lying and call her crazy. How was Eric going to understand without her having any proof to show him but the emergency responder? The little box looked like a generic electronic component—nothing worthy of time travel known to the general public as impossible.

The fun-loving grandpa had warned her—'If I don't have their trust, I have nothing'. Kiko needed Eric's trust more than anything. Since he was currently swollen, bruised, and suffering side effects of a concussion, telling him something in his current state might ease the blow. Kiko inhaled a deep breath, bracing herself for the worst possible reaction. "Where I've spent the last seven years won't make a lick of sense to you."

"The wilder the better." Eric kissed her arm.

Kiko closed her eyes. He didn't mean that, and she didn't want to lose him or his respect. She chose her words carefully. "Our late Thanksgiving dinner, the day you kissed—"

"I remember that clearly."

"Don't interrupt." Kiko exhaled. Trembling began in her arms. She rubbed her skin to stop it, but it didn't help. "I accepted a job offer promising I'd help people—people incapable of helping themselves."

"What kind of employer knocks on doors with cryptic offers?"

Eric's skepticism was in full swing.

Kiko narrowed her watering eyes at him, but he kissed her hand.

"I didn't mean for it to come out like that. I'm living with regrets and dealing with a migraine."

When Eric's attention was on her hand, Kiko swiped away the tears. "He wasn't just any employer. He gave me the ability to travel extensively."

"And they didn't have phone service?" he countered.

"Many of the places didn't, actually."

"Like the Cambodian jungle?"

"Not quite." Kiko chuckled nervously.

"What does this traveling and helping people have to do with writing? I get the feeling you're being obtuse on purpose."

"I am. This is difficult to explain and accept."

"Hey." Eric kissed her hand and smiled reassuringly. "I spilled my worst secret and you stuck around. I'm not going anywhere. I only want the truth."

With those words, Kiko mustered up the guts to spit it out. "I time traveled." Her face scrunched at how ridiculous it sounded.

Eric's face showed his thoughts flickering. "You ditched me for seven years to time travel while writing three hundred novels? How was this helping people?"

It sounded even more absurd as he spoke it. "I was actually gone much longer than seven years, and I was helping people fall in love."

Eric shook his head, and his words were soft, tired. "You're the writer. I hope someday you'll trust me with the truth."

"It is the truth."

Her wheat-haired protector patted her hand dismissively, and his eyes closed. He was disappointed, but in his current state, at least he didn't overreact. Even from experience and bracing herself for him to not believe her, it still hurt. Eric drifted off to sleep and tears formed on her lids.

Kiko slipped off the couch, and parts of her naked body jiggled while she crossed the foyer to the stairs, intent on finding clean clothes. The front door behind her opened, and she screamed.

Paul Woodson stood in the entry way, gathering way too much information about her. Kiko covered herself the best she could with her hands.

Eric yelled a painful epithet and rushed naked into the foyer, swaying on his feet. The moment Eric understood the situation, he spun and covered himself. Paul finally turned around.

"Shit. Doesn't anyone call first? How did you get in here?" Eric asked, annoyed.

"I forgot to lock the door after getting the mail," Kiko admitted. And a stupid mistake it was, having thought of it. Paul wasn't the worst person who could've wandered inside.

"Well, now that's settled. Can you give us some privacy, Dad?"

"I'll wait outside. Come get me when you're decent."

When Paul left, Kiko rushed up the stairs to dress.

Eric returned to the library, and while she was still upstairs, Eric invited Paul back inside, and she listened.

"Repeating history I see," the old man said. "Didn't you learn your lesson about the company ink?"

"This is different."

"Well, here's your preemptive 'I told you so'."

Kiko had a feeling they were discussing her, and the elder Woodson wasn't being polite about it.

"Please tell me you came here for a real reason," Eric said.

Kiko climbed down the stairs and plastered a smile on her face as if she'd heard nothing.

"I believe so," Eric's dad said. "Got any coffee?"

"I'll get it," Kiko offered and strolled toward the kitchen, shamelessly listening to any other tidbits Paul wanted to drop about her.

The men's steps echoed against the tile as they entered the sitting room. Kiko followed moments later with a tray of steaming coffee mugs. She offered them both one, and they accepted. Kiko dropped into a firm upholstered chair with wood trim as if she were invited.

"What happened to you this time?" Paul said, observing Eric's bandaged hand. "Don't tell me you were wailing on someone. You want to get yourself arrested again?" Paul shot a glance at Kiko, but she darted her eyes away. If Eric wanted to explain, that was on him.

"You didn't bail him out, did you?" Paul asked her accusingly.

Before Kiko could defend herself, Eric cut in, "Drop it, Dad. What are you here for?"

"I warned you something was going on at Blue Feather." Paul shifted the mug from one hand to the other. "And now I won't be able to tell you anything."

"Why?" Eric sipped his coffee.

"The board felt it was in Blue Feather's best interest if my influence was no longer primary."

Eric leaned forward in his chair, forearms resting on his thighs, and Kiko set her coffee down. "Are you saying they removed you from your position?" Eric asked.

"I was fired." Paul tipped his head down into his hands as he fought the emotional impact of his passion being stripped from him.

"They can't fire you. It's your company." Anger rose in Eric's voice.

"That's what I thought." Paul's voice broke, and Kiko wanted to reach out a comforting hand, but she refrained, still pissed he helped Amanda with that contract manipulation and wary about that company ink comment.

Eric stood, anger and resolve in his voice. "Who's responsible?"

"You can't stop them, son. The system is set up the way it is, and I made sure it was unbreakable."

"Them?" Eric repeated, emphasizing the word.

Paul sighed. "The news was delivered by Fred Carter, my trusted goddamn friend."

"Amanda," Eric inferred.

"I can't confirm or deny."

"I'm going to make this right. Come on, Kiko. Don't worry, Dad."

Eric insisted on taking the Ducati, but Kiko refused. She didn't trust his head yet, nor his hand strength. She'd never had a concussion before, but a not-so-quick internet search told her he could be woozy for a few days after. So Eric and Kiko arrived at the office with Stan's limo assistance.

Holding hands, they charged into Blue Feather. Eric was confident he could save the day. Kiko only hoped things didn't get worse.

Chapter 31

AFTER THE NIGHT HE had and the infuriating news he'd received, Eric marched ahead, holding Kiko's hand loud and proud and with zero shits about what anyone thought. He glanced at her several times to reassure himself she was still with him; the feeling in his hand wasn't all there yet. He brought her to Amanda's office, but it was empty. He tracked down Caroline at her desk, and the opportunistic sprite had her nose in a pile of documents on her lap.

"Caroline." Eric's voice was clipped, but he didn't care. She didn't deserve respect.

"Hi, Eric, how are...you?" Her eyes flicked to Kiko, and she dropped her friendly façade.

"Where's Amanda?"

"Well, I don't know. I work for you." Caroline smiled, an empty pull of the lips.

"Don't give me that line. Where is she?" The woman angered him to no end, and he was not in the mood.

"Fine." Caroline crossed her arms in a huff. "Conference room

C."

"Let's go," Eric said and gripped Kiko's hand tighter—or he thought he did.

Eric barged into the conference room and found Amanda, Fred, and Cece's agent Todd Stammer in deep conversation with a stack of documents. Their heads turned toward the intruders, and Amanda's face darkened at Kiko's appearance. All he could see was red, and he needed Kiko's presence to keep him grounded.

"What are you doing here?" his ex demanded.

"I work here," Eric said with a sharp tongue.

A knowing smile crossed her lips, and he wanted to slap it off her face. "Ri...ight." Amanda's eerie drawn out use of the word chilled him, as if she'd done something more, something that would turn his life so far upside down, it would be unrecognizable.

"What's going on in here?" Eric asked, patience dwindling rapidly.

"Since you're no longer representing any portion of Cece's release, it doesn't concern you."

"As the vice president of finance in this company, all contractual amendments concern me, whether or not I earn any bonus. Furthermore, what business do you have in firing my father?"

Todd slipped lower in his chair, but Eric didn't care what he heard.

"Me?" Amanda laughed. "Oh, no, honey. It wasn't me."

Fred stood, his chair scraping on the floor. "It's highly inappropriate to hold this conversation before a colleague. Please see yourself out the door."

Eric's turn to laugh. "Todd, can you give us a minute?"

Todd eagerly scrambled out the door, and Kiko closed it gently behind him.

"Now we can have this conversation." Eric stood resolute, unwilling to leave until he had answers. "What's going on around here?"

"We still have a pair of ears unqualified to listen." Amanda referred to Kiko.

Eric's anger surged through his veins. He needed her here for strength, for grounding, but most of all, he didn't want to be anywhere without her ever again. "She works here, so she's qualified to listen. Now stop dodging the question."

Fred closed the distance between them in an obvious challenge of authority. "Paul Woodson was let go by a vote of the board."

"So I hear. Why?"

"Well, after his…indiscretion a number of years ago, Paul brought on investors, thus losing his majority share in the stock."

"That's how not why, Fred. What the hell is going on?"

Eric's ex-father-in-law held out his hands in a placating gesture. "Calm down, there's no need to be upset."

And now Eric was pissed. "Upset? I'm beyond upset, Fred. My father bought this company and turned it around, saving dozens of jobs but losing his marriage in the process. You can't take that away from him."

Fred smiled. "That's where you're wrong. Amanda?" He nodded to his daughter, who now had a smug smile on her ugly face, and she stepped out of the conference room.

A pit settled in Eric's stomach. "What's the end game here? You destroyed my dad's life for the CEO position?"

"No." Fred Carter chuckled. "Two lives." He leaned around Eric to make a point. "Well, now three."

Kiko's hand found his, and he squeezed.

"What are you talking about?" Eric demanded.

Amanda walked back into the room and handed Eric papers.

"What's this?"

"Your termination notice. I don't have one for your little fling here, but I think it's clear enough. Kiko, you're fired, too," Amanda said cheerily.

Eric's heart stopped in his chest for a few beats. His head spun, and Kiko grasped his arm, steadying him on his feet. "You can't fire me and Kiko for no reason."

"Sure we can. It's called at-will employment. Maybe you need to have a chat with Derek to brush up on your labor laws."

Eric shook his head. He couldn't believe this was happening. "You need us to run this place. What do you gain by eliminating all of us?"

Amanda sat in her chair, leaning back, while Fred stood behind her, arms still crossed. "For starters," Amanda said, "There's now two less people to share the bonus with. New management hires will no longer be privy to that arrangement. Oh, and Kiko, that new contract you signed took away most of your bonus and all of his so thanks for that."

Regardless of that destroyed contract, steam boiled his skin. "You wanted money? All of this was for money?"

"Well, yeah. I've got all your cash and all your current and pending bonuses. Dad has Paul's position, and I have complete control over my department. The new finance guy will be vetted to be a doormat."

Eric refrained from slapping her. She intentionally destroyed his life for money. There was one more thing he needed to know. "And the birth control was for…?"

"Because I didn't intend to stay with you. Kids would've been too…permanent."

The words knocked the wind from Eric's chest, and his knees suddenly weren't sturdy.

"Toodles," Amanda said.

Kiko led him from the room, and she closed the door behind them. Eric leaned against her until they reached her office. He dropped into a chair, and Kiko sat next to him. Her hands rested on his lap. "I'm so sorry," she said.

"You didn't do anything wrong, and they fired you just for being with me."

"Likewise," Kiko said solemnly. "And all the rest was carefully planned from the start."

Eric could hear Dad's 'I told you so' ringing in his ears. And here he thought his ex was harmless—all bark and no bite. Showed how much he really knew her.

"I can't believe the balls on that woman," Kiko said.

Eric sighed. "I can."

The door opened and slammed against the wall. Amanda stood in the door frame with a smirk on her smug face. "Payroll says I need your forwarding address for your last check."

"You know where I live, Amanda. Get out."

She walked away, heels clicking on the tile and leaving the door wide open. Kiko packed her office and followed Eric to his, where he did the same. With boxes in hand, Kiko said, "Let's go to your house."

Without his job or his bonus, it wasn't going to be his house for much longer. Amanda had literally taken everything away from him, and he was blind to see it until it was too late. Now what was he going to do?

KIKO WOKE UP BRIGHT and spunky for a change, probably because Eric was tangled in the sheets next to her. While his breathing shifted in and out evenly, she inspected his knuckles. They were much cleaner, so she removed the bandages entirely. Her hands flexed his fingers and kissed them one at a time to encourage faster healing. Kiko leaned over and brushed locks of hair from his face and kissed his forehead.

Eric stirred and sunk back into sleep.

She dressed quietly and sneaked off with her cell phone. Down the stairs, she made a call. "Derek, it's Kiko Takai."

"Eric's Kiko?"

Her cheeks heated at the description. "Yes, hi. Eric and I were fired yesterday, so I no longer have access to a contract I signed with Amanda and Paul. Blue Feather doesn't deserve my business anymore. Can you tear it up entirely?"

"You did your best to rectify the situation," he said sincerely. "And as Eric's attorney, I've become accustomed to bailing him out of situations that weren't of his doing. I would be happy to make certain papers disappear...unofficially."

"Thank you." Kiko hung up giddy with excitement, because she was able to fix something. After everything Blue Feather had pulled on her and Eric, there was no way those thieves were getting their hands on any of her books.

"Everything okay out here?" Eric asked. He stood above her at the second-floor balcony, naked above the waist. Such a beautiful sight.

"Just fine."

"We need to talk." The ominous tone in Eric's voice worried her.

She took the steps and followed him into his room. She sat on the bed next to him. "What is it?"

Eric exhaled a deep breath. He wrapped his hand around hers, but he failed to meet her eye. Whatever he needed to say pained him, and Kiko wanted to brush away all his burdens. "There are no other publishing houses here."

Kiko didn't like the sound of that.

"There aren't many vice president of finance positions open, and without a job, I can't afford the house. So I need to move out, sell the house, and job hunt elsewhere. I don't know what you plan on doing, but I'd love for you to join me." Eric's green eyes found hers.

Kiko's lips lifted in a soft smile. "I'd follow you anywhere."

"Even a broke fool like me?"

"You're not a fool. Anyone could've fallen for Amanda's shenanigans. I'm sure you're not the first, nor the last."

Eric scrubbed his head with his hand. "I don't think that makes me feel better."

Kiko chuckled. "I can try something else."

"And what's that?" A hungry smile creased the corners of his eyes, and Kiko melted.

What would it be like to wake up in bed next to Eric every morning? In all her years of travels, she'd only lived with roommates or all alone, never with someone she'd loved.

What if he said no? She braced herself for the disappointment while holding onto hope like a lifeline. "You're out of a place. I happen to have an empty house. Move in with me."

Eric's pupils dilated, and his eyes flicked to her lips. "I see zero downsides to that plan, after we install a security system, and maybe get a dog. A big one."

"Dogs and cats don't usually mix," Kiko said.

"Well, a watch cat isn't as effective as a watch dog." Eric sent her a lopsided grin. He tilted his wrist to read an imaginary watch. "So...my schedule happens to be wide open. What do you say we move today?"

Kiko's heart roared in her chest. "Are we really doing this?"

Eric grinned, feeding off her excitement. "We are."

He must've forgotten about her crazy time travel story, but at this point, he didn't seem to care, and she hoped it stayed that way. "Today is good for me. I'll swing by my place, get it cleaned, and make space in my closet for you. You pack up and call a real estate agent?"

"That's a deal. I'll even give Ted and Barry a call for some extra hands. Stan could help, too. What about all my extra furniture? Your place isn't big enough for most of it."

"I have a storage unit. It's small, but I can transfer to a larger one."

Eric beamed. "This is going to work. Thank you." He kissed her lips, and Kiko's heart swelled with pride. She loved him so much. How had she gotten so lucky?

Eric dressed and made calls. Kiko collected her things and filled her duffel. She called for a cab and shouldered a bag. "Don't forget to pack those beautiful photographs in the foyer."

"Those are the second most important things in my life." Eric tipped her chin up. "The first being you." He kissed her slowly, arms embracing her with promises of more.

A car's honk pulled them apart. Despite not wanting to leave his touch, she was giddy with the possibilities of their future.

"That's my ride."

"Be safe and keep me updated. I hope to be swinging by with the first load in a couple hours. Stan will be along to transfer the house's security system to yours."

Kiko lifted onto her tippy-toes and gave him a kiss on the cheek. "That's the plan, Stan."

"No, that's Stan's plan."

She chuckled and shook her head. Soon she'd be living with her love while enjoying all his security. Then all she had to do was keep Eric alive until Roger's future murder at The Wounded Soldier. Any day now would be great. Quickie Dick waited at the curb.

Chapter 32

Ted brought his pickup truck and backed it up Eric's driveway, and he and Barry jumped out to help. Stan pulled over curbside with a moving truck. No fancy moving service for Eric any longer. Stan unloaded stacks and stacks of brand new flattened boxes, and lined up tape, markers, and several rolls of bubble wrap. Then he proceeded to dismantle the security system.

"Damn shame I have to take down those canvases right after I got them up. Next time plan better, son," Stan said, while unscrewing the faceplate off the wall.

Eric's eyes widened at Stan's crude tone and casual language. "Are you okay?"

"I'm great. Since I don't work for you anymore, I can be myself instead of the stiff butler-type your dad wanted."

"But you've been a stiff butler-type my whole life."

"Only when I was around you and your family." Stan dropped a screw and picked it up.

"Ouch."

Stan shrugged, wearing jeans and a casual T-shirt that fit him well. "It was a job, and I was grateful for it. I still think of you as family, but I'm happy to be myself now."

"I'm touched. Really, Stan. Thanks." Eric placed a damaged hand on Stan's shoulder and squeezed. "I appreciate the help, all of you. It means a lot." Eric swallowed a lump in his throat at their generosity.

"Hey, it's okay," Ted said. "But you're still coming to the tournament at The Wounded Soldier this weekend?"

"Of course. Can I bring Kiko?"

"I already invited her."

Eric's brows lifted, and he smiled deviously—rematch. "Great. I'm looking forward to it."

"Same here," Barry said. "With a face like yours, Ted and I have the chance of talking to a woman. I'm excited."

Eric shook his head with a chuckle and unfolded boxes and taped their bottoms. Ted and Barry lifted furniture into the moving truck.

The real estate agent rapped on the open front door. "Hi, Eric? I'm Shelly."

Eric shifted a box in his arms and shook her hand. "Hey, Shelly. I'm just getting everything out now."

"I'll take pictures when you've emptied it out. I have my lock box here, and if you don't mind, I'll hang it on the knob."

"Sounds good. I need this place sold as soon as possible." After everything his ex put him through, a foreclosure would be the cream on top of the shit pie.

"Well, we happen to have an inquiry at the office already." Shelly tucked a lock of hair behind her ear and smiled, probably thinking this was the easiest commission she'd ever earned.

Eric's brows lifted in surprise. "Really?"

"The potential buyer was very insistent on having an offer ready to go. I'm not even sure how she heard about it so fast, but she seems very motivated. I think we're going to get lucky with a quick sale, just like you want."

The wind was sucked from Eric's lungs. That scheming, no-good bitch. He couldn't hide the anger from his tone. "Amanda Carter, right?"

Shelly frowned. "How did you know?"

"Lucky guess. What was her offer?" He'd paid top dollar for the area, because Amanda wanted the best he could give her. Knowing his precarious situation, he imagined she'd low-ball him out of spite.

"I came prepared in case you didn't like the offer, and I don't suspect you'll take it, but like you expressed, it would be a fast sale. One hundred even, cash."

Eric laughed because crying was not something he wanted a stranger to see.

"If it were me, I'd laugh in her face too, but you did express a desire to sell quickly above all else," Shelly said.

Eric had no cash. That amount would give him a small cushion wherever he moved to. He didn't have time to wait for a better offer. Paychecks were stopping next week, and his bank balance was on the verge of overdrawing. Foreclosure was next. "That goddamned bi—"

"Everything okay in here?" Stan interrupted.

"Amanda just pulled another one of her tricks."

"I see. Sorry about that." Stan took the box from Eric's hands, and immediately Eric stuffed his fingers into his hair.

"Yeah, me too. She cleaned me out in the divorce, and she's taking the house back for a steal, knowing I can't wait for a reasonable offer. Such a lovely final insult."

"I bet she's going to flip it for full price," Stan said.

Eric gritted his teeth. "She pushed me to buy the most expensive place, but oddly, she never wanted to be here, so that wouldn't surprise me." Eric sighed, wishing none of this had happened, except the divorce. "Take the offer," he told Shelly.

"Will do, Eric."

"Stan, let's get out of here."

Eric had the place emptied and cleaned. After all the bad memories, he never wanted to step foot in this cold mansion again. Even though the idea was foreign to him, a cozy home and modest life with Kiko was better than anything he'd ever imagined or wanted. And despite his life falling apart, Kiko was a ray of light—a beacon of sanity keeping his mind and his heart focused.

KIKO NEEDED SPACE IN her small rental for Eric's stuff. She loaded up her Bronco with boxes and boxes of her journals from her bedroom and delivered them to her self-storage unit. The fun-loving grandpa with his 1950s music was just as she left him, except this time he didn't have a shotgun in his hands.

"Good day, miss—you look familiar. What can I do ya for?"

Kiko blushed. "I need another storage unit, one bigger than the one I have, number 214."

"Why not transfer units? It'll save you some money."

Kiko had already paid for her little unit in the present year. She needed to cover that gap from now until then, and still have a place for Eric's stuff. "I'd rather have two units."

"If you insist." His crooked, veiny hands worked on the paperwork while his head bobbed to the music.

When it was complete, she loaded her stuff into her smaller unit. After she arrived home, she organized and shifted furniture around to make room. Kiko was dirty, sweaty, and ripe, just in time for the U-Haul to pull up. She flung the door wide open to greet her love moving in.

Stan climbed down from the truck and opened the back. A pickup truck arrived and pulled into her driveway. Ted jumped out of the pickup with a box in his arms, and Barry came to help too. Eric waved to her from the back of the moving truck. Surrounded by people who cared, who knew who she was for the first time in decades, felt amazing—light, full of hope, a place of belonging. Kiko had friends, and the thought made her tear up. She blinked them back and rushed out to help unload Ted's truck.

"Where do you want the boxes, Kiko?" Ted asked.

"Stack them against the walls. We'll sort later."

"Right on."

Kiko, Ted, and Barry methodically unloaded his pickup while

Eric and Stan brought in a few pieces of furniture that Kiko hadn't purchased herself yet. Her house finally looked like a home—cozy, warm, and inviting, although buried in boxes.

Eric panted and wiped his forehead. "I think the rest will have to go to storage. There's a buffet, China cabinet, settee, console table, foyer table, various round tables, rugs, that sort of stuff. Any of that sound interesting to you?"

"If there's room and we need something, we can always get it later."

"Good point. Stan! Let's bring it over."

"Here's the key." Kiko unlooped the padlock key and handed it to him.

Eric gave her a salty kiss on the lips. "Come on guys, one more stop. Then I'm buying beer."

"Deal. Let's go," Ted said.

The lumbering truck rumbled away from the curb with Ted and Barry following in the pickup. Kiko wrapped her arms around herself, staring at the pile of boxes overwhelming her small house. She had friends to thank and nowhere for them to move around in here, not that her house was ready for entertaining yet.

"What a chore!" She exhaled a massive breath and dug through the pile, searching for something easy. She found one labeled clothes and carried it to the bedroom.

The box was packed in a clear rush. Clothes were stuffed inside as if Eric couldn't wait to get over to her. She smiled. After surviving Roger's attacks, they had years to savor together, and the idea was calming. They'd get to have a family, argue about toilet training and kids' schedules. They'd take family vacations and wear silly hats while taking photos. Kiko would get to be a normal human, living life like all those around her whom she'd envied all those years, and the two of them would grow old together. No longer the ghost flitting through time, she'd exist, she'd make a difference in someone's life. And when her time was up, she'd move on with Eric too. Never again to be alone.

They hadn't been together that long and they'd never discussed the future, but Kiko could dream.

Kiko finished sorting all the clothing boxes she could find, several labeled for the kitchen, and one marked for the bathroom before crashing on her couch.

The unmistakable rumble of a motorcycle rolled up her driveway. Kiko couldn't move her limbs. Exhaustion kept her butt planted on the cushions. The motor cut out and Kiko dragged herself up to greet Eric.

She flung the door wide, and a very sensual Eric sauntered up the driveway with a sexy red helmet in his hands, matching his Ducati. Despite her exhaustion, she grinned, her heart warming at the sight, and Kiko dashed into his arms. He caught her, and they spun with her leaping force.

"We did it," she whispered in his ear. He was home.

"In one day," Eric said. "A little slower than movers, but there's something satisfying about doing it yourself. I need a shower. How about you?"

"Count me in. I just need to muster the energy."

Eric carried her across the threshold, and Kiko kicked the door closed. Her lips began on his neck, the salty sweat teasing her. Right now he was here and happy, and that mattered the most to her.

"Where's everyone else and the beer?" she asked.

"They were too tired, but I'll see them tomorrow, and it will be my treat at the lanes. Ted told me you were invited."

"I was, and I can't wait." Kiko brushed damp hair off Eric's forehead while he swung her legs clear of boxes on the way to the bathroom.

"I challenge you to a rematch. I don't lose to former gutter ball queens so easily," Eric declared and set her feet down on the linoleum.

"I don't know. It was pretty easy last time." Kiko winked.

"We'll see about that." Eric kissed her forehead while lifting her shirt up.

"Yes, we will." Kiko unbuttoned Eric's jeans. She liked the casual look on him. Heat surged through her body, and the only thought on her mind was getting him naked…and whipped cream. She wished she had whipped cream.

"Until then, shower and—hey, is the bed buried?" Eric's sweaty hands slipped over her damp skin.

"The bed is clear and ready for use."

"Perfect. Thou art as wise as thou art beautiful." Eric mimicked an English accent, and Kiko blushed with the compliment.

Kiko and Eric took turns stripping each other down while the steam billowed, filling the bathroom with a humid haziness. The first night of their new lives together was so very exhausting.

But amazing.

Chapter 33

Eric closed his cell phone and slid it along their coffee table. Their table. He liked the sound of that. Every day with Kiko in his life was a dream come true. All those years he'd searched for her, wished for her, and then—poof—here she was. If this was a dream, he never planned to wake up.

"I've got some news, but I'm not sure if it's good or bad," Eric said, satiated and exhausted after moving, during which he'd almost twisted an ankle, but Kiko shifted her weight at the last second, and he avoided a trip to the emergency room.

"Whatever it is, we can figure out a solution," she said.

Eric chuckled. "I like the way your brain works. So—reasonable."

"I've had many years of practice."

That reminded him of the silly tale she'd told while he was recovering from a knock to the head. "Right, when you time traveled to match couples and then wrote novels about it?" Eric teased. He didn't believe a word of it. She was hiding where she really had been, but he didn't want to push. She must've been ashamed to not come clean. A small part of Eric felt rejected at her inability to trust him with her secret.

Kiko blanched.

"I'm kidding." It was simply light banter with the hopes that she'd spill.

"What's...What's your news?"

"My house sold. I have to pop in at the agent's office and make it official."

"We just emptied it yesterday," Kiko said, perplexed.

"Amanda put out feelers with a preemptive offer. When Shelly told me, I just said to take it, not knowing if it were an honest offer or not, but Amanda actually meant it."

"I thought she didn't want the house. Why didn't she take it in the divorce then?"

"Because she wanted to low-ball me and flip it."

"Money," Kiko clarified. "Sounds like her."

"You got it," Eric said.

"I hate to judge, but my brain went there. I still can't believe you married someone like that."

"Believe it or not, she wasn't that bad when we were dating." He refrained from telling her the worn adage of hindsight.

"Or you were struck with lust blindness." Kiko stood from the couch.

"Hey!" Eric said, feigning insult. "Do you think I'm lust blind to you too?"

"I hope not."

Eric stood up to meet her, and he tilted her chin up. "Let me boost that confidence. Seven years is far too long for lust blindness to affect me. I love you, Kiko. I always have and don't forget it."

A bright smile and lovely color rose to her cheeks. He loved that color. "You ready to knock some pins?" she asked.

"While we're there, we can celebrate cutting ties with Blue Feather, and I owe some guys beer."

Kiko smiled. "We should celebrate moving in together."

"It's on the list."

Kiko rejected the idea of taking his bike, so Eric insisted he drove her Bronco, and memories hit him of driving her to Yoshi's funeral. Tears sprung to his lids, and he blinked them away. In a pit of fresh darkness, one warm memory floated to the top, bringing a soft smile to his lips. He'd shared a box of mixed chocolates with her afterward. They'd bitten off little pieces and, depending on the scale of awesomeness, they'd swapped for their favorites.

He navigated through the city, and hit the freeway, seeking her hand. Eric's fingers entwined with hers and rested their clasped hands on her lap.

"Where is this place?" Kiko asked with a strange wariness on her tongue.

"Greenleaf. Why?"

Kiko's body tensed, and she patted her jeans pocket, as if seeking reassurance of something. "Are you sure this is such a great idea?"

"We have friends waiting for us, and we'll have fun, but if you don't want to go, we can turn around," Eric said.

"No, it's okay. You're right." She sent him a tight smile.

Eric wasn't convinced. Something was bothering her, but until she wanted to explain, he wouldn't push—another one of those secrets of hers. Eric drove them through the small town as dusk settled in. Kiko's body turned rigid under his hand while he steered the Bronco into the parking lot of The Wounded Soldier. "I've heard the lanes here are awesome," he said.

"I didn't realize there was bowling here. Are you sure this is a safe place?"

"It's a sports bar with lanes," Eric said, puzzled. "Why wouldn't it be?"

"I just heard things. That's all."

They unbuckled, and Eric held the front door open for her. Music pumped through the sound system. Laser lights beamed across the ceiling, floors, and walls, and pins rattled down the lanes. Eric inhaled a deep breath, competitive juices already flowing.

"Over there, I see the guys." Eric grasped Kiko's hand and guided her past the bar and lounge to the lanes. It was packed full of people. Pool cues snapped against billiard balls, bowling pins crashed, sports fanatics cheered whatever game was on the large screen, and the music charged him.

Stan's head bobbed to the music while he waited his turn.

"Are you guys in the tournament?" Eric asked.

"No, just rolling for fun. Hi, Kiko! Glad you could make it," Stan said.

Kiko smiled and nodded. Eric squeezed her hand while her eyes scanned the place as if looking for someone.

"Mind if we join you?" Eric asked.

"Not at all, we were just finishing this game. Hop on in." Stan waved at the empty seats. Eric liked this new relaxed Stan.

"Let's choose our balls, and I'll get us set up," Eric said to Kiko. She broke off from his hand in search of the perfect fit among the racks of balls. Eric dug out his loose change to cover their game. How was he going to buy the guys a round of drinks? He still didn't have a credit card. Maybe, just maybe, he could swallow his pride and ask Kiko to cover it until he could pay her back.

Kiko racked up, and Eric was right behind her. Ted reset the game and took the short steps down to the lanes. "Hey, Kiko, do you need bumpers?"

Kiko laughed, a sweet melodic sound that Eric loved and hadn't heard since they left the house. "No, Ted. Not anymore. Tell him, Eric."

Eric grinned. "Careful, she'll kick your ass. She beat me last time we played."

"Really?" Ted's brows popped with a mischievous smile. "Ten says I win."

"I'll take that bet," Kiko said.

"What about you, Woodson?" Ted asked.

Eric didn't have the funds to participate, leaving a lump in his belly, but he smiled anyway. He felt like a failure and a fool for being duped out of everything he'd worked for. Now instead of enjoying the view at the top of the world, he was stuck worrying about pinching pennies and watching the budget for things he never thought of before—like taxi rides, haircuts, and a round of beers. Even for a simple bet he'd never hesitate before, but now…he was shamefully broke. "I think I'll skip the bet."

"Awe, come on, man," Barry egged him on.

Kiko came to his rescue. "Eric is in also." She winked at him. "But make it fifty."

The guilty shame lump in his gut just doubled.

"Oh, high roller here," Stan teased.

"Money where your mouth is," Ted said.

Eric loved the camaraderie. Someday, he'd have the funds to treat everyone well and join in on the fun. Always the proud provider, it pained him to have Kiko spot him cash.

Kiko's jitters stopped her from enjoying the first half of the evening as much as she wanted, and she hoped she hid it well. Every second her group of friends turned away, her eyes were scanning. The hairs on the back of her neck kept her on high alert.

Roger had already attacked.

They had already survived.

She knew Roger was destined to die here some time this year, but he lived in Milwaukee, and they were currently an hour from Green Bay. What were the odds that he'd show up here tonight? Kiko must've changed something in the layout of the events. Roger had never hounded her about her bags left in his trunk, and maybe he'd finally given up. Maybe he gets killed by three mysterious suspects somewhere else. Or maybe he gets killed by those three mysterious suspects here, but on a day when she and Eric weren't around.

Every time she heard a loud guffaw from up by the bar, her hand patted her pocket for the emergency responder, just in case—a comfort while her nerves were on fire.

"That's a great strike, Kiko. Didn't know you had it in you," Ted said.

"I did," Eric cut in.

"You know what they say about assumptions," Kiko mindlessly retorted.

"Well, now you're assuming I know your assumption." Ted smiled.

"Touché, but your first assumption, that I'm an inadequate, easy-to-defeat bowler was premeditated solely on my sex and age, and now you've revised your assumption, once again assuming that I'm entertaining Lady Luck when in fact, my skill is far beyond yours. Make the bet a hundred."

"Oh! You did not just go there. Hundred it is, skirt." Ted laughed and fished in his pocket for his wallet.

Gummy worm Ted surprised her with his sharp banter. Kiko scoffed playfully, finally pulled out of her wary state. "For that derogatory remark, make it two hundred."

"Got it," Ted met her challenge.

"Whoa, it's just a game," Stan said with an amused lift of his lips.

"Short stuff," Eric whispered to her and gestured for her to come closer.

Kiko leaned close, backing down from the banter. "What is it?"

He whispered into her ear. "I can't afford a two-hundred-dollar bet."

Kiko found shame in his eyes, but she respected him telling her the truth and admitting it. "We're here to have fun, and I'll spot you the whole night. In fact, why don't you go order a round for us. It'll be on me, but they don't have to know that." She slipped a credit card out of her back pocket and discreetly passed it to him.

"You are a doll," Eric said and kissed her forehead.

"Don't call me a doll."

"You are an amazing, generous, wonderful woman."

Kiko smiled, and Eric rushed up to the bar.

Kiko picked up her chosen ball and prepared herself on the approach. She steadied her feet, shifting them slightly, and lined the ball with the pins. The camaraderie happened only between rolls. Everyone kept silent as Kiko swung her arm and released the ball with a hook, sending it curving down the lane. Another strike. Kiko pumped her fist in the air. Stan, Ted, and Barry clapped, but with real money riding on the game, Ted's enthusiasm lacked the others. She wanted to smear the alley with Ted—in a friendly way.

Three men walking by caught her eye. One had a backward baseball cap. She recognized him as Sean, the man right in front of her Bronco when Chaos first sent her back to 1995. The other she recognized had been carrying an armful of stuff during the robbery of the storage unit, Travis. The unfamiliar one must've been the driver of the getaway cranberry Geo Metro. She stared at them wondering why they were here, of all places, when Sean saw her and pointed her out to his friends. They walked over, motioning to talk, and Kiko met them at the stairs since they didn't have bowling shoes on.

"You're that girl that saved our asses at the storage unit," Sean said.

"That was me."

"How'd you do it? Appear like that, I mean. I never seen anything like it."

"Special tricks." Kiko gave him the truth, in a way. "What were you guys doing there? Why was the old man trying to make Swiss cheese out of you?"

Kiko didn't expect them to blatantly answer, but Travis said, "Our Gramma died, and we had the key, but turns out no one paid the bill, and we didn't know. We were just gettin' some stuff that meant a lot to us, and he tried to shoot us for it."

Kiko couldn't fault them for that. "I'm glad you got what you needed."

"Can we buy you a drink? As a thank you?" Travis asked, and the two others nodded in agreement.

"I'm already well-stocked but thank you for the offer."

"We owe you one, lady," Sean insisted. "Hey, what's your name?"

"Kiko."

"That's a pretty name," the driver said.

"Thank you. Have a nice evening, gentlemen."

Sean snickered. "Oh, lady...Kiko, we ain't gentlemen, but thank you for the compliment."

Kiko gave them a friendly smile, and Eric walked toward her carrying a tray full of beer. She helped him bring it down the stairs without spilling. The three robbers—or not robbers?—watched them together.

"I love you," Eric said and flexed his wounded knuckles. She set the tray down for him, and he embraced her, kissing her lips with a heated desire, while sneaking her credit card into her back pocket.

Cat calls and hoots surrounded them, and Kiko pulled back and grinned.

The driver called out, "Kiko, get a room with your sexy man."

"Hell yeah," Travis said.

"But we don't mind watching," Sean said.

Eric glared at them with a protective stink eye.

Kiko pulled his jaw so he faced her again. "Ignore them. They're harmless."

"You know them? They look like hoodlums, you know, if there was a 'hood around here."

"I accidentally helped them out. I'd consider them friendly at least for tonight," Kiko said.

"I can live with that."

"You're up, dude," Barry said to Eric.

"Hold on to your scoreboards folks, I'm about to blow yours away." Eric released Kiko's back pockets, and she stuffed the card down further so it wouldn't fall out. He collected his ball, lined up his shot, and released it down the lane with a practiced hook.

The pins crashed, echoing through the lanes, but the dreaded seven-ten split remained.

Kiko gasped with a smile.

"Oh, that's too bad, loser," Stan said.

Eric frowned. "I liked you better when you were a suit."

"Get used to the new me now, son. I don't see you or your dad getting back into Blue Feather any time soon."

"No, you're right. Not as long as that psycho is running the place."

"Who are you calling a psycho?" Amanda Carter said with a sneer. What the hell was she doing here?

Chapter 34

The moment his evening was going amazing, his damned ex-wife had to make an appearance. She'd never bowled a day in her life.

"What the hell are you doing here? You're going to break a nail," Eric said. He had no love left for her and had no shame in spiting her. The laser lights shifted and twirled over her and for once, he wished one was a light saber, ready to chop her down.

"I was invited, same as you."

Eric looked at Stan, Ted, and Barry with as much anger as shock and hurt.

Ted stepped forward, both terrified and red in the face. "I invited the whole office, actually. There was a posting in the lunchroom, but since you and Kiko never eat with us, I invited you personally. In my defense, I didn't think she'd show up."

"I'm surprised myself," Eric said, "since she was never supportive of my bowling hobby and never had interest in being in smoky bars."

Amanda laughed mockingly. "Of course I would show up. Since you no longer work at Blue Feather, how else was I going to let you know my plans for your house?"

"I don't care." Eric turned away from his ex-wife and hugged Kiko's shoulders.

Stan stepped up to the approach with his ball lined up in the air. Barry and Ted stared at Amanda as if seeing a new side of her, and Eric smugly smiled at feeling vindicated.

"I think you do," Amanda countered.

Eric's patience circled the drain. "Then I'm going to spell this out for you. I don't care what you do with the house. I don't care that you managed to get me fired and steal my bonus from under my nose. I don't care that you've destroyed our sham of a marriage with cheating and lies, because there is one perfect thing in my life you cannot take no matter what bullshit you pull. So, give up your twisted obsession and move on."

"Obsession? Oh, honey, no. You're not worthy of obsession. I just wanted to destroy you."

Eric's lips pressed to a thin line. He didn't realize her issues with him were so personal. "Why?"

Amanda chuckled. "I seduced you because you were a good lay, but when I figured out you were the son of moneybags, I married you as quickly as possible. But why did I systematically ruin everything in your life? Now that's something that will bother you forever."

Eric's body tensed with contained fury. "I shouldn't be surprised you don't have the decency to explain. I'm done with you." Eric turned away.

"Because, you halfwit," Amanda said and paused to recapture his attention. It worked. She put a hand on her hip, her face curling in anger as she pointed at Kiko. "You put her above me. Her precious picture, her precious memories. I'd had enough and wanted a divorce. I was going to take half of everything until the moment that hussy strolled into your office—it was on."

"You need help," Eric said.

"I needed to prove I wasn't a fool, and I have."

"Great! So, then you're leaving?"

Amanda grinned with a glint in her eye, as if she had one more trick in her bag, but she didn't answer.

"Whatever, we're having fun down here," Eric said. "Since you'd never take off your heels, good luck watching from up there." Eric turned away from her and tried to shake off the anger. He hated that she got under his skin.

It was his turn, long overdue, but the guys and Kiko were

appreciatively patient. He stuffed his fingers in the ball, lined it up on the approach, and released it on a spin down the lane. All the pins went flying in a crashing echo. *Eat that, bitch,* Eric thought, half expecting some pins to shatter from his festering rage. Not that Amanda cared about his score. He sat down next to Kiko while the machine realigned the pins for Ted's turn.

"Are you okay?" Kiko asked.

He rested a hand on her thigh and a calming wave soothed his anger. "Yeah. Yeah, I'm okay. Nothing like having your dirty laundry tossed around in public, by a sniveling...I'm okay." Eric released a deep breath and it helped...a little.

Kiko pressed a finger against his chin and tilted his face toward her. "She doesn't matter. There's nothing she can do to hurt you any longer."

"You're right. I know you're right. It's just raw right now."

Kiko nodded and then took his lips. At first he resisted, not wanting to unleash his remaining anger on Kiko, but quickly he relented, his desire and passion for Kiko wiping away the festering anger from Amanda. Heat, warmth, and love blossomed in his chest, and his hands found her, pressed her closer, desperate to never let her go.

Laughs, hoots, and catcalls resounded around them, and

Eric backed up just enough to speak. He whispered, "I think everyone's watching."

"I assume so."

Eric whispered, "You're the best. I don't know what I'd do without you here."

"Probably something you'd regret." Kiko kissed his lips in a quick touch, and Eric smiled. She was probably right.

"Eric, you're up," Stan said.

"You're going to need strikes from here on out if you have any hope of beating me, mister seven-ten split," Kiko teased.

"Oh, you wait and see. It isn't over yet." Eric grinned at the challenge.

Eric spit into his hands and rubbed them together. Kiko cringed, and he winked at her. With a flash of his gut, he scanned the open space for Amanda, but he didn't see her anywhere. Eric rotated his head to relax his neck, selected his ball from the return, and lined it up on the approach. Kiko was the best thing in his life—always had been. She was sweet, generous, and always there for him, except when she disappeared for seven years. While waiting for the truth, Kiko showed him a new life—one where he was richer in friends than money, and he wouldn't trade it for anything.

Eric rolled a strike to cheers from his friends, and a blown kiss by Kiko.

KIKO CHECKED OVER HER shoulder. Amanda was hiding just over by the bar, giving her a creepy death stare. The woman was nuts. She'd admitted to everyone exactly what she'd been doing to Eric, and rather than leave shamefully, Amanda sat at a round table above the lanes, nursing a mixed drink and checking her watch regularly. Her face darkened whenever Eric rolled and pinched into disgust when he earned a strike.

Whatever Eric saw in her, Kiko would never understand. Despite the unwanted supervision, the five of them were having a great time. Too bad no one else from the office joined them. With only three frames left to roll, Kiko and Ted were tied in first place, Eric came in second, and Stan and Barry last, but only by a couple pins. Kiko hadn't enjoyed a game this closely matched in...well, ever.

"Does anyone want another round of beer, on me?" Kiko offered.

"If you're buying, sky's the limit," Stan answered.

"You think you can beat me with more beer in your system?" Ted asked.

"Are you feeling threatened, Ted?" she asked playfully. "Two hundred bucks got you nervous?"

Ted scoffed. "Bring it on. Loser buys dinner."

"Deal."

Kiko strolled past Amanda with a smug smile on her face. Was it immature? Sure, but Kiko was satisfied in knowing that Amanda was incapable of breaking Eric's spirit entirely. Kiko ordered a pitcher of beer and a round of new mugs. On her careful journey back to their table, trying not to bump into anyone coming and going or drunkenly zigzagging, the expression on Amanda's face changed from impassively annoyed to cunningly excited.

Kiko stabilized the tray and handed out drinks. While the men imbibed, Kiko picked up her ball, not able to see what changed Amanda's disposition, and an easy roll gave her a strike. Despite the end of the game nearing, an uneasiness settled on her shoulders, but she still smiled.

"One more frame guys. It's not looking good for you, Stan," Ted said.

Stan scratched his head with solely his middle finger raised, and Ted laughed.

Stan lined up his shot and rolled a strike.

"Not bad, rookie," Ted taunted Stan. "But we'd all have to roll gutter balls for you to win at this point. Pony up the cash."

"Yeah, yeah. Gloating winner." Stan dug out his wallet while Ted stepped up for his final roll.

Kiko held Eric's hand while they sat next to each other on the plastic seats. Eric chugged the rest of his beer. Kiko didn't want hers any longer.

Ted rolled a seven-ten split. "You gotta be kidding me!"

"Can't take the pressure, eh?" Stan made a point of stuffing his bills back into his pants pocket.

"Your turn. Knock 'em dead," Kiko whispered to Eric with quiet encouragement. "Win or lose, you're still my best man."

"Check your confidence. It's not over yet." Eric's lips lifted with a glint in his eye, and he collected his ball one last time. He stood on the approach, lined up his shot, and in mid-release, a shout across the bowling alley messed his concentration. The ball thumped out of his fingers, lopsidedly rolling over into the gutter and earning him no points.

A chill shuddered through Kiko's body at the familiar voice.

Stan poured out another mug for each of them, while Kiko stood to see what the commotion was about—a blond brute strolled inside. Images of Roger attacking Kiko in the hotel broom closet filled her mind's eye. Her stomach dropped, and the sudden urge to vomit took over all her other senses. She placed a steadying hand on her forehead and inhaled and released a jagged breath.

Amanda stood up and sashayed on her heels over to him—a man who Kiko hoped would never appear in her life again. It was as if Fate was somehow mocking her or testing her. Why? Just why?

"What's wrong?" Eric asked. His large hands enveloped her shoulders, and he followed her gaze. Eric tensed against her skin, and Kiko knew he saw Roger Meyer in a sporty track suit with designer shades propped on top of his head.

Amanda grinned broadly and touched his arm in a familiar way. They whispered to each other, and then they turned their attention toward her and Eric.

"Shit," Kiko said.

"I like your articulation when situations are dire."

Kiko frowned at him. "Our fun is over. We need to go."

"The likelihood of Roger being dumb enough to try anything in a crowded public establishment is slim. And Stan is packing," Eric said.

Having a gun on their side didn't give Kiko confidence, but the way Amanda and Roger were being chummy had her interested. Kiko patted her pocket to reassure herself the emergency responder was at the ready. Eric was right; it wasn't

Roger's M.O. to do anything public. The risk still weighed heavily on her chest, and her palms started sweating.

"You don't think they're involved, do you?" Eric asked with a twist of disgust.

Her gut reaction was no. Then Kiko remembered even when Roger had a girlfriend—Jessica—he still pursued Kiko. "I don't know, but if so, they're made for each other."

Stan, Eric, Ted, Barry, and Kiko were watching the mismatched couple with wariness—Kiko far more than the others. Would their fate be different now with all that had changed? She couldn't see any weapons on Roger, but he didn't need them to do serious damage.

Kiko was last to roll her final frame to end the game, but no one cared at the moment. Roger sauntered over with a smirk on his face and Amanda on his arm. Only bad things were going to happen with a free and angry Roger and an encouraging rat alongside him. The only thing keeping her calm was knowing Roger would die tonight.

And she hoped she hadn't changed that part of the future.

Chapter 35

"Well, well, well. Thanks, Ted for assembling the team," Roger said, his steps sounding like plastic bags rubbing together.

Eric and Kiko stared Ted down. His hands went up in defense. "I only posted an offer for a fun night out. I don't know who this guy is or why he's here." Ted scrambled away, sensing danger like a wise field mouse. Barry chased after him.

Stan remained. "Do you want me to get the limo ready?"

"You don't work for me anymore," Eric said, but he appreciated the offer.

"Doesn't mean we aren't friends."

How could he turn that down? "Sure, bring the limo around, this won't take long."

Stan left.

"But," Kiko whispered in Eric's ear, "he has the gun."

"It's not going to come to that," Eric whispered. Besides, Stan would be right back.

Eric's fists were still healing, but to his benefit, they were mostly numb anyway. His disadvantage was the two frosty mugs of beer in his system. Had he known he was going to face Roger this evening, he wouldn't have partaken. Eric blocked Roger's descent at the head of the stairs. "Rodg, we're having a private party here, if you don't mind."

"Kiko and I have plans for bowling and a movie," Roger said, leaning against the railing.

"Kiko," Eric said to her, "roll your last frame." He only wanted her farther out of arm's reach while they waited for Stan to return with the getaway vehicle and gun. He'd put any money on Stan using the limo's phone to call the local police. Roger couldn't have these cops in his pockets too.

"Are you serious?" Kiko whispered back.

"Trust me."

Kiko hesitated, but she collected her ball.

"Hey, getting warmed up," Roger said while watching Kiko. "Excellent. I'm going to buy us a game. The four of us. Me and Amanda against you two."

"I don't think that's a good idea," Eric said.

Kiko turned her head toward him while sizing up her roll. Eric nodded at her to continue, and he watched her score a strike. A dancing turkey fluttered across the scoreboard. She won. Damn woman won again. If he didn't gutter ball the last frame, he would've still had a chance. He needed a rematch, but not tonight and certainly not with Amanda or Roger in the vicinity.

Kiko grasped his arm like a buoy. He wished he could move her away to safety, but he couldn't come up with another excuse. Eric asked, "How do you two know each other?"

"We're cousins, dipshit," Roger said.

Eric frowned. "Then how did I not know this when we made our guest list?" he asked Amanda.

"I was in prison," Roger cut in. "Did you forget, because I didn't." His menacing eyes groped Kiko's body, and Eric shifted her behind him slightly. Eric tensed. He might have to swing his injured fists after all. Considering how he whaled on Roger earlier, any sane person would walk away.

Roger wasn't sane.

Amanda tossed her locks over her shoulder. "When Roger mentioned you and Kiko all those years ago, I thought nothing of it until I saw a picture of you with her on your desk, I put two and two together, and had a chat with Roger. Kiko attacked my cousin."

Eric shook his head in disbelief. "If you'd have been at the trial, you would've heard Kiko's written statement, and you would've learned she was acting in self-defense."

Eric had been there, and he wished Kiko was too, but at the

time, he figured she just couldn't face him. Now he knew that was part of her seven-year mystery.

Roger turned to Amanda. "Yeah, why didn't you come?"

"I was working," she answered simply.

"Too busy to support Roger in his time of need?" Eric tried to turn this whole situation back toward her, trying to delay them for Stan and hopefully a parking lot full of police.

If the big brute turned half his brawn into brains, he wouldn't have fallen for any of Amanda's bullshit. And that was where Eric stopped his train of thought. He considered himself to be a bright guy, but he still fell for it.

"I said I was working," she repeated sternly. "Besides, Daddy got the best attorneys. I really didn't think you'd serve time."

Eric had no reason to stick around for whatever additional bull they wanted to string along. "On that point, Kiko and I will be going." Eric tugged Kiko by the wrist. Stan hadn't returned yet, but fresh air sounded good right now.

"Not so fast." Roger pressed his first two fingers against Eric's chest and anger spiked immediately.

"What do you want, Rodg?"

"Kiko and I have a date. So, if you would step aside and stop interfering, I'd appreciate it."

Eric glanced back at Kiko for confirmation. He couldn't believe she'd go along with it.

Kiko said, "I've told you 'no' more times than I can count, and I thought smashing you in the head with a chair made my feelings clear."

Eric would've laughed if the situation weren't so tenuous.

Roger's face pinched into a line of fury, and Eric released Kiko's wrist. It was only a matter of seconds before Roger came swinging. His predictability was an advantage, but still, Eric didn't want to be the first to charge.

"I'd leave you alone now, but this is too much fun to watch." Amanda pulled up a chair at the table nearby and crossed her legs with a smirk on her face. Kiko stood behind Eric, and the brick wall of Roger towered over them at the top of the carpeted stairs.

"Kiko," Eric turned to face her. "Take the other stairs and find Stan."

A blinding snap of pain registered through Eric's skull, and after being knocked off his feet, he rubbed his jaw. Another cheap shot.

Roger wanted to play dirty?

So be it.

Eric leaned against the row of plastic seats bolted to the floor as if catching his balance and panted for show. Roger stalked down the stairs, and when he stood within range, Eric slammed the larger man straight in the gut with his better fist. Roger folded over with a heave of breath. Eric recovered and clocked him in the jaw, turning his head on its axis. Roger lost his balance, and Eric stepped back as the tornado of Roger crashed to the floor.

The customers inside the bar and around the bowling alley gathered to watch. The bartender was on the phone, likely calling the cops. He hoped they arrived before one of them ended up in the hospital.

Eric shook his hand and checked for damage. His still-healing knuckles split open again, but it was no big deal. He searched for Kiko, but he couldn't see her, and in craning his neck around, Roger nailed him in the jaw.

Eric went down.

KIKO BACKED AWAY FROM the fists while digging the emergency responder out of her pocket. Someone grabbed her arm. Instinct was to yank her arm free, but the grip was surprisingly strong.

Amanda tried to drag Kiko back toward the fight. The tall, slender woman on heels had no chance against her, and in a few more seconds, Kiko would no longer be gentle.

"Let me go," Kiko demanded.

"No way. As long as you're in sight, Eric is distracted."

"Why do you want Roger to hurt Eric? Haven't you done enough damage already?"

"I told Roger where Eric would be tonight. He insisted on coming and on me staying out of his way. Tonight is all Roger. Would you tell him no?"

"Yes, and I have."

"I see that worked out well."

Kiko grunted in frustration because she was right. Roger never accepted no. "Let go of me."

"You're staying here until this is over. Roger's orders. For some reason he still wants you. I don't see why. There's nothing special about you," Amanda said, looking down her nose at Kiko.

"I don't know what Roger wants with me either, considering he's a murderous asshole, and you're not many branches away from him on the family tree. Let me go. I'm not warning you again."

Amanda chuckled. "Such strong words from such a small girl."

"I'm not a girl." Kiko wasn't fighting to free herself. She was fighting for the future she wanted, the future she deserved, the future Chaos had promised her. Kiko wrenched her arm away and slammed the unsuspecting taller woman with an uppercut to the chin. She barely connected with their height difference, but it felt amazing to put her in her place.

Tears sprung to Amanda's eyes and she bent over, touching her chin and looking for blood. "What the hell is wrong with you, bitch?" And her tone changed just like that from sniveling weasel to frightened mouse.

"You don't tell me what to do. You don't imprison me against my will, and after all the shit you pulled against Eric, you can go to hell." Kiko kicked the downed woman in the ribs with her sneaker. Amanda cried out, but Kiko was all out of shits to give. She rushed over to Eric the split-second Roger's fist connected, snapping Eric's head back. Kiko screamed while Eric crashed to the floor.

She avoided Roger on her path down the stairs, and cocooned Eric with her body. Her vision turned blurry as tears of worry consumed her. She felt his throat for a pulse, totally believing Roger could one-punch someone to death. Eric had a strong pulse, and Kiko smiled. Her fingers brushed his locks away from his eyes as a shadow loomed over them.

"Enough of this," Roger said, hands shaking with rage. He stuck his hand into the waistband at the small of his back. Kiko heard the unmistakable click of the hammer being retracted on a pistol.

Voices of concern and panic flooded the bar. People ran screaming.

"Roger, please leave us alone! We haven't done anything to you," Kiko begged.

"We? No. You humiliated me. Eric just pissed me off. Both of those are equal in my book." Roger leveled his pistol in point-blank range at Kiko's back while she covered Eric.

Her fingers fumbled the lid on the emergency responder. Without a second's hesitation, she gripped Eric's body and pressed the button.

Two gunshots rang out at the same time Kiko's vision wavered and her stomach dropped out from under her. All she could do was hold onto Eric with all her might.

When the queasiness stopped, Kiko opened her eyes. She checked Eric, who, gratefully, was in her arms. His pulse was still strong, and she found no blood on him besides some minor cuts over bruises and swelling where Roger's fist had connected.

Kiko breathed in and out, checking her own body. Her hand

patted her chest, but she didn't feel any sharp pains or burning heat. Wherever those shots landed, it wasn't on either of them.

Eric's eyes fluttered and then closed.

"Eric?" she said his name softly. "Wake up, it's over."

"Don't wake him yet," a booming familiar voice said—Chaos and an ironic gleaming smile. "I hear my Mystic Cloud of Dread is…unpleasant for humans."

Kiko smiled and stood up, brushing her pants clear out of habit. The bowling alley was dark and empty. The lanes were splintered, rotted, and the varnish peeled. The scoreboards were off, one of them broken, and the musty carpet was torn. The cracked walls had plaster falling down.

"Back to the future?" she asked Chaos.

He nodded.

Kiko sighed in relief. "Thank god."

"Excuse me?"

"Never mind." Kiko passed him the time travel device. "I won't be needing this anymore. I have everything I need right here."

Chaos accepted it. "Good job, kid. I was worried for a moment there."

"Really?"

"Uh, no. That was a joke."

"Funny, almost." Kiko considered carefully, remembering the words of the cab driver who was impossibly fast. "Quickie Dick. That was you watching out for me."

"I can neither confirm nor deny those allegations."

"No human can drive like Quickie Dick. I also didn't miss the humor of it. So now what?"

"Well, since you were one of my best Love Curators, I gave you a favor. Just one. Your house and storage units had the rent paid for all these years."

"Thank you. I assume my Bronco was impounded again. How about a ride out of here?" Kiko asked with a fiery smile on her lips.

Chaos held one finger in the air as if to remind her, just one favor. He disappeared in a blink.

She'd never see him again. She didn't even thank him properly for her chance at a happily ever after, that chance she'd never fathomed having after Yoshi's murder, and that happily ever after laid partially conscious at her feet. Kiko slipped her two phones out of her pocket. She lopped the old flip phone across the bowling alley, never to be needed again. She wasn't sorry for it either. Kiko used her modern smartphone and called a cab.

"Yes, The Wounded Soldier. Or what used to be. Yes, Greenleaf. Really. I don't care how much extra; we need a ride home. Yes, really." Kiko hung up. She figured The Wounded Soldier had been abandoned for at least twenty years. After all the history this place had seen, good riddance.

Eric groaned. "What happened? And why do I have to ask that again?"

Kiko smiled. "Let's get home first. You've taken a good knock to the head."

Chapter 36
Present Day, Green Bay, Wisconsin

Kiko held Eric's hand while they rode in the backseat of a cab. She tossed him way more money than the fare, and helped Eric into their house. It was the same as they left it—filled with boxes of Eric's stuff that hadn't been unpacked yet, only now it was dusty. Kiko set Eric down on the couch, which could use a good vacuuming. She had no other choice but come clean now, and Eric had no other choice but to believe.

Kiko had broken the news to her matches hundreds of times over the century, and one thing was guaranteed—a panic. But they'd always come around...eventually. Still, she hoped telling him the truth didn't cost her Eric's respect and trust.

"Shit, I didn't get to sell my dot com stock," Kiko said. Oh, well.

"What?"

"We have to talk," Kiko said.

Kiko made Eric a mug of hot coffee and sat next to him on the couch. The grounds were a little expired, but they tasted fine.

"What happened to Roger? Why didn't Stan take us home?" Eric sipped and shook his head as if clearing away the cobwebs.

Kiko exhaled a deep centering breath and explained, slowly, because Eric took a good knock to the head—again. "I'll find out. One minute." Kiko slipped her smartphone out of her back pocket, waited for a data signal and searched online for the news article that detailed Roger's death.

There was more information now, and she read out loud while Eric eyed her phone suspiciously. "Greenleaf, Wisconsin. Convicted felon Roger Meyer from Milwaukee was shot dead at The Wounded Soldier sports bar during an altercation. Several witnesses detailed a man and woman also involved in the battery had vanished, but sources say that was a hoax. Meyer had served seven years for the slaying of Kiyoshi Takai. One woman, Amanda Carter, was arrested for assault and battery and further charged with resisting arrest. Three suspects were also arrested..." she trailed off.

Eric didn't move. He stared off as if processing the information.

Kiko pulled up another story. "Sean Trejo, the shooter from The Wounded Soldier pleaded not guilty in a motion for self-defense. Forensics confirmed the trajectory of the bullet matching Roger's pistol, and Trejo was charged with misdemeanor possession of an illegal handgun and fined five hundred dollars."

"Why are you reading this as if it happened in the past? And what are you holding?" Eric scooted a few inches away, and

Kiko's chest squeezed. No, no, no. I can't lose him now, she silently pleaded.

"Take a deep breath, okay? This is a cell phone from the current year."

"That doesn't make sense."

"Hear me out, please," Kiko asked gently. "Roger shot at me, intending to kill me, and you were his collateral damage. I had no other choice, so I brought you here."

"How is this any safer? Roger will be here soon, and Stan didn't finish installing the security system," Eric said.

"Roger is dead. He was killed in 1995."

Eric frowned.

"Amanda is probably on the verge of retirement."

Eric leaned back on the couch and rested a hand against his forehead. "I must've been hit harder than I thought. Amanda is in her thirties, how is she nearing retirement?"

Kiko grasped his hand and said, "I've brought you almost thirty years into the future."

"What in the hell are you talking about?" Eric stood and swayed on poor balance. Kiko tugged him back down onto the couch, and dust billowed up in their faces. Kiko waved it away and coughed. Definitely vacuuming later. Although she expected the outburst, it still hurt that he didn't believe her, but he was in no condition to flee.

"You knew I was missing for seven years," she explained carefully. "That's not entirely accurate. I've actually spent the last hundred years matchmaking couples from the present to the past. I wrote those three hundred novels over the course of a century, not seven years."

Eric's mouth parted, and his brows lifted. "Time traveling while writing."

"Precisely."

Eric stood again, surer on his feet, and Kiko let him go. He stared out the picture window and newer model cars moved down the street. He saw Kiko's 1995 television, and she turned it on for him to see the date on the news. Shockingly, it picked up a local station without a converter box.

"It's real. All of it is." Kiko rubbed her sweaty palms on her jeans. "You're here with me now, and I'll understand if you're angry."

"Why would I be angry?"

Because it was normal for people ripped from their lives to be angry. Plus, there was something else that happened when you shift into the future.

"Paul Woodson..." Kiko trailed off, resisting having to break the news. Her matches always did the heavy lifting while she watched, but now it was her turn to pick up the broken pieces.

Eric weaved his way back through the boxes and sat next to her. "Add thirty years…and he isn't alive anymore."

Kiko shook her head and regret pressed heavily against her. "And you can't go back."

Eric's head hung.

Kiko pulled him into a hug and said, "He never knew what happened that night. The witnesses insisted that we vanished, and Paul obviously never made contact with you again."

Eric's shoulders shook softly, and a wet gasp jerked against her. This was awful, so much worse than watching from the outside. She hated not only ripping him from his life, but also tearing apart his family. Sure, his was fairly dysfunctional, but at least he had one. Now Eric only had her. But there was more news, and she hoped at the end of it, he'd stay.

"That's not all. There are so many consequences to time travel. Stan retired to Florida with his grandkids. Ted and Barry quit Blue Feather immediately after The Wounded Soldier incident of 1995, and now they do public relations for an online tabloid. And I checked on Caroline."

"How do you know all this?" Eric dashed tears from his eyes.

"Internet search. For a few bucks you can learn anything about someone, but you'd be surprised what people offer freely."

"That's unsettling."

Hopefully this was the last gut punch. "Caroline married and had two kids. She stayed at Blue Feather...until the publishing house closed."

"Blue Feather closed?" A look of horror crossed Eric's face and pain stabbed her fresh. Had she made the right move?

"It only stayed open a couple years. Fred Carter wasn't capable of running it. He passed away a few years back. Amanda does social media marketing for a local restaurant chain."

"I can't believe this. I can't believe any of this. It's like some wild dream." Eric pulled away from her and paced the cramped living room, pausing when a vehicle rolled by. He was going to be okay, she told herself. Eric was just processing in his way.

"It took me a while to believe, and a lot longer to adjust," Kiko admitted.

"Why do you still look twenty years old?" Eric put his hands on his hips, and Kiko didn't like his defensive position.

Tears filled her eyes and she blinked them back. It was her job to be strong for him, no matter his decision. She wasn't the one whose life was turned upside down and inside out. "I didn't age while fulfilling the Love Curator role."

"So you're really a hundred and…"

"Twenty years old. Yes," Kiko finished.

"Wow." Eric's mouth gaped, and then curved into a swollen smile. "You look good for your age."

A return of his sense of humor brought her hope back. "And you could use some time to heal."

"Speaking of which, my head's pounding. What do you have?" Eric asked.

"Ibuprofen and water." Kiko went to the kitchen cabinets. The ibuprofen was expired, but it would have to do for now, and she filled a glass of water, thankful the bill had been covered.

"What no cool future stuff?"

"The future isn't that much different. Car shapes, clothing, internet. Everything's online. Smartphone apps."

"What's an app?"

Kiko handed him the glass of water and dropped the tablets into his palm.

"I'll teach you everything to get you up to speed. Diving into the world of the internet and smartphone capabilities is for another day. But I'm afraid your old Motorola doesn't work here. We're on a Five G network now."

"I don't know what that means." Eric swallowed the pills and handed her the empty glass. "But I appreciate you telling me the truth."

Kiko smiled warmly. "It means, take some time to get acquainted before you worry about everyday stuff."

Eric stared off beyond her shoulder as if another thought just struck him. "Shit, I don't have a job, and I'm flat broke. I need job listings. Where do I find a newspaper these days?"

"Don't worry about it." Kiko gripped his shoulder to calm him down. "Take your time to heal and learn the future."

"I don't have time. I've got bills due and no cash."

"Eric," she sat him down. "You have the house sale proceeds plus thirty years of interest, but there's something else I haven't told you."

"What's that?" His brow lifted, and he leaned back an inch. He was right to be wary after all she'd told him, but this should cheer him up, or make him feel wholly inadequate.

"I have a lot of money."

Eric gave her a suspicious sideways glance. "What do you consider 'a lot'?"

"Well, I didn't get a chance to sell my dot com stock in 1999 or 2000, but it's okay. I can take the hit."

"How much did you lose?"

Kiko's crafty smile lit up the room. "Sixty million."

Eric jumped to his feet and then pressed a palm to his forehead. "You lost sixty million dollars and you aren't concerned?"

Kiko shook her head.

"How? Were the Love Curator wages astronomical for those hundred years?"

"No. Unpaid gig, but wise investing is easy when you can see the future."

"And now I've got to ask—" Eric's crooked grin lit up her heart.

She knew exactly what he was thinking. "Sorry to burst your bubble, but all my abilities ended when I retired. So, we're just going to have to survive on my current nest egg."

Eric sat back down next to her. Kiko took his bloody hands in hers.

"When did you retire from the time traveling?" he asked.

"When I fell back into your life."

Eric leaned in for a kiss, and Kiko gently pressed her lips to his, not wanting to cause any pain on his bruised skin. As if doves were released overhead, Kiko's heart soared with his acceptance. She knew he would be okay—they would be okay. Eric's mouth took hers with a need so profound they spent the rest of the day in bed, carefully.

ERIC ROLLED OVER AND found a beautiful sight on his arm. He must be dead, because he felt dead. Everything ached. But today was a new day in a new world, and Eric had exploring to do. Kiko had explained everything so well that his mind was slowly wrapping around the idea. It was surreal to know his entire life as he knew it was over. He and Kiko had a fresh start. A real second chance.

"How about breakfast?" Kiko asked when Eric sat up.

His stomach growled. "Food? Yes, please."

Kiko lit up the screen—color screen!—of her cell phone and pressed some buttons. "What do you want?"

"I'm not picky." His hand caressed her clothed thigh.

She tapped some buttons and turned off the screen. Shortly after, an unmarked car arrived at the curb and a young man rushed to the door with a bag of food. Kiko tipped the man and brought the bag inside.

"Wow. The service is faster," Eric said, unwrapping a croissant sandwich and taking a bite. "But the food is not as good."

"I've had worse," Kiko said.

He couldn't wait for all her stories. They ate quickly as if it were a task to get out of the way rather than leisure. Afterward they both unpacked his boxes and got him settled, while Kiko tried to explain things from the future. Some of it was great—like electric cars. He saw that coming from miles away. Other stuff was terrible—school shootings, government surveillance, and pandemics. At the end of the day, they were beat but happy. And Eric was glad to have a warm, welcoming home and loving arms wrapped around him.

"Now what?" he asked, meaning what was he supposed to do with his life now?

"Well, I happen to have three hundred unpublished novels sitting in storage."

Eric leaned forward. "They're still in storage?"

"My boss covered the tab for us as a parting gift, and speaking of which, we need to unload our stuff."

Eric rode along with Kiko in the cab and they rented a pickup truck. Eric helped her load the boxes of books into the rental and back into the house.

"What are you going to do about the Bronco?" he asked after Kiko returned the rental and came home in a new car.

"It's probably a pancake in a salvage yard somewhere. I'd managed to retrieve it a couple times, but I think it's best to let it go. I picked this up quick at a dealership, but I'll get you what you want later."

Eric didn't like handouts, but he wasn't going to argue about it. He carefully turned pages of her red journals, marveling at her handwriting. Some, now that he knew the truth, where clearly written with a quill. It was beautiful. Kiko slipped the book out of his hand and said, "There's someone I want you to meet."

They pulled into the parking lot at Animal Care of Wisconsin. They didn't have pets. "What are we doing here?"

Kiko smiled. "Come."

Inside, a freckled young woman with wild hair and piercing green eyes sat behind the desk. "Good afternoon, what can I help you with? Oh, Kiko! Hi. Oh my goodness. Let me get Matt." The spitfire dashed off through an office door and returned with a tall man in a white lab coat with blue eyes and a gentle smile, which quickly brightened when he saw Kiko.

Something about him was familiar.

"Kiko, hi! How have you been? You need a pet so we have a reason to see each other regularly."

"I'm great. Really great. I want you to meet Eric Woodson. Eric, this is Verity and Dr. Mathew McCall."

Eric's jaw dropped open and he stared, starstruck. The stories were real. This place was real. He'd read the last three of her novels, and it was then he realized all three hundred of her novels were really real, not that he didn't believe her, but how could anyone believe such a tale?

"You escaped the wrath of Jaime Perez?" Eric turned to the doctor. "And you saved April and Sam's puppy? It was all real?"

Dr. McCall stuck out a hand, and Eric reluctantly shook it, still in awe of meeting the character who was a tangible human. A small dog rushed up to greet him, tail wagging so hard his little body shook. "Just Matt. And Snoopy says hi. How did you know about our story?" Matt glanced at Kiko suspiciously.

"I wrote the stories down. Yours, your sister's, Becca's, everyone's. If it's okay with you, we'd like to publish them. They'll be marketed as fiction, of course." Kiko hugged Eric's waist.

Verity and Matt exchanged warm looks with broad smiles. Matt said, "Of course. The story is probably better as fiction than living through it was."

"Wow." Eric's fingers threaded through Kiko's in awe. The stories she must've seen. Eric couldn't wait to read them all. "It's unbelievable." All those books. Hundreds of books—all true. "I know it's true. It's just not sinking in yet."

"Don't worry. It just takes time." Matt laughed, and Verity rolled her eyes at his lame pun.

"Mommy, my dinosaur been eaten by the fish water," a tiny voice said. A toddler pointed to the office fish tank. There was, indeed, an orange dinosaur sunk to the bottom.

"This is Sammy," Matt said. "Little Sam McCall. He was named after my brother-in-law from 1853."

"I know," Eric said. "I read all about it."

A woman and her puffy dog entered, jingling the bell on the door.

Matt said, "I have to get back to my patients. It was so good to see you again Kiko, and to meet you, Eric. If you want to chat about your experiences, feel free to make an appointment."

Eric waved goodbye, and Kiko followed him outside to the new car. "I feel like this is The Twilight Zone. What a story this would make!"

"Yes, I've been writing it. Story number three hundred and one," Kiko said.

"Let's get to work. We've got books to publish."

"Only if you'll be the new vice president of finance."

"Sure thing, CEO and chief talent person. That's not a thing, but it should be."

Kiko grinned.

Eric's mouth found hers with a rejuvenated excitement. He never imagined how his life would change the day Yoshi introduced him to Kiko. And the day she appeared in his office he would hold dear. Now he had a new brilliant business partner, a cozy home, and the love and trust he'd always wanted. He had a feeling she'd be more open to suggestions than his dad had been. They might not have seen eye-to-eye, but Eric would always miss his dad.

For now, they had work to do, and Eric was ecstatic to have found true happiness.

Epilogue

One year later...

Knuckles rapped on Kiko's office door. She no longer sat in a dingy corner office of Blue Feather with a tiny window. Kiko's new penthouse corner office featured rows of books on two walls and a sheet of glass on the other two, giving a bird's eye view of the city skyline and of all the bustling activity of her and Eric's publishing company, Many Feathers Publishing.

She had a team working around the clock on edits, covers, and formatting of her three hundred and one books. She'd given vast freedom for the editing team to make changes, because there was no way she was ever going to complete the edits herself in her lifetime. While she'd enjoyed being temporarily immortal—except for the hand tingles—she was much, much happier having a family and running a business with the man she loved.

"Come in." Kiko released the computer mouse and spun the rings on her finger. Eric had been so shy when proposing, which surprised her. Turned out he was a little ashamed at how much the ring set he'd chosen would be, and he asked her to front the financing for it. She was a modern woman and had no issue with buying her own, but she insisted on a small intimate ceremony. They'd eloped in Jamaica and stayed at the condo Paul Woodson owned there and since passed to Eric.

Her husband stepped inside, looking dashing as always, and held out a bouquet of tropical flowers in a glass vase and a strawberry cheesecake. Kiko's heart blossomed at his sweetness and her hand rubbed her growing belly. Sixteen weeks and counting. Kiko couldn't wait.

"What's the occasion?" she asked.

He set the round pan of cheesecake down. "I thought you and the baby would like a treat."

A black furry cat, their office mascot, jumped up on her desk to inspect the treats. She gave the feline, her first ever pet cat, a few head scratches and set him on the floor. "You have your own food and you know it, Chaos."

He wasn't the real Chaos; she just named him that. Although after the Quickie Dick thing, Kiko would never be one hundred percent certain he wasn't looking out for her.

"Baby and I always want a treat," Kiko said to her love. "But that's it? No crazy sales, new acquisitions, or shocking projections?"

"No." Eric smiled with a beautiful green twinkle in his eye, and he held out a hand in invitation to help her to her feet. Braced in his arms, he said, "No other reason than I love you."

"I love you too," Kiko said.

"And you look sexy as hell sitting in the CEO's desk carrying my child. We're going to make good use of that couch on your lunch break." Eric kissed her, and a hard dick swelled, pressing near her belly. She throbbed in all the right places.

Chaos had been right—the real one. This was her happily ever after with a job that gave her purpose, friends in the company and at the veterinary clinic, and surrounded by her own growing family. It was better than anything she could've ever imagined.

Eventually Eric convinced her to try snails. They were gross.

DEAR READER,

Like pirates? Chaos has an agent working at the Tall Ships festival. Check out the Pirates in Time trilogy, and discover how a group of friends in their late 30s and early 40s survive the high seas, treasure hunting, and swashbuckling men with broken hearts and dangerous secrets. The complete series is now available! Grab **Pirate's Prize (Pirates in Time Book 1)** or pick up the complete **Pirates in Time** trilogy!

Pirates not your thing? No problem! I've got vampires too, or check out my other titles at StephanieFlynn.com.

As an indie author, I'm thrilled you decided to share your time with me, exploring the crazy worlds residing in my head and keeping me up at night. Your reviews are very important to me, so if you enjoyed this book, please consider leaving some stars for Kiko and Eric's story, **Years to Savor (Matchmaker in Time Book 4)**.

If you found any typos or errors, I blame my cat. Rat her out at: support@stephanieflynn.com.

Thank you for your support!

Also By Stephanie Flynn

Find my catalog at StephanieFlynn.com

Immortal Protector series
0.5 Vampire's Distraction
1 Vampire's Deception
2 Vampire's Secret
3 Vampire's Promise
3.5 Elf Bound
4 Vampire's Demand

Immortal Protector Side Tales
Deer Holiday
Love Claws
Depths of the Heart

Matchmaker in Time series

0.5 Minutes to Live

1 Seconds to Act

2 Hours to Arrive

3 Days to Hide

4 Years to Savor

Pirates in Time series

1 Pirate's Prize

2 Pirate's Treasure

3 Pirate's Plunder

Time Travel Romance Shorts

Fateful Time

One Crazy Time

If you like your urban fantasy without the romance, too, check out Stephanie Flynn's other name, Marie Flynn!

About Stephanie Flynn

Stephanie Flynn writes action-packed paranormal romance filled with adventure, suspense, and danger. She lives in Michigan, USA, with her husband and kids, and she spends her writing time surrounded by a herd of normal cats who bat everything off her desk, including her coffee. Check out her website for more books: StephanieFlynn.com